10/14

SHATTERED TIES

NEW YORK TIMES AND *USA TODAY* BESTSELLING AUTHOR

K.A. ROBINSON

OTHER BOOKS BY
NEW YORK TIMES AND *USA TODAY* BESTSELLING AUTHOR
K.A. ROBINSON

THE TORN SERIES

TORN
TWISTED

Cover Photo by Think Stock Photos

Cover Designer: RBA Designs

Editor and Interior Designer: Jovana Shirley, Unforeseen Editing

This book is a work of fiction. Names, characters, places, and incidents either are products of the author's imagination or are used fictitiously. Any resemblance to actual persons, living or dead, events, or locales is entirely coincidental.

K.A. Robinson

Visit my Facebook page at http://www.facebook.com/KARobinson13

ISBN-13: 978-1492293293

CONTENTS

PROLOGUE

Every child puts his or her parents up on a pedestal. Parents could do no wrong, and their opinions were your opinions as well.

At the tender age of six, I felt the same way. My mother, the famous supermodel, Andria Bellokavich, was my idol. I wanted to wear her clothes, make my hair look the same as hers, and share her opinions with the world.

"I can't *believe* they let that kind of riffraff in this park," my mother said as she wrinkled her nose in distaste.

I followed her gaze to see a boy around my age and his mother playing by the sandbox. "What's wrong with them, Mommy?"

"They're low-class white trash, and I don't see why they feel the need to invade *our* park."

I stared at the boy. I saw nothing low-class about him, but what did I know? My mommy knew everything, and if she said they were icky, then they must be.

"Can we make them go away?" I asked, eager to please my mommy.

"I wish, but unfortunately, this is a public park, so there's nothing I can do. I will say this—we will not be coming back here anytime soon."

I loved this park, and it made me sad that we couldn't come back. I instantly hated the boy and his mother for taking away my favorite place in the world.

"Can I go play on the slides?" I asked, not wanting to waste a minute of my time here since it would be my last.

"Of course, honey, but don't go anywhere near *them*." She sniffed as she pulled out her BlackBerry and started punching buttons.

I hated that thing. Mommy was always on it, and she never paid attention to me when she was. Daddy had one, too, but he always put it down if I wanted his attention. I didn't mind Daddy's so much.

"Thank you, Mommy!" I said as I leaped off the bench we were sitting on and ran for the slides.

I looked back once to see if Mommy was watching, so I could show her just how fast I could climb up the slide, but of course, she wasn't looking. She still had that stupid thing glued to her hand.

I sighed in defeat and slowly climbed the ladder. I was so proud of myself when I made it to the top. Not every six-year-old could climb this high without being afraid, but I could. I'd been doing it forever or at least since I was five and Mommy had started to let me run around the park on my own. She always told me that I was a big girl now and that I could take care of myself while she worked.

I sat down and pushed myself down the slide, giggling when I got to the bottom as I felt the static in my pigtails. I loved the slide. It was my favorite part of the park—after the sandbox, of course. I glanced over at the sandbox to see that the boy and his mommy had moved on to the swings.

Now's my chance! I jumped off the slide and ran as fast as I could to the sandbox. Once I made it there, I sat on the edge, so I wouldn't make Mommy mad by getting sand all over my dress. I picked up the bucket and started filling it with sand to make my very own fairy princess castle. One day, when I was all grown-up like Mommy, I would find a prince who would build me my very own castle.

"Whatcha making?" an unfamiliar voice asked.

I looked up to see the boy from earlier standing above me. I wasn't supposed to talk to him, but how could I not when he'd asked me a question?

"Making my princess castle," I replied, hoping he would lose interest after the princess part and leave me alone. If Mommy saw us talking, she would be so mad at me.

"Can I help?" he asked as he sat down right in the middle of the sandbox.

I looked around, expecting his mommy to yell at him for getting his clothes dirty, but she was just watching us and smiling as she sat on one of the slides.

"I can do it on my own," I replied shortly, hoping that he would take the hint and leave me alone.

"Don't you want to play with me?" he asked, sounding hurt.

"I'm not supposed to play with you. My mommy said so."

"Why not?"

"Because you don't belong here, and you're trash."

His eyes widened at my words, and he frowned. "I am not trash!"

"Well, my mommy says you are, and she's always right. She says you shouldn't even be allowed to play here."

"Well, your mommy is wrong. My mommy says that we are welcome here, just like everyone else."

I shrugged. "I don't care what your mommy says. My mommy is right, and you shouldn't be here. Go away."

Before he could respond, I heard my mommy calling my name.

"Emma Bellokavich Preston! Come here!"

I glared at the boy as I stood. "Now see what you've done? I'm in trouble all because of you!" I turned and ran back to my mommy. I felt a twinge of fear as I saw the angry sneer on her face.

"What did I tell you? I do not want you around people like that!"

I hung my head, ashamed that I'd disobeyed her. "I'm sorry, Mommy. I told him to go away, but he wouldn't listen."

"I don't want to hear it! If you can't listen to me, then you don't need to be here. Come on, we're going home."

I sighed as I followed her out to the parking lot where her brand-new Mercedes was parked.

All I wanted was a princess castle.

1
EMMA

Eleven Years Later

"Emma! Are you ready to go?" my mother shouted through my door.

"I'll be ready in a minute!" I shouted back as I applied eyeliner around my green eyes.

I needed complete concentration to get the smoky look that I was going for, and my mother yelling through the door wasn't helping matters. I finished applying the liner and reached for the brush sitting in front of me. I ran it through my strawberry blonde hair until it looked perfect.

Today was the first day of my junior year in high school, and I wanted to look perfect. I needed to *be* perfect. I'd managed to snag a spot on the varsity cheerleading squad my freshman year, but this was the first year that I was co-captain. I needed to set the standards for the rest of the girls on my squad. Anything less than perfection was unacceptable for the girls of Hamrick High School's State Champion Cheer Squad.

I set down the brush and grabbed my bag on the way out of my room. As I started down the stairs, my phone rang. I smiled as I listened to Ke$ha's "Die Young" playing. I had that ringtone reserved for one person and one person alone—my dad.

My parents had divorced when I was eight. My dad, Alexander

Preston, traveled a lot with his rock band, Seducing Seductresses, so I rarely got to see him anymore, and I cherished every phone call that I would receive from him.

"Hi, Daddy," I said as I held my phone up to my ear.

"Hey, baby girl. Are you ready for your first day?" he asked.

"Yep. I'm getting ready to walk out the door now."

"I wish I were there to see you off," he said sadly.

I knew that he'd meant it, but like always, he was thousands of miles away from the home I shared with my mother in Santa Monica.

"Me, too. How's England treating you?"

"It's great. It's far rainier than I remembered though," he replied, sounding truly distraught about the weather.

I laughed. "You're such a dweeb, Dad."

"Did you just call your rock-god dad a *dweeb*?"

"I did. Listen, I need to go, or I'm going to be late. I'll talk to you later?"

"Of course, baby girl. Enjoy your day."

"Thanks, Daddy. I love you."

I disconnected the call and walked into our kitchen to find something quick to eat for breakfast. Our chef, Razoule, was standing by the island, holding a granola bar and smiling.

"Thanks!" I said as I grabbed the bar from his hand.

"You are very welcome, Miss Emma," he replied as he turned back to whatever he had been working on.

Razoule was one of the best chefs in the country, and my mother had managed to snag him a few years ago. After living off of his cooking for most of my life, I wasn't sure if I could handle it if he ever left us.

I walked to the front door, but just as I put my hand on the knob to open it, I heard my mother calling my name.

"Emma! Don't forget that I have a committee meeting tonight, so I won't be home until late."

"I know, Mom. You've only told me about it twenty times since last week."

"Don't use that tone with me. This is a very important meeting, and if all goes well, we will have a new and very well-known celebrity on our side."

My mother was on every committee from here to San Francisco. Since she'd walked away with a huge chunk of my dad's fortune when they divorced, she could afford not to work. Instead, she spent all her time climbing the social ladder around here, and she expected me to do the same. She only liked my friends if their parents were rich or famous or both. I loved my mom, but she was conceited and power hungry, not two things that you want to put together.

"Have a good day!" she called after me as I opened the door and walked out into the bright sunlight.

I slipped my sunglasses over my eyes and smiled as I walked to my car. I loved California. The weather was perfect, the beach was just a short drive away, and the entire place was beautiful. I'd traveled some with my dad over the years, but no place could ever come close to California.

I attended a private school, Hamrick High School, with most of Santa Monica's finest. Rather, I attended it with the demon spawn of Santa Monica's finest. When mommy and daddy were gone most of the time and they supplied you with endless amounts of cash, the perfectness that surrounded our school and the students attending all but disappeared. Underneath were wild parties, drunken fights, and more than one crashed sports car. Lucky for me, I was at the heart of it all.

I played the perfect daughter and the perfect student by day, but when the parents disappeared and the alcohol flowed, I liked to party with the best of them. Chalk it up to my mommy and daddy issues, but I used the parties as an escape from reality. After all, who is really perfect when it comes right down to it?

My school was less than ten minutes from my house, and I arrived before I'd even managed to finish my granola bar. I parked my brand-new Mercedes-

Benz next to my best friend, Lucy's, Jaguar and stepped out. Students were everywhere. Most were standing by their cars while others, the more responsible ones, were walking up the steps to the school.

I caught sight of Lucy's dark brown hair in a crowd of people next to the stairs. I snuck quietly over and launched myself onto her back. Her squeals of terror had everyone laughing as she tried to throw me off. I finally gave up and released her after I thought she'd suffered enough.

She turned to glare at me. "That was so not cool, Emma!"

"It might not have been cool, but it was funny," I said as I giggled.

She rolled her eyes as she linked her arm through mine, and we started walking up the steps to the school.

"Lookin' good, Emma," Todd Bex said as he walked past us.

I sighed dreamily as I watched him walk by. Todd was a senior and the captain of the football team. Add in his good looks and charm, and he was the most sought-after guy in our school. I rarely wasted my time on boys, but he wasn't a boy. He was a man. He kept his dark hair cut short most of the time. His eyes were a beautiful baby blue, and that, coupled with a strong jawline and full lips, made every girl turn to mush at his feet. The fact that he had talked to me, a lowly junior, sent thrills through my body. Maybe this would be the year that someone finally tamed him, and that someone could be me.

"Wipe the drool off your face," Lucy teased.

I stuck my tongue out at her. "Shut up."

She opened her mouth to reply, but she was cut off when we heard a loud backfire coming from the parking lot. Both of us turned to see a beat-up Jeep pulling into the lot and parking beside my car.

I raised my eyebrows in disbelief. *Who on earth is driving something like that around here? And why do they feel the need to park next to me?*

"Who is that?" I asked as we watched a guy climb out of the Jeep and walk toward us.

"I have no idea, but I wouldn't mind finding out," Lucy replied as she stared at the new arrival with lust-filled eyes.

I squinted, trying to see him as he walked toward us. He looked vaguely familiar, but I couldn't place him. Lucy squeezed my arm as he looked up and noticed us staring. I thought my arm was actually going to fall off when he approached us and stopped directly in front of me.

"Hi. I was wondering if you could tell me where the office is," he said politely.

Now that I could see him up close, I understood Lucy's excitement. *Wow. Just wow.* I had been ogling Todd not two seconds before, but I had to admit that this guy was far better than Todd. His hair was a shaggy mess of blond curls, and his eyes were the brightest emerald green that I had ever seen. His upper lip was a bit thin, but his bottom was full and just begging to be kissed. He was wearing a fitted polo shirt, and it stretched to its limit every time he moved due to the muscles that it was concealing. Several tattoos covered his arms, and they were a total contradiction to how he was dressed. This boy looked like a fallen angel and a surfer boy all rolled into one, and I wanted to wrap myself around him.

I blushed as I pictured us together, both wearing nothing but a smile. *Dear Lord, what has gotten into me?* Yes, I was a partier, but I'd never been in *that* situation before. Virgins didn't imagine total strangers naked, yet here I was, picturing him naked.

"I'm Lucy," she said as she held out her hand for him to shake.

He took it and smiled. "I'm Jesse. It's nice to meet you, Lucy."

She gave him her brightest smile as I stood frozen.

"And this is Emma," Lucy introduced me.

He held out his hand to me, and mine rose on its own to meet his. When our hands touched, I felt like I'd been shocked, and I pulled back quickly.

"It's nice to meet both of you," he said politely.

"Uh, yeah. You, too," I said lamely. I knew Lucy was going to have a field day with this later.

"Anyway, can you point me in the direction of the office?" he asked again.

"Oh, right. Of course." I turned and pointed to the doors where several students were walking through to go to their first class. "Just go through those doors and make a left. It's right down the hall."

He smiled. "Thanks so much for your help."

I watched as he walked around us and made his way through the doors.

"Holy shit. I think I'm in love," Lucy groaned as she stared at the empty spot where he'd just been standing.

"Wow," was all I could manage to get out. My brain wasn't functioning at the moment.

"Yeah, wow. I don't think I've ever seen you freeze up like that," she teased.

"I just…wow. I don't know what happened."

"I think we both have it bad," she said as we walked up the rest of the steps and headed into our school.

I remembered him pulling in with his piece of crap car. "I wonder who he is. He has to be a new student since I've never seen him before, but I don't see how since he drove up in that thing."

"Maybe he's one of the scholarship kids," she suggested.

"Scholarship kids?" I asked stupidly.

"Do you ever pay attention? Coach Sanchez was just talking about it the other day at practice. I guess the school awarded scholarships this year to two or three kids from across town. They normally attend the public school over there."

"Oh," I said.

"Yeah, oh. That has to be it. I would have remembered seeing that guy before now. He's not exactly someone you can forget."

"So, if he went to the public school, he must be poor," I said, sounding disappointed. There was no way I would ever be able to get to know him. My mother wouldn't allow it.

"Do you realize how snobby you just sounded? I swear to God your mother's voice just came out of your mouth."

I rolled my eyes. "You know what I mean. My mom would never let me associate with someone like him."

"Because he isn't rich?" Lucy asked sarcastically.

"Because he isn't rich."

"Your mom is a bitch."

"And so is yours. They both run in the same circles, you know."

She sighed. "Don't remind me. I swear our mothers run some super-secret organization of stuck-up bitches."

I laughed even though it wasn't really funny. While my mom was far worse than Lucy's, they were both rather…selective of who they associated with. At least Lucy had her dad around to keep her mom straight.

We walked the rest of the way to our first class in silence, both of our minds on the new boy, Jesse. I loved that name. I found it sexy, but I knew my mother wouldn't agree. She would think it was too common, too plain. Everything had to be the best when it came to her. While my first name was fairly common, instead of having a normal middle name like most people, she'd given me her maiden name. It was always the best for us.

When we finally arrived to our first class, trigonometry, all of the seats were taken with the exception of a few in the front. I hated sitting in the front of the classroom, but it didn't look like I had any other options unless I wanted to sit on someone's lap.

I sat in an empty seat next to the door, and Lucy sat down beside me. It looked like we were the last two to enter since Mr. Kester walked to the door and shut it seconds after we had taken our seats.

"Good morning, students. I hope you're as excited as I am to start a brand new school year," he said happily as he walked to his desk and sat down.

That was doubtful. I hadn't made it an entire day yet, and I already missed summer vacation. Hopefully, this year would pass by quickly, or I might lose my mind. It wasn't that I hated school. I just hated playing into the popularity games that were played here.

Sure, I was on the cheer squad and right at the center of the popular crowd, but that didn't mean that I always liked it. It was great to have so many friends until you realized that most of them were fake and just using you for your popularity. I didn't trust any of them with the exception of Lucy. I knew that she was my best friend because she wanted to be, not because I could get her more friends.

Lucy and I had met in elementary school, and we had bonded instantly. Since our mothers were together so much, they had often brought us along, and we'd played together constantly. I might not like my mother or the games she played with the power players in this town, but I appreciated the fact that if it weren't for her, Lucy and I might not have ended up as best friends.

Mr. Kester was taking attendance when the door swung open, and Jesse walked in. He scanned the room before walking to the teacher's desk and handing him a piece of paper.

"I'm Jesse Daniels."

"So glad that you could join us, Mr. Daniels. Why don't you take a seat over there by Emma?" Mr. Kester said pleasantly.

My eyes snapped to Lucy just as she looked at me and grinned. This class just got a whole lot more interesting.

Jesse glanced around the room. His eyes stopped on the empty seat beside me, and he smiled. I held my breath as he crossed the room and sat down beside me.

"So, we meet again," he said as he settled into his seat.

I couldn't hide the grin that was plastered on my face. "I guess so."

I fidgeted for the rest of class, trying to keep my eyes glued to the board in front of me. Instead, they kept glancing over at Jesse of their own accord. He really was something else to look at, even from the side. I couldn't help but stare as he seemed oblivious to my constant scrutiny.

I shook my head to clear my thoughts. *What am I doing?* According to Lucy, this guy was here on a scholarship, and his piece of crap car all but confirmed that he wasn't up to my mother's standards. He wasn't someone who I needed to involve myself with. My mother would never allow us to be friends, and she would absolutely kill me if she knew I was crushing on someone like him.

I glanced over at him one more time, determined to push him out of my thoughts. That was a bad idea. *How the hell am I supposed to stay away from someone who looks like him?*

"I think I've covered everything we need to today. If you want to talk among yourselves for the last fifteen minutes of class, feel free," Mr. Kester said.

Mr. Kester was one of only two math teachers at our school. I'd had him my freshman year, so I knew that he would usually let us hang out during the last few minutes of class. For teaching one of the worst subjects, he was pretty cool.

I turned to Lucy, determined to ignore Jesse, so he wouldn't try to talk to me.

Lucy raised an eyebrow as she noticed my obvious attempt to ignore Jesse. "What are you doing?"

She'd whispered the words, but I tensed, afraid that Jesse had heard her. While I was ignoring him, I didn't want him to realize that I was doing it on purpose. I didn't want to look like a stuck-up bitch even though I knew I was being one.

"Nothing," I whispered back.

She rolled her eyes but said nothing. We just sat there and stared at each other, both of us unable to think of anything else to say.

"Hey, Emma?" Jesse said from behind me.

I closed my eyes and mentally groaned before turning to face him. "Yes?"

"Can you tell me where Ms. Mason's class is? It's my next class, and the lady in the office wasn't very good at giving directions."

He gave me a smile, and I felt my heart speed up. "Yeah, sure. It's actually my next class, too, so I can just show you."

Did I really just say that? I was supposed to be pretending that he didn't exist, not walking him to class.

"That would be great. Thanks," he said sincerely.

I studied him closer. This guy seemed to be exceptionally polite, and I wasn't used to that around here. Most of the guys were raging idiots. I wasn't sure if it was because he was nervous and a bit shy or if he was just this nice in general. Surely, this hot guy covered in tattoos couldn't be shy. His demeanor and his physical appearance were complete opposites.

"So, what's your story?" I asked, unable to stop myself.

He looked confused. "What do you mean?"

"I was just wondering where you were from." I gestured to his tattoos. "You don't fit the mold for most of the guys around here. Did you just move here or something?"

He hesitated for a split second before I saw determination fill his eyes. "Nope. I attended the public school across town all my life. I'm here on a scholarship. As for my tattoos, I like to be creative, and sometimes, I use my body to do it."

I felt my cheeks turn red from embarrassment. I was sure he could get very creative with that body of his.

He seemed to sense my discomfort, and he laughed. "I didn't mean for it to come out like that."

"It's fine. I was just embarrassed for being so nosy," I lied.

"You weren't being nosy, just curious. But you were right about one thing—I don't fit in around here. My mom kind of forced me into coming here."

That surprised me. Hamrick High School was one of the top private schools in California. I had no idea why he wouldn't be jumping for joy at the chance to attend when so many would kill to be in his position.

"Why don't you want to be here?" I asked.

"I thought it would be obvious. I'm not one of the rich kids, like you. My *kind* tends to be looked down on."

"Oh," I said, unable to think of anything else to say.

He gave me a small smile, and I noticed a dimple in his left cheek. *How did I miss that?*

"You don't have to feel awkward or anything. It's just the facts of life. I've been looked down on my entire life by this entire town because my mom works as a waitress instead of being married to some rich guy."

I added *blunt* to the list of notes I'd made about him in my head. The kid didn't beat around the bush. He got straight to the point.

"My mom isn't married to a rich guy." I pretended to glare at him, but I couldn't keep a straight face. "Well, she isn't married to him anymore."

He looked shocked at first, but then he realized that I was kidding, and relief flooded his face. "I thought I pissed you off there for a second."

"Nah. I was just messing with you!" I said as I giggled.

The bell rang to signal the end of class. I grabbed my trig book and threw it into my bag. Lucy waved good-bye as she left for her next class on the opposite side of the school from mine. I knew that the two of us couldn't have every class together, but I hated the ones that she wasn't in. School was boring without Lucy around.

I glanced over to see Jesse waiting for me to lead the way to our next class. *Maybe history won't be so boring after all.*

We walked side by side out of the classroom and down the hallway to our next class. As soon as I entered the room, I heard someone shouting my name from the back of the room. I looked up to see two of the girls on my squad, Andrea and Vanessa, waving their hands and pointing to an empty seat in front of them. I smiled and waved back as I started walking toward them.

Remembering that Jesse was still with me, I turned to look at him. "Do you want to sit back there with us?"

He seemed unsure, but he finally nodded. "Sure."

I watched Andrea's and Vanessa's eyes widen as they took Jesse in. I smiled to myself. Leave it to the broke kid to make every girl at Hamrick High turn into a puddle on the floor.

2
JESSE

This place was everything that I had expected and not in a good way. I had known coming here was a mistake, but my mother hadn't listened to me when I told her that I wouldn't be welcome here.

"Nonsense. You snagged that scholarship, and you have just as much right as the rest of them to be there," she'd said this morning, standing in the kitchen of our single-wide trailer.

I had tried to make one final attempt to make her see reason, but she'd refused to listen to me. It wasn't that I cared what those stuck-up rich kids thought of me because I didn't. I just had no desire to attend Hamrick High and pretend to be something I wasn't. Public school was fine by me, but my mother had all but begged me to apply for the scholarship.

I had agreed, not expecting to even be considered. When I came home from school one day last spring, I had been shocked to see my mother sitting at our kitchen table, holding an acceptance letter in her hand. Since then, I'd tried to find every excuse out there not to attend, but she'd refused to let me get out of it. She thought this was my chance to make it somewhere in life, to escape the mobile home park I'd grown up in.

I hadn't been able to tell her that I had no desire to attend college. Art was my thing, and I'd found my calling when I picked up a tattoo gun my freshman year in high school. For someone who had no formal training, I was damn good at it, too.

I'd spent the past two years working at a local tattoo shop. I was the slave boy since I obviously wasn't old enough to do tattoos legally, but I'd learned a lot from my boss, Rick, and his guys. I had hoped that after I turned eighteen and graduated, I could get an internship there, so I could be fully licensed. I knew now that it was never going to happen. This trailer-park kid was going to end up going to college like all the respectable kids.

I knew my mom would be disappointed if she found out all I wanted to do with my life was tattoo. She would see it as staying where I was in life, and she wanted so much more for me. My dad had left when I was only a few years old, and since then, she had worked her ass off to provide for me, so I could go out into the world and prove myself. And in her eyes, that meant going to college. I hated the idea of college, but I knew I would go just to make her happy. I'd worked hard in school, so that maybe, just maybe, I could snag a scholarship. There was no way that I would let her take out loans to put me through school.

I'd finally given up this morning, and I'd driven the twenty minutes to my new school. I was here for her and her alone.

Of course, when I pulled in, the first person I'd seen was *her*. I didn't even know her name, but I'd remembered her just like it was yesterday when she had sat in the sandbox and told me I was trash. I should have thanked her really. She had been the first person who showed me what the world was really like.

She still looked the same, only older. Even at six, she was the prettiest girl I had ever seen. Her eyes were a deep shade of green, and her hair was a light strawberry blonde.

On that afternoon, my mom had decided to take me to the really nice park across town to celebrate the end of kindergarten. I had looked up to see her sitting by herself in the sandbox, and I had wanted to go play with her. She had looked so lonely and sad, and I had been determined to cheer her up.

Instead of being happy to have someone to play with, she had cut me with words no six-year-old would ever know to say. *I was trash. I didn't belong there.* I'd toughened up after that. At six years old, it had become clear to me that the world was not a nice place to live in, so I should be ready for whatever it threw at me.

I pulled myself back to the present as I followed Emma down the aisle to sit with her friends. I had purposely stopped to talk to her outside this morning, hoping that she would remember me. Of course, she hadn't, but I had been shocked at how nice she was then and again in our first period. I had expected a stuck-up bitch, but instead, she had helped me, and she'd even been friendly to me. I wasn't sure if I liked that. I had always portrayed her as a villain in my mind, and without it there to make me see reason, I couldn't help but notice again just how beautiful she was.

She was obviously an athlete of some kind. Her body was toned, and she had been blessed with a figure most girls could only dream of. The skin-tight shirt and shorty shorts she was wearing today did nothing to hide it, and I found myself wanting to see what was underneath. I blamed my damn teenage hormones as I tried to get a grip on myself. This would lead to nowhere, so I needed to get my head back into the game. I was here to get good grades and hopefully a scholarship, not stare at Emma's ass like I was doing right now.

"Hey, girls. This is Jesse. Jesse, this is Vanessa and Andrea. They're both on the cheer squad with me," Emma said as she sat down.

So, I was right about her being an athlete. It was obvious that cheerleading had done wonders for her.

I walked around her desk and took the one next to her. "Nice to meet you."

They were both staring at me like they wanted to eat me alive, and it took everything I had not to roll my eyes at them. I wasn't interested in their type, so they really didn't need to bother undressing me with their eyes. However, it did seem I *was* interested in one girl like them even if I didn't want to be.

I kept glancing at Emma as I pulled a notebook from my bag and set it on my desk. I caught movement out of the corner of my eye and looked up just in time to see a guy sitting down in the chair on her other side.

"Good to see you, Emma," he said as he looked over at her and smiled.

I wasn't sure if I wanted to laugh or punch him in the face when Emma blushed as she told him good morning. It was obvious that she had a thing for this guy and that should be reason enough for me to leave her alone.

"Hey! This is Jesse. He's a new student," Emma said as she introduced me.

I nodded my head in greeting. That was all this guy was going to get.

"Nice to meet you, Jesse. I'm Todd."

Again, I nodded but said nothing as I stared straight ahead at the chalkboard at the front of the class. I wasn't interested in making friends here. Any friends I had were back at my old school, and even there, I had very few. I wasn't the most sociable person, and it took a lot for someone to gain my respect and trust. Besides the guys at the tattoo shop, I could count on one hand the number of people that fell into that group. Most of them were kids who lived in the park with me, including my best friend, Andy, and his sister, Ally.

I had to admit that I missed the guy. We'd grown up in the park together, and I thought of him more like a brother than a best friend. I usually tried to stay out of trouble, but he was always the first one to dive into it, and I was often found guilty by association. We and the other boys we hung around with were branded by most as the troublemakers in school and in the trailer park. It didn't bother me though because it meant that most people left me alone.

"Don't take offense. He's just shy." I heard Emma whisper to Todd.

He had obviously picked up on my unfriendly attitude and had taken it as a personal insult.

I wanted to laugh when I'd heard Emma say I was shy. I was the furthest thing from it, but I tended not to get wrapped up in bullshit things like being social, so I often came off as shy or an asshole. I hoped that the latter would apply around here, so everyone would take the hint to leave me alone.

They both turned their attention to the front of the classroom as the teacher entered. She was an older woman, and I could already tell that she was going to be strict. She just put off that dreaded no-nonsense vibe.

"Good morning, class. I'm Ms. Mason for those of you who don't know me. For those of you who have had me before, you know what I expect out of my classes. Those of you who are just now getting the privilege of taking one of my classes, I want to be clear now. I won't put up with any of your silly little games that so many students like to play. If I give you an assignment, I expect you to do it and have it turned in by the due date. No excuses. Yes, I am strict, but I'm also fair. Just don't cross me."

I rolled my eyes. *Isn't she just a breath of fresh air?* It looked like this class was going to be one that I needed to focus a lot of my attention on.

"Let me take attendance, and then I'll pass out your books," she said as she sat down at her desk.

I didn't miss the disapproving look she'd given me when she called my name and I raised my hand. My tattoos were obviously not going to be very popular with most of the staff around here, but I was used to it. Everyone always thought that if you had ink, then that automatically made you a criminal.

She wasted no time in passing out our books as soon as she'd finished with attendance.

"I would like to speak with you after class," she said as she handed me a book.

"Sure, no problem," I grumbled as I took it from her.

Emma glanced at me worriedly, but I gave her a small smile, hoping to reassure her. I could handle whatever Ms. Mason wanted to dish out.

We spent the rest of class working on chapter one, and she even assigned the questions at the end as homework. She obviously didn't care that it was practically a rule that no one should give out homework on the first day of school.

When the bell rang, I threw my books in my bag and stood up. Emma grabbed my arm just as I started to walk to the front.

I gave her a questioning look. "What?"

She seemed uncomfortable, but she hid it well. "I just wanted to tell you where the cafeteria is. When you leave this class, just turn right and then left at the end of the hall. Just go straight after that, and you'll find it."

I was surprised that she was trying to help without me asking for it.

"Thanks," I said as I looked down to where she was still holding my arm.

She looked down, too, and she quickly pulled her hand away when she realized that she was still touching me. "You're welcome."

I continued walking up to the front. I stood next to Ms. Mason's desk as the rest of the class disappeared out into the hallway.

"Thank you for staying, Mr. Daniels," she said once everyone was out of the room.

"Sure, no problem. What did you want to talk to me about?" I asked, already knowing that it probably had something to do with the tattoos covering my body.

Everyone might as well get used to them. It wasn't like I could take them off while I was here. I had even made an attempt to look somewhat civilized with this damn polo shirt I'd found at the local thrift shop, hoping that it would make them happy.

"As you know, this is the first year that we have done this scholarship program. All of the teachers were given a file to look over for the new students, so we would know what to expect. I have to say that you completely shocked me when you raised your hand today. From what was in your file, I was expecting someone a bit…tamer. It's quite obvious that you are a very intelligent young man based off of the fact that you're standing here now in addition to the grades that your old school sent to us. I just want to make sure that we aren't going to have any problems since you're not what I had envisioned."

"Are you profiling me?" I asked, unable to stop myself.

People like this woman pissed me off, and if she were anyone besides a teacher, I would have told her to *fuck off* by now. Instead, I was forced to hold my tongue and be semi-polite.

She frowned. "I am not. I just want to make sure that we're on the same page."

"No, you are. You think that just because I have tattoos that I'm some lowlife with anger issues and a drug habit. I can assure you that I am not. Like you just pointed out, I have very high test scores, and my transcripts are damn near perfect. I was never suspended from my old school either, so it's obvious where your concern lies." I held out my arm, so she could see the tattoos on my right arm. "This doesn't change who I am. I'm that guy in your little folder. I just happen to like color."

I swore that I'd seen her mouth turn up in a grin, but a second later, it was gone, and I wondered if I had imagined it.

"That's good to hear, Mr. Daniels. You've been blessed with a great opportunity, and I'd hate to see it go to waste."

"You don't have to worry about that. I understand what being here means, and I will continue to keep my grades up, just like I always have."

She stared at me for a moment before speaking. "I'm glad we cleared things up. I look forward to having you in my class this year. Maybe you can teach some of these idiots how to be a proper student."

"I doubt that," I said as I turned and walked to the door.

As soon as I was outside of the classroom, I all but growled in frustration. I was hoping that the rest of the teachers wouldn't decide to judge me before they even had the chance to know me.

I followed Emma's directions and found the cafeteria easily. I would have to be deaf not to hear the roar of the voices coming from inside it. Even if she hadn't given me directions, the place was hard to miss. Just like everything else in this school, the cafeteria screamed money. My old cafeteria had been plain, just a room filled with marked-on tables and plastic chairs. This place, however, reminded me of a restaurant more than a high school cafeteria. The tables were all identical in the same polished wood with matching chairs. I looked around, but I didn't see one chair that was broken or any tables with graffiti on them.

I had to admit that this was a nice change of scenery. The table that Andy and I had claimed back at my old school wobbled from where one of the legs was ready to fall off, and the chairs were all those uncomfortable plastic ones that made your ass hurt after two seconds of sitting in them.

I was one of the last to arrive, so the line for food was almost completely deserted. I moved through it quickly and started looking for an empty table. Hamrick High was a highly selective school, and there were less than three hundred students total, yet there wasn't a single open table to be seen. I ignored everyone as they stared at me and whispered while I looked for an empty seat. I wanted nothing to do with any of them.

I noticed a table in the far corner of the room that had only two male students sitting at it. They looked like outcasts to me, and I decided that they were the best option I had. They were both watching me as I approached, and they traded glances as I stopped in front of their table.

"Is this seat taken?" I asked as I pulled out a chair and sat down.

The boy sitting across from me shook his head. "No, you can sit there if you want."

"Thanks," I said as I looked both of them over.

The one who had spoken up was the typical nerd with glasses and a bad haircut. He was skinny while the other guy was overweight with a bad case of acne. *Just as I suspected—outcasts.*

I started eating as they continued to stare at me. I had to admit that this school did have at least one perk. The food didn't taste like ass, like my old school's did. It was actually kind of good. If there was one thing that I liked above all else, it was food.

"Why are you sitting with us?" the chubby one asked.

I looked up to see him staring at me with a confused look on his face. "What do you mean?"

"It's just that you're not like us, and no one ever sits with us."

I glanced behind me to see the rich brats watching me. "Trust me, I'm just like you."

"You're a scholarship kid, aren't you?" the skinny boy asked.

I nodded. "I am."

"You could fit in with them if you tried." the chubby one said.

"Don't want to," I said before shoving food in my mouth.

Skinny smiled. "I think I like you already." He held out his hand, and I shook it over the table. "I'm Charles."

"Jesse."

Chubby held out his hand, and I shook it as well. *What is up with seventeen-year-olds shaking hands?*

"I'm Sean."

"Good to meet you guys," I said as I wiped my hands on my jeans.

"Likewise. Where are you from?" Sean asked.

"Public. I'm a poor bastard." I grinned as I watched both of their mouths hang open in shock. "Don't act so surprised. I'm sure you knew already. I know what this whole school thinks of me."

"Actually, I haven't heard any poor bastard comments. I *have* heard a lot of the girls talking about you though," Charles said.

"Same here, and we hear everything. No one even pays attention to us, so we hear all the good gossip," Sean added.

"They can keep talking. I'm not interested in rich bitches."

I heard someone suck in a deep breath behind me. I turned to see Emma standing behind me with a hurt look in her eyes.

"I'm assuming you heard that?" I asked.

"I came over to see if you wanted to sit with me and my friends, but I think I have my answer." She turned and stomped off, leaving me to feel like an ass.

I wasn't sure why I cared that I'd made her feel bad, but I did. I was out of my chair in a flash, hurrying after her, before I even realized what I was doing.

"Emma, wait!" I yelled as I caught up to her.

She had all but run from me, and we had ended up in one of the empty hallways leading away from the cafeteria.

"What?" she asked as she spun around to face me.

"I didn't mean to hurt your feelings," I said, realizing that it was the truth. I didn't want to hurt this girl, but I wasn't sure why I cared.

"Don't worry about it. You didn't."

"Then, why did you run off on me?" I asked skeptically.

"I, uh…I remembered that I needed to grab a book from my locker."

"Couldn't you do that *after* lunch?" I asked, calling her out on her lie.

We both jumped as the bell rang, signaling the end of lunch.

"Look at that. It *is* after lunch. Later, Jesse," Emma said as she waved and disappeared around the corner.

I stood in the hallway for a split second before I forced myself to start walking to my next class. *Why did I chase her? What the fuck did I care?* She was a spoiled rich bitch, and I didn't need her screwing with my head. I was here to get good grades and keep my mom happy—nothing more. Sure, Emma was attractive, but so were most of the girls in this school. There was no reason for me to give a shit about her.

I spent the rest of my day searching for my classes. The building was small enough that I could figure out where I was going most of the time, and if I couldn't, there was always someone around to ask.

Each time I walked into a class, the teacher would give me a disapproving look as soon as he or she saw me, but I didn't really care. They could think whatever they wanted to about me as long as they would give me the grades I worked for. If they didn't, then we would have a problem.

I was worn out by the time the final bell rang, but I was looking forward to working my shift at the tattoo shop. Rick had been working on a back piece for a guy, and today was his final session. I couldn't wait to see the end results. So far, it looked sick.

I threw my books into my locker and walked out to my car, happy that I was free. I threw my bag in the backseat, and then I slid into my car. I was trying to hurry so that I could get to the shop in time to see Rick finish the session, but when I turned the key in the ignition, the only sound I heard was a click.

"You've got to be kidding me!" I groaned as I hit the steering wheel.

Today was really not my day. I tried a few more times before finally accepting that I was going to have to call Andy and see if he could come pick me up. I pulled my cell phone from my pocket, and I nearly threw it out the window when I realized it was dead. *What good is the stupid thing if I can't use it when I need it the most?*

I hung my head in defeat as I realized that I was stuck. I was either going to have to walk across town or ask someone here to use a phone. Both options sucked in my opinion.

3
EMMA

Why is it that on the only night this week when I don't have cheer practice, Jesse is sitting in his obviously broken-down car parked next to me?

I'd been standing on the stairs, watching him fight with his car and then his phone for the last few minutes. I was still mad about what I'd heard him say at lunch, and I didn't want to help him. I wanted to let him sit in his hot car and turn into a puddle. *Okay, maybe I don't want that, but still.* He obviously didn't think very much of me. *So, why do I feel like I should help him?* I *should* just get in my car and drive away, but I knew that I couldn't. He needed help, and I was going to offer it to him.

I took a deep breath and walked over to his Jeep. "Need some help?" I asked him through the open window.

He nearly jumped through the roof before he looked me over carefully. "My car won't start. Can I use your phone?"

I pulled it from my pocket and held it out to him. "Sure, go for it."

"Thank you." He dialed a number and waited. "Andy, it's Jesse. Listen, I'm broke down at school. Can you come get me?" His face fell as he listened to his friend talk. "No, it's fine. I'll figure something out. Thanks."

He hung up the phone and handed it back to me without a word. He was obviously still in need of help even if he didn't want to admit it.

"Did you get a ride?" I asked, pretending that I didn't already know the answer.

He shook his head. "No, he has to take his mom to the doctor, and my mom is working right now. I'll just have to wait until one of them is free."

"Where do you need to go?" I asked.

He glanced up. "I was supposed to be at work in ten minutes. I don't see that happening now."

I motioned to my car. "Get in. I'll take you." I wasn't sure what I was doing, but I'd already offered, and I couldn't take it back now.

"You don't have to. I'll figure something out," he said stubbornly.

"Oh, for God's sake, get in my damn car, and I'll take you where you need to go. Not all of us rich bitches are heartless, you know." The words had come out of my mouth before I had a chance to think them over, and I instantly regretted them.

He didn't say a word as he climbed out of his car and slipped into mine. Instead of making me feel better, the fact that he hadn't commented made me nervous. I walked around to the driver's side and got in, careful not to look at him.

"Where do you need to go?" I asked.

"Rick's Tattoos over on *my* side of town."

"You tattoo?" I asked.

I backed out of my parking spot and pulled onto the main road. I had no idea where Rick's was, but I knew where the lower-class part of town was. He could just give me directions when we got closer.

"Nah. I'm only seventeen, so I can't legally. I just work there as the shop bitch."

Again, I couldn't help but admire him for saying exactly what was on his mind. "Do you like it?"

"I do. Rick and his guys are great, and I've learned a lot from being there."

"That's great. I'm glad that you found something you love."

The seconds ticked by slowly as we both stayed silent.

"I hurt you, didn't I?" he asked suddenly, destroying the silence.

"I have no idea what you're talking about," I replied, hoping that he would believe me.

The truth was that he *had* hurt me. I wasn't sure why, but the fact that he had labeled me a stuck-up bitch bothered me. Sure, I could be one if I wanted to, but that wasn't usually the case.

"Don't lie to me," he said as he stared at me.

"I'm not lying to you," I said stubbornly

"Yes, you are. I can see it in your eyes."

I had no idea how he could be in my head like this. There was just something about him that made me care about what he thought of me. I'd lived my entire life not caring what others thought, yet here he was, pushing his way into my life without even trying. I couldn't deal with this.

"What gives you the right to ask that?"

"I don't have that right, but I want to know. I didn't mean to hurt you, and if I did, I really am sorry. I grouped you in when I shouldn't have. You've been nothing but nice since I got here this morning."

I glanced back and forth between him and the road, unsure of what to say. "Yeah, it did hurt a little."

He turned away from me. "I knew it did, and I'm sorry. Sometimes, I speak before I think. Listen, I don't want to start out like this. Can we start over?"

"Does it really matter that much to you?" I asked.

"Yeah, I guess it does. I'm just not sure why," he said as he turned to face me.

"Well, I'm willing to ignore this afternoon if you are. You could use a friend since you're so antisocial, and I'm willing to be that friend if you let me."

He grinned. It was the first one I'd seen since he'd gotten in the car.

"I am *not* antisocial."

"Yes, you are. You completely ignored Todd in class today."

"I did not ignore him. I nodded when he said hi."

"That doesn't count. You're supposed to be sociable, you know, as in, like, talking to someone," I said as I grinned back at him.

"Whatever. Maybe I prefer not to be around people."

"Why would you say that?" I asked, confused.

"Because people are assholes. I learned long ago that the only person I can trust is myself."

For someone so young, he was definitely jaded. I had no idea what had happened to him previously, but it was obvious that he didn't care about others or what they thought of him. Someone had hurt him, and for some reason, I cared.

"Not everyone is an asshole. Some of us still care."

"If there's anyone out there that cares, I've yet to meet them, besides my mom. It's just her and me against the world. Fuck everybody else."

He had just given me a bit of information about himself without even realizing it. I smiled as I glanced over at him.

"You're close to your mom, I take it?"

He nodded. "Yeah, my mom is the only one I have left. It's been me and her for years, and I like it that way."

"Where's your dad?" I asked.

"No clue. I can barely remember him. The bastard left us when I was little."

"That sucks. My dad travels a lot, but at least I still get to see him. If not, I might go crazy without him."

He raised an eyebrow. "Why is that?"

"My mom and I don't get along. She's too busy planning committee events to be a mom."

"You said before your parents are divorced. Where is your dad?"

"He's in a band, so he travels a lot. It's been like this my entire life, so I'm used to it. I just wish he was home more to help me deal with her."

"Make a left here," he said, effectively ending our discussion.

I gave my signal and turned left at the light. We were in the slums of the city, and I was glad that my car had automatic locks. I had no idea how Jesse could stand to work here. I would be afraid of getting mugged. Although, since he was a pretty big guy, that probably wasn't a problem for him.

A few buildings down from the turn off, there was an old brick building with a sign out front that said *Rick's Tattoos*. It was weathered and broken down on the outside, but the inside looked brightly lit. I pulled into the parking lot and shut the car off.

"Well, this is me. Thanks for the ride," Jesse said as he opened the door to get out.

"Wait!" I yelled.

He turned back to me. "What?"

"So, we're starting over tomorrow? Clean slate?"

He smiled, and my stomach flipped as I saw the dimple in his cheek.

"Yeah, we can start over. Maybe next time, I won't be such an ass."

I laughed. "Something tells me you're good at being an ass."

"That, I am. Have a nice night, Emma."

"You, too!" I called as he walked away.

I waited until he went inside the building before I finally pulled out. There was just something about this boy that kept me intrigued, and I was determined to find out what it was, mother be damned.

The house was quiet as I closed the door behind me. I had to admit that the peace was kind of nice. I knew as soon as my mom came home, there would be never-ending chatter about her meetings, and I just didn't have it in me to listen tonight.

I walked up to my room and threw my bag on the bed. I didn't have any homework tonight since I'd finished it at school, so I fell down on my bed and stared up at the ceiling.

Today had been interesting to say the least. Jesse had come out of nowhere and completely thrown me off balance. I needed to pull myself together. I didn't get nervous over boys. They got nervous over me—with the exception of Todd, but every girl in the school got nervous when he was around.

I should be focusing on Todd, not Jesse. Todd was safe. Todd was someone who my mother wouldn't commit murder over if she found out we were together. He was who I was supposed to be with. Or, at least, I should be with someone like him, not a guy like Jesse. He was too poor, too common.

So, why am I staring up at my ceiling, thinking about him? I wondered. I needed to get a grip and control my hormones. That was all this was. Jesse was attractive, and I couldn't help but notice that. I was a hormonal almost eighteen-year-old. There was no other excuse for it. I couldn't be crushing on the poor boy, no matter how attractive he was.

I groaned as my phone started ringing. I pulled it from my pocket to see that it was Lucy calling. "Hello?"

"I saw you leaving school with the new guy. Start talking."

"There's nothing to say. His car broke down, so I gave him a ride to work. That was it."

"You didn't bang him in the back of your car?" she asked, sounding disappointed.

"No, I didn't bang him. Sorry to disappoint," I said sarcastically.

"A girl can hope. What happened when you drove him to work?"

"Nothing. We talked, and I dropped him off."

"You're seriously crushing my dreams right now. I was picturing him naked."

"We were both fully clothed." *Unfortunately.*

"Well, that just sucks. Maybe next time…" she hinted.

"I'm not interested in him like that."

"Are you a lesbian?"

My mouth dropped open. "What? No!"

"Then, you're interested in him. I'm pretty sure every girl at our school is interested in him. Everywhere I went today, all I heard was people talking about the new kid."

"There are other new kids though, so maybe it wasn't all about him," I said.

"I saw the other new kids. Trust me, they were talking about Jesse."

"Oh."

"Yeah, oh. But I have to say that he didn't even glance at anyone all day, except for you. I think he has a thing for you, too. You could totally snag him if you wanted to."

"I don't want to snag him," I lied. "I want Todd. Did you see him talking to me today?"

"Todd is nice, but he's no Jesse, and yes, I saw. He's definitely into you, too."

"I hope so. Todd is just what I need."

"I don't care who you *need*. It's who you *want* that matters. So, do you want Todd or Jesse?" Lucy asked.

"I want Todd," I answered automatically.

Even I knew it was a lie, but I couldn't help it. There was no way that I could get involved with Jesse. My mother would make my life a living hell.

"Whatever. I'm going to go. I'll see you tomorrow."

"Later." I ended the call and threw my phone onto the nightstand.

I definitely want Todd…maybe.

That lesbian option was starting to look pretty good.

When I pulled into the parking lot the next morning, Jesse was under the hood of his car with some guy I'd never seen before. I parked a couple of spaces down from them and got out. Jesse was oblivious to my presence as he tinkered with the engine.

"I'm telling you, it's the starter. The engine is fine," the unknown guy said.

"It can't be the starter," Jesse argued.

"Why not?"

"Because I can't afford a fucking starter right now. I just cut back on hours at the shop for school."

My heart went out to him. He was trying so hard, trying to work as much as possible and go to school, and he couldn't even afford a part for his car.

"Listen to me. I know cars, and you don't. It's the starter. Talk to Rick. Maybe he can pay you early or something."

"I'm not asking him to do that for me. I'll figure something out," Jesse snapped.

I cleared my throat to let them know that I was standing behind them. Jesse tensed before glancing over his shoulder. He seemed to relax when he noticed me.

"Hey, Emma."

"Hey. Did you figure out what's wrong with your car?" I asked.

"It's the starter," the unknown guy said.

"Oh, is that easy to fix?" I asked, sounding like a total girl. I knew nothing about cars, except for how to put gas in one.

"It is if we can get the part. They're expensive though."

"I'll figure something out," Jesse said as he closed the hood and wiped his hands on a rag.

"What year is it? After school, I'll check around at a few of the junkyards to see what I can find," unknown guy said as he took the rag from Jesse and wiped his hands on it.

"It's a '98 Jeep Cherokee," Jesse said as he took the rag back and glanced up at me. "By the way, Emma, this is Andy. Andy, this is Emma."

I held out my hand, and Andy shook it. "Nice to meet you."

"You, too," he said as he looked me over.

I stared back, taking in his appearance. He had the same surfer guy look as Jesse, except where Jesse's hair was longer and blond, Andy's was a dark brown and cut short. His eyes were dark brown, too.

Both guys were both extremely tan and really attractive. Standing next to each other, they made quite the pair. Andy seemed nice enough, but there was just something about the way he looked at me that made me think he was a player.

"Well, I'd better get to class. I'll see you inside, Jesse. It was nice to meet you, Andy," I said as I looked away from Andy.

"See you in a few," Jesse said as he walked to the passenger side of his car and pulled out his bag.

I knew just what to do to help Jesse. I smiled as I pulled out my phone and dialed the number to the repair shop that my mom had me take my car to for services.

4
JESSE

Frustrated, I slammed my books down on the desk. I had no idea how I was going to come up with the cash to get my Jeep fixed. It pissed me off even more to know that every single one of these kids had enough money in their pocket to pay for the repairs without even thinking about it. I wasn't usually a whiny asshole, but that really sucked. I hated them all for it right now.

"You okay?" Emma asked as she took the seat beside me.

"I'm fine," I grumbled. I wasn't in the mood for small talk.

"No, you're not. You're upset. Do you want to talk about it?" she asked.

"Not really."

She sighed as she set her books on the desk. "Fine, I'll leave you alone. I was just trying to help."

I instantly felt bad about being a dick to her. She was only trying to be a friend to me. "I'm sorry. I'm just in a bad mood, and I'm not the best company right now."

"It's fine. Seriously, don't worry about it. We all have those kind of days."

I looked up to see her smiling at me. She really needed to stop doing that. I'd spent half of my night talking myself into ignoring whatever I felt when she was around. When she smiled, she made that really hard to do.

"It seems like I have more of them than most. I can never catch a break," I replied.

She opened her mouth to speak, but the teacher walked in just then, and we were forced to pay attention to him instead of our conversation. I caught her glancing over at me several times throughout class, and I couldn't help but grin when she'd look away quickly, pretending that nothing had happened.

Instead of having the end of the period free like last time, we worked right up to the bell, leaving no room for conversation. I was actually kind of glad. I didn't want to have to explain to the rich girl that I didn't even have enough money for a fucking car part. It was embarrassing.

I had no idea what I was going to do. I needed to pick up more hours, but I didn't see how I could with school. It wouldn't be such a big deal if I were at my old school, but this one was so much farther away, and it took me longer to drive there.

As soon as the bell rang, I grabbed my books and started walking to my next class. I was completely zoned out, and I didn't even notice when Emma started walking beside me.

"Jesse? Hey, Jesse? Anybody home?" she asked as she poked me in the side.

"What? Oh, sorry. I was in my own head there for second."

"Yeah, I noticed. What are you thinking about?" she asked.

"Nothing, just thinking." There was no way I wanted to tell her that I was broke, not that she didn't already know that.

She frowned but said nothing as we continued to walk down the hallway. I started walking a little bit faster, hoping to avoid her. She finally took the hint and left me alone as we settled into our seats in our second class. I ignored her as she turned in her seat and started talking to her friends behind her, and she did the same to me. My aggravation increased when I noticed Todd walking in before he sat down beside her.

"Hey, Emma," he said as he looked over at her.

Her cheeks turned a light shade of red, and I couldn't help but groan. I had no idea what she saw in the guy. He was nothing more than the shallow, stereotypical jock, and she could do better than that.

"Hey, Todd," she said.

"Are you doing anything this evening?" he asked her.

I clenched my teeth to keep from saying anything. It wasn't my place to tell her that he was a douche bag. Not that I was sure he was a douche bag, but he just seemed like he was.

"I have practice after school, but other than that, I'm free," she said shyly.

"Cool. Do you want to grab something to eat after you're finished with practice?"

"Sure, that sounds great."

"Perfect. I'll meet you by your car in the parking lot then."

Out of the corner of my eye, I watched as Todd turned around to talk to someone on the opposite side of him, and Emma started doing a silent screaming fit with her friends. I just wanted to hit something, but I wasn't sure why. It shouldn't matter that she was going on a date. I didn't even know this girl.

Ms. Mason walked in just then and instructed us to open our history books. *Thank God.* I could focus on school instead of stupid shit, like where Emma was going after school. I ignored everyone around me for the rest of class, and I was the first one out of the room when the bell rang.

I walked to the cafeteria and grabbed my lunch before sitting at the same table as yesterday. Charles and Sean were sitting at the table already. I mumbled hello as I sat down, but other than that, I ignored them both. I wasn't in the mood to be sociable, and they could just deal with it. I shoveled food in my mouth quickly. I was in a hurry to escape the noise of the people around me. I just wanted to be alone. First, my car, and then Emma and

Todd—today was not my day. The sooner I could get out of this place, the better. I finished my food and said good-bye. I stood and dumped my tray.

I spent the rest of the day just like the morning as I ignored everyone. *I just want out of here.* As soon as the final bell rang, I was out the door and walking to the parking lot to look at my Jeep again. Maybe there was something small I could do to keep it going until I could afford a new starter. *Yeah, right.* I knew my luck, and I knew that I would need a new starter regardless. Too bad money didn't grow on trees for me like it did for the rest of these assholes.

I didn't even bother to lock up my car this morning. I mean, come on, who would steal my Jeep with all these other fancy cars around? As soon as I reached my car, I opened the glove compartment and pulled out my keys. I stuck them in the ignition and turned, expecting nothing. To my surprise, my car started instantly.

"What the fuck?" I said as I stared at the steering wheel.

I shut my car off and got out. I ignored the strange looks I received as I got down underneath my car. Andy had shown me where the starter was this morning, so I knew where to look. My eyes widened in disbelief as I stared at a brand-new starter. *What the hell is going on?*

I knew that there was no way Andy had found one already. He was still in school, so that left only one other culprit since I hadn't even told my mother about my car breaking down. I knew she would try to help pay for it, and I didn't want to put any extra financial strain on her. Only Emma and Andy had known what was wrong with my car. She had to have been the one who had it repaired for me.

But the big question was...*why? Why would she do this for me when she barely knows me?* I wasn't used to people helping me, and I wasn't sure what to do. Normally, I would assume that whoever had helped me had done it with ulterior motives, but I doubted that was the case with Emma. There was nothing I could give her that she didn't already have. I was stumped, but I was determined to figure out why she had helped me.

I had to be at work soon, but I would corner her tomorrow before school and ask her why she'd helped me. I stood back up and grabbed a notebook from my bag. After scribbling a quick note on a piece of paper, I ripped it out and walked to Emma's car. I stuck it under the windshield wiper and returned to my car, satisfied that she would know she had been busted. I pulled away from the school and floored it to make it to work on time.

I sighed as I stared out the window at the ocean beside me as I drove. It had been too long since I'd been out there on a board. Next to tattooing, surfing was my life. There was nothing like being out there—just you against the ocean. I had crashed and burned a lot when I first decided to try it, but now, I conquered it most of the time. I made a mental note to get Andy after school tomorrow and go surfing since I wasn't scheduled at the shop.

I pulled into the shop's parking lot and shut off my car. I'd been wound tight all day, but at the familiar sight of the shop, I felt myself relax. This was where I belonged. This was home. I'd made no attempts to fit in at Hamrick High, and I didn't plan to. I had nothing in common with those people, and I was okay with that. I didn't need a bunch of stuck-up snobs to tell me how I wasn't good enough to be at their school.

The bell above the door dinged as I opened it and slipped inside. As soon as I was walked in, I could hear The Amity Affliction's "Open Letter" playing. They were one of my favorite bands, and I instantly perked up.

Rick was sitting behind the counter with a pencil in his hand. He glanced up at the sound of the bell. "Afternoon, Jesse."

"Rick." I nodded as I walked past him to go into the room we used as our employee room.

It was small to begin with, but with the table, two chairs, and lockers that Rick had shoved in, there was barely enough room to walk around. I threw my bag in the locker that I used, and then I slipped off my school shirt to change into one of the shirts with *Rick's Tattoo* written across the front of it.

I walked back into the shop and stepped behind the counter with Rick to see what he was working on. As usual, his artistic ability blew my mind. The piece he was messing around with now was so real that it practically jumped off the page. It was of a young girl, no older than ten, sitting on a beautiful white horse.

"That's amazing," I said as I watched his hand move across the paper, shading around her face.

"Thanks. It's going to be a back piece. My client's daughter was big into horse riding competitions, and she was killed while performing. Something spooked the horse, it threw her, and she was trampled while her mother watched," Rick said as he stared down at his work.

"Shit," I said. I couldn't even imagine watching that happen to someone I loved, especially a kid.

"I know. I wasn't sure I could even do it when she asked me to, but I knew I had to. This piece is too important to pass up," Rick said.

"Yeah, I can see why you were conflicted," I said.

This tattoo was a perfect example of why I wanted to go into this business. People looked down on those who were inked, but the truth of it was that for most people, their tattoos represented something major in their lives—a birth, a death, a marriage, or anything that was important to them. Their tattoos were a way of remembering, of dealing with the shit-ass hand they had been dealt in life. They shouldn't be looked down on. They should be praised for having the balls to put their lives on their skin for the world to see.

Getting tattooed was bliss masked by pain. Sure, it hurt to have a needle go deep into your skin and leave a mark, but the feeling was also about the pleasure and euphoria of it as well. At least, it had been that way for me. The pleasure of feeling the needle go deep into my skin was like nothing I'd ever felt before.

I pulled myself from my thoughts as I looked up at Rick. "What do you want me to do today, boss?"

"We're kind of slow, so just clean up a bit, and then you can watch the front when my six o'clock appointment comes in."

"Sounds good to me. I have some homework in my bag. Is it okay to work on it while I watch the front?" I asked.

He smacked me across the back of my head. "You know better than to ask me that. You can always work on your school shit here."

"Thanks." I rubbed the back of my head. "And ouch. You don't have to get physical with me."

He grinned as he grabbed his sketch and walked to his office, leaving me alone to start cleaning. I hated nights like these. When the shop was slow, time seemed to drag by. He had apparently already sent the other guys home since none of them had come out of the back to talk, so it was just the two of us for the night.

I grabbed a broom and started sweeping the front of the shop. I cleaned everything nightly, so it was always pretty clean. It only took me a few minutes to finish. I started gathering up the garbage bags from the front and then the rooms in the back to take out to the dumpster. I glanced at Rick's closed door as I walked by to go outside. Surely, we wouldn't have a customer come in while I was throwing the bag in the dumpster behind the store.

I pushed the back door open and walked over to the dumpster to throw all the bags in. When I started walking back to the shop, my phone dinged, and I pulled it from my pocket, expecting Andy or my mom to be texting me. Instead, it was an unknown number.

Unknown: Jesse?

Me: Yeah, who's this?

Unknown: It's Emma. I got your note about wanting to talk to me about something. What's up?

I grinned as I read her texts. When I left my number on the bottom of the note, I hadn't expected her to actually use it.

Me: Yeah, I do. I'll talk to you about it tomorrow. Just wait for me by your car if you get to school before I do.

Emma: Okay…if you say so. You're okay though, right?

Me: I'm fine, but I need to go. I'm at work.

Emma: Whoops. Sorry. I'll see you tomorrow.

Me: It's fine. Talk to you later.

I slipped my phone back into my pocket as I walked back inside. I couldn't help but grin over the fact that Emma had to be on her date with Todd by now, yet she was texting me. Something as stupid as that shouldn't make me happy, but it did. I was trying my hardest to avoid her, but for some reason, she kept pulling me back in. I didn't belong in her world, but she didn't seem to care about that. She was the one bright spot I'd found at my new school even if I didn't act like it.

I walked back to the employee room and grabbed my bag. I made my way back out to the counter and started pulling my books out. Within a few minutes, I was working on my homework as I waited for Rick's six o'clock to arrive.

Sure enough, a few minutes later, a woman walked into the shop, looking around nervously. She was a first-timer, I could tell. They always looked like they wanted to bolt before the door even closed behind them.

"Can I help you?" I asked, trying to put her at ease.

She stepped up to the counter and looked at me. "I have an appointment with Rick."

I pulled out a clipboard and put our new customer form on it, not even bothering to ask if she'd been here before. "I'll let him know you're here. Just fill that out while I go get him."

"Thanks," she mumbled as she took the clipboard from me with shaking hands.

The woman was terrified.

"Ma'am?" I called as she turned to walk to the empty couch in the waiting area.

"Yes?"

"I'm sorry if I'm being presumptuous here, but I'm betting that this is your first tattoo, and you are terrified."

She gave me a weak smile. "Is it that obvious?"

"Yeah, a little bit. I just want you to know that Rick told me a little bit of your story, and I think that your daughter would be so proud and honored by what you're doing. You're keeping her spirit alive even if her body is gone."

Her eyes filled with tears, and I suddenly felt uncomfortable. I wasn't good with handling tears.

"What's your name?"

"Erm, Jesse."

"Well, Jesse, I just want to thank you for what you just said. I wasn't completely sure that I could go through with this, but now, I am. I want to remember my baby girl always, and I want to make her proud."

"You're welcome, and I'm sure she was proud of you before. You were her mom, so that made you her idol."

She put the clipboard down and walked around the counter to stand in front of me. "Thank you, Jesse. You're a good soul. I hope you know that."

When she wrapped her arms around me and hugged me, I froze, unsure as to what to do. I'd never had a customer hug me before, and I wasn't exactly the type to like physical crap like this.

I patted her on the shoulder gently until she pulled away. "You're welcome."

Rick appeared out of nowhere and stood beside us. "Hi, Martha. Are you ready to get started?

"Yes, definitely," she said. She finished filling out the forms, and then she followed him back to one of the rooms.

I breathed a sigh of relief when she disappeared. I was glad that I'd helped her realize just how important her tattoo was, but the hugging wasn't cool. I didn't like people to show me their emotions, especially when they did it physically. *Unless it's Emma.* She could get physical with me any day. I groaned to myself as I pictured us getting physical together. *Way to give myself a hard-on at work.* Hopefully, Rick wouldn't come out of the back for a while until I could get my dick in check.

We didn't have another customer the entire night, and by the time the shop closed, I was ready to bolt. I'd finished all my homework two hours ago, and I wasn't good at sitting still and doing nothing.

I couldn't help but smile when I started my car. I really owed Emma for helping me. What could I do to thank her though? I was pretty sure she'd laugh at anything that I could offer. *Maybe I could buy her a burger or something? Yeah, that'll work.* I'd offer to buy her dinner as a thank-you.

The lights were on in our trailer when I pulled into the driveway. I was glad to see that Mom had actually made it home on time tonight instead of being stuck with a double again. As soon as I walked inside, I saw her standing in the kitchen.

She glanced up and smiled when she saw me. "Right on time, kiddo. I made us dinner."

I glanced at the clock on the wall as I walked to the table. "At ten o'clock at night?"

"Oh, shush. We never get to eat together anymore, so I thought this would be nice."

I kissed her on the cheek before I sat down. "It is nice. Thanks, Mom."

"You're welcome. I made your favorite—chicken and dumplings."

My mouth watered as she set a plate down in front of me. Even though I'd grown up in Santa Monica, my mom was originally from Kentucky. When I was younger, all the kids in the trailer park would come to our house because my mom would always make Southern comfort foods. It was something that none of them were used to. My mom was an amazing cook, but over the years, she'd started working more, so she didn't have time to make dinner very often.

After my mother said grace, I grabbed a fork and started shoveling food into my mouth. "This is awesome."

She laughed, and then she started to eat as well. "I thought you would like it. I wanted to talk to you about something while we have a chance."

My fork stopped halfway to my mouth. *So, that's why she took the time to make my favorite food. It's a bribe.* "Okay…"

"It's nothing bad, honey. It's just…I met someone."

"Met someone?" I asked, confused.

"Yes, his name is Mark. He just moved here a few weeks ago, and we met when he came into my work for lunch one day."

"Wait. You met a guy? Are you dating him?" I didn't like this—at all.

My mom and I were a team. We didn't need some asshole coming in and screwing everything up.

"I've been on a couple of dates with him, yes. He's really sweet, and he wants to meet you."

I stared at my mom, really stared. Even though she was close to forty, she was still pretty. Her hair was blonde and curly, like mine, and her eyes were an unusual mix of green and blue. I must have gotten my height from my dad because I stood a few inches over six feet while my mom had barely managed to reach five feet. She was tiny and cute, and I hated this bastard for noticing her.

"I don't want to meet him. I'm sure he's an asshole, just like every other guy out there."

"That's not fair, Jesse. You can't judge him before you even give him a chance. He's been really sweet to me, and it's been nice to have a guy around."

"I'm a guy," I said stubbornly.

"Yes, you are, but it's nice to have someone besides my seventeen-year-old—"

"I'm almost eighteen. There are only a couple of weeks until my birthday."

"My apologies. It's nice to have someone besides my *almost* eighteen-year-old son to look after me. I've been alone for a long time, Jesse."

I sighed as I put my fork down. I didn't like the idea of my mom dating some douche canoe, but I didn't want her to be alone either. "Fine. I'll meet him, but I'm not promising to like him."

"That's all I'm asking of you, but I really do think you'll like him once you meet him."

"So, I'm assuming you already told him yes. When are we meeting?"

"Well, the tattoo place is closed on Sundays, so I thought he could come over then, and we could all have lunch together."

"Sounds exciting," I said sarcastically.

"You'd better not be rude, or I'll take my mama's paddle to your ass," she scolded.

I couldn't help but laugh. My mom had threatened to use that paddle more times than I could count when I was a kid, but she'd never used it.

I saluted her. "Yes, ma'am."

She shook her head. "I don't know what I'm going to do with you."

I arrived at school early the next morning, hoping to beat Emma there. As soon as I pulled in though, I saw her sitting in her car. I parked next to her and shut off my car.

She smiled and stepped out of her car when she saw me. "Morning, Jesse."

I got out and walked around my car to stand beside her. "Morning."

I knew she was waiting on me to start talking, but I was enjoying watching her squirm too much. She shifted her weight from foot to foot as she waited. Finally, she couldn't stand it anymore.

"You said you wanted to talk?" she asked.

"Yeah, I did." I didn't elaborate. Messing with her was too much fun.

"Okay, about what?" she asked impatiently.

"Oh, I don't know. Maybe about the fact that you had my car fixed for me. Why would you do that?"

Her eyes widened. "I have no idea what you're talking about. I didn't have your car fixed."

"Bullshit. I know it was you."

"How do you know that?"

"Because you and Andy were the only ones who knew what was wrong with it. I talked to him last night after I got home from work, and he confirmed that it wasn't him."

"Oh," she said as she looked away.

"Yeah, oh. So, tell me why you did it."

"Fine. Yes, it was me. I knew you needed help, and I wanted to help you. I heard you talking to Andy about not being able to afford the part, and I didn't want you to have to worry."

"You don't even know me. Why do you even care?" I asked, truly curious as to why she would help me.

"I don't know. I guess it felt like the right thing to do."

Wrong answer. I didn't want to be a charity case for anyone. "So, you did it out of pity?" I asked, getting angry.

"What? No! I just wanted to help a friend."

"But I'm not your friend. I'm nothing to you."

"That's not true! You're my friend…or at least I thought so."

"I don't have friends here." I knew I was being an asshole, but I couldn't help it. I didn't want the rich girl to befriend me out of pity.

"You would if you tried, but instead of trying to meet new people, you ignore everyone."

"I'm not here to make friends with the rich kids. I'm here to get good grades and get a scholarship for college."

"Can't you do it all at once? I know you well enough already to realize that you always put what you want last. You're a teenager. You need to have some fun."

"I have fun," I replied stubbornly.

"Really? What do you do for fun?"

"I work at the tattoo shop. I consider that fun."

"See—you *work* for fun."

I wanted to beat my head against my Jeep. This conversation was not going where I had planned. "Look, I just wanted to talk to you to thank you for helping me, and I was hoping to repay you in some way. Since we both know that I can't afford the damn part, I was going to see if you wanted to get something to eat after school."

"Like a date?" she asked with a small smile.

Shit. I hadn't intended for her to think of it like that. Then again, I guessed it could be considered a date. *Since when did I date?*

"Uh, I guess you could call it a date if you wanted to. If not, you could think of it as the poor kid trying to break even with the rich princess."

I realized my slipup as soon as the word *princess* was out of my mouth. I'd been referring to her making her princess castle in the sand the first time I'd ever met her. I was praying that she still didn't know that I was that little boy. Hopefully, she assumed that I was just being an asshole by calling her princess.

"First of all, I am *not* a rich princess. My parents have money, not me. When I graduate, I plan on running as far away from my mom and her money as I can. And second, we won't call it a date. We'll call it two friends getting something to eat."

"Sorry, *princess*. Do you want to do it tonight?" I asked.

When her face turned red, I realized how that sounded. "I mean, do you want to grab something to eat tonight?"

She snickered. "I'd love to do it tonight. Want to meet here after I finish my cheer practice?"

"Works for me," I replied.

She started walking up the steps to the school. "Great. It's a date."

5
EMMA

My legs couldn't carry me fast enough to get to Lucy to tell her about my not-a-date plans for this evening. I wanted to jump up and down and scream like a girl right there in the middle of the hallway, but I didn't want to take the chance that Jesse might see me. There was no need for him to realize how excited I was. He had seemed less than enthused when I asked if it was a date, but I was going to ignore that and focus on the fact that I was going out with him tonight. *This day is going to drag by.*

I hurried to Lucy's locker, but she wasn't there, so I made a beeline for class. Luckily, she was sitting in her seat, and Jesse was nowhere to be seen.

"Guess what?" I whisper-shouted.

"What?" she asked as she eyed me curiously.

"I'm going out with Jesse tonight."

"*What?*" she shouted.

"Shh!" I glanced around the room to make sure that no one was listening. "He just asked me to go get something to eat after school."

"Like a date?"

"Yeah, I guess so."

"That's great, but I thought you weren't interested in him."

That stopped me in my tracks. I wasn't supposed to be interested in him. I was supposed to be ignoring him and focusing my attention on Todd. Todd and I had gone out last night, and it had been fun, but it didn't make me nearly as excited as going out with Jesse. *I must be losing my mind.* I'd ogled

Todd for two years, and when he finally paid attention to me, I didn't even care.

"I, uh…" I stammered, trying to think of a way to cover myself.

"Emma, chill. It's okay to like him. Honest."

"No, it's not. My mom will freak if she finds out."

"Who cares? He seems like an okay guy, and he's smokin' hot. Just go with it," Lucy replied as she grinned at me.

"I care. I don't want to have to deal with her."

"She won't find out. Didn't you say she left this morning and won't be back until tomorrow?"

"Well, yeah…"

"Okay, so then you're safe. She never has to know."

"I guess you're right."

"I *am* right. You always worry about what your mom will think. Well, I say, fuck her. She's nothing but a stuck-up bitch."

My mouth dropped open. "Lucy!"

"Sorry, but it's true, and we both know it. If you like this guy, go for it. She can go suck a fat one."

"What are you sucking?" Jesse asked as he settled into the chair next to me.

"Uh, nothing," I muttered, praying he hadn't heard anything else from our conversation.

"A big fat dick," Lucy said matter-of-factly.

I dropped my head to my desk and prayed that the ground would swallow me whole. I couldn't believe she'd just said that to him.

Jesse snickered. "Well, if you insist…"

I raised my head from my desk and glared at him. "Don't even finish that sentence."

Lucy and Jesse both laughed at my embarrassment.

"What? We've all done it…well, everyone, except you," Lucy said as she stuck out her tongue.

I didn't think I'd ever hated my best friend, but in that moment, I did. "Will you shut up already?"

"Sorry." She snickered as Mr. Kester walked in.

"Sure you are," I grumbled as I glanced at Jesse.

He was smiling, and I felt my heart melt a little. *Why does he have to be so damn gorgeous?* His personality sucked most of the time, so if he were ugly, I could ignore him. *No, that's a lie.* There was just something about the guy that made me want to get to know him, regardless of what he looked or acted like.

The rest of the day passed in slow motion. I must have checked the time at least twenty times in each class, only to see that a minute or two had passed.

When the final bell rang, I grabbed what books I needed from my locker and walked to the gym for practice. It was normally my favorite part of the day, but today, I wasn't looking forward to it. It was just another obstacle that got in the way of my date…or rather, not a date with Jesse.

All of the other girls had already arrived by the time I walked in, and I hurried to the locker room to change into a pair of shorts and a tank top. By the time I finished changing and made my way back out to the gym, my girls were already lined up and waiting on me.

Jennifer tapped her foot impatiently as I approached. She and I were both captains of the team, and she was my least favorite person on it. It wasn't that she was a bad cheerleader because she rocked at our routines. It was just that she came off a bit cold sometimes. We had butted heads more than once, and

I often wondered if Coach had lost her mind by putting us together to run the team.

"Are you ready, princess?" Jennifer asked sarcastically.

I liked it much better when Jesse had called me princess even if he was being sarcastic about it.

"Yeah, I'm ready when you are," I replied, ignoring the iciness in her tone as I started stretching.

"Great. Everyone ready?" she shouted.

The girls nodded and prepared for the start of the routine. I grabbed the remote next to the CD player and hit play. As soon as I heard Nicki Minaj's "Roman's Revenge," I relaxed my body and prepared to start. This was my thing. Cheering was everything to me, and I loved it. It was like breathing. I couldn't live without it.

My eyes met Lucy's, and off we went. We'd perfected this routine over the summer, and I could do it with my eyes closed. We both did two cartwheels that put us in front of the rest of the girls. I took a deep breath. We started off small with a toe touch jump, and then we did two more cartwheels past each other. Next, it was tuck, tuck, back up, get a running start, then an aerial, and end with a handspring. *I. Loved. This.*

We continued to do our stunts until we finished up our routine with two basket tosses. I was sweating, and my muscles were burning, but I loved it. I'd been cheering since I was three, and it was such a huge part of my life. Thankfully, my mom thought it was good for me to keep in shape, so she fully supported me.

"That was great!" I said to the rest of the girls.

They had all performed flawlessly. We were a hell of a team.

"Okay, let's do it again, and then we'll move on to the next routine!" Jennifer shouted from beside me.

We spent the rest of practice doing our routines over and over until we were sure that we had them. Even though it was Friday, our school didn't have a game until the following week, so we decided to add an extra night to our practices for the week. When we were finished, I showered and pulled my hair back into a ponytail. I was nervous over the fact that Jesse was probably out in the parking lot already, waiting for me.

I waved good-bye to the team and left the gym. As soon as the parking lot was in view, I saw Jesse leaning up against his Jeep, waiting, just as I'd expected. My stomach churned nervously as I approached him. I wasn't sure why I was so nervous, but I was. I wanted tonight to be perfect even if it wasn't a date in his eyes.

"Hi," I said awkwardly as I stopped in front of him.

"Hi back," he said casually.

I wanted to kick him for being so at ease when I was a giant ball of nerves.

"You ready?" I asked.

"Sure. You want to take my car or yours?"

"It doesn't matter to me," I replied.

"Okay, we can take mine. This isn't a date, but I can be a gentleman and all that crap." He grinned, and that damn dimple appeared in his cheek.

"You're off to a good start, talking like that," I teased.

"Right? Anyway, hop in, and I'll take us to grab some food."

I walked past him and slid into the passenger seat of his Jeep. It was very strange to be in a car that didn't have all the luxuries I was used to, but I kind of liked it. Life was boring when you had everything you wanted.

Jesse started the car and switched on the radio to some rock station. I found myself bopping my head to the song as he pulled out of the lot.

"Who is this?" I asked.

"Breaking the Hunger. They're a really cool rock band from West Virginia. They just came onto the scene a few months ago, and I'm already a huge fan."

"I don't listen to rock, but I like this."

"Whoa, wait a minute. You don't listen to rock?" he asked incredulously.

"Nope. I usually listen to pop music. I like stuff that I can dance or cheer to."

"So, you don't listen to Linkin Park? Metallica? The Doors? Seether? All That Remains?"

I shook my head as he continued to name off bands. "Nope. I have no idea who any of those bands are, except Linkin Park. They play on the pop stations occasionally."

"I'm not sure if I should feel sorry for you or kick you out of my Jeep at this point. You poor, sheltered child. How have you survived in this world without rock?"

"By being awesome?" I teased.

"I feel like I should educate you. You've missed out on so much, young one."

"Hey, I'm not that young. I'll be eighteen in a month. I'll be legal and all that jazz."

"Wait, in a month? When's your birthday?"

"October third. Why?"

"You've got to be shitting me. We have the same birthday."

I smiled from ear to ear. *What are the odds?* "That's too funny. Will you be eighteen, too?"

He nodded. "Yep. I can't wait."

"Me either. Nothing will change for me until I graduate next year, but there's just something about being an adult that sounds so exciting."

He laughed. "Yeah, I can barely contain myself for when I have to pay bills."

"Oh, shut up. You know what I mean."

"I'm just kidding. I'll be glad when I turn eighteen, too. So, back to music. I feel the need to make you fall in love with at least one of my favorite bands before the night is over. Flip down the visor and pick any CD up there."

"Sure, why not?" I pulled the visor down and started looking through his collection. He had a ton, and I wasn't sure which to pick. There was one with an apple on it, and I pulled it out. "Let's try this one."

"Good choice. In This Moment kicks ass, and their lead singer is a woman."

I popped the CD in and waited for the first song to start, but before it could, Jesse skipped to the second one.

"The first one sucks. The second is much better."

I stayed silent as the music started. A woman's voice came through the speakers seconds later, and I concentrated on the lyrics. I wasn't sure how I felt about the screaming, but I tried to act interested for Jesse's sake.

"What do you think?" he asked.

"They're not bad. It's just not something I would normally listen to," I answered truthfully.

"They're not for everyone. Andy hates them."

"I think if I listened to them for a while, I could get used to it."

"Take it with you tonight, and listen to it over the weekend. I bet you'll be singing along by the time Monday rolls around."

"You'd trust me with your precious music?" I asked.

"Surprisingly, yes. And if you scratch it, I'll just make you buy me a new one."

I laughed. "Way to abuse the rich girl."

"Might as well put Daddy's money to good use," he said as he glanced over at me.

I knew he was teasing, but there was a darkness behind his eyes that I couldn't ignore.

"Listen, while we're out, I'm not the rich girl, okay? I'm just a girl you're taking out for dinner. I hate how you categorize us. We're just people, regardless of what our parents have in their bank accounts."

"Wow, you sound all wise and shit," he joked, and I felt the tension in the car ease.

"I *am* wise, believe it or not."

I hadn't been paying attention to where he was taking us, and I was surprised when he suddenly stopped the car. We were sitting in the parking lot of a restaurant on his side of town. The building looked surprisingly clean for being in the bad part of town.

"Welcome to Joe's. They have the best burgers in town," Jesse said as he got out of the car.

I followed closely as we walked across the lot to the entrance.

There was no hostess to seat us, and Jesse walked straight in and took a seat in one of the booths in the back. I sat down across from him and picked up a menu that was already on the table.

"So, you said they have good burgers?" I asked.

"Yep. Anything they make is good, but their burgers are amazing. I would commit murder for one."

"Then, I guess I'll have a burger," I said as I glanced down at the menu. I looked through their burgers, trying to find the cheapest one. I felt bad for doing so, but I knew Jesse didn't have a lot of money, and I didn't want him to waste it on me.

"Hello, are you ready to order?" a young girl asked as she stopped beside our table.

Jesse glanced at me. "You ready?"

"Yeah, can I have just a regular burger and fries with a water, please?"

"I'll have the same, except I want a Coke," Jesse said as he closed his menu.

"Sure. Give me just a few minutes."

"Thanks, Lisa," Jesse said as the girl turned and walked away.

"Come here often?" I asked, noting that he knew the waitress's name.

"Usually once a week if I have any cash to spare."

If I have any cash to spare. I felt horrible. Here I was, driving around a brand-new car that probably cost more than his house, and he could barely afford to eat at a hole-in-the-wall burger joint. The more I was around him, the more I realized just how different we were.

"What has you in such deep thought over there?" Jesse asked.

"Nothing. Just wondering if you're telling the truth about these so-called amazing burgers," I lied.

"You don't trust me? I'm insulted."

I laughed. "I'm sure you are."

We sat in an uneasy silence as I tried to think of something to say. I wanted to get to know him, but I wasn't sure how. We were so different.

"So, what do you like to do when you're not working or in school?" I asked.

"I like to surf."

I raised a brow. Jesse was full of surprises. I'd pegged him as a surfer when we first met, but this was the first time he'd mentioned surfing to me. "Really?"

"Yep. I've been doing it since I was ten, so I'm actually pretty good at it."

"I'm impressed. I've always wanted to try it, but I'm too scared of falling or something."

"It's not that hard once you get the hang of it. You'd probably be pretty good since you're in great shape from cheerleading."

"You think I'm in great shape?" I asked, half-teasing and half-fishing for compliments.

"You know you are, so don't act all surprised."

"You're such a charmer, you know that? If you think you're so good at it, why don't you teach me?"

"To surf or charm people?"

"To surf, smart-ass. I'd love to give it a try."

The waitress appeared just then, and she set our food and drinks in front of us. "Here you go. If you need anything else, just let me know."

"Thank you." I picked up my burger and took a bite. *Sweet mother of God, he wasn't kidding.* It was like a mouthgasm—yes, a mouthgasm. It was so good that it needed a new word to describe it.

I moaned a little bit, and he grinned.

"Good?"

"Um, yes! How did I not know about this place before now?"

"Because you've never been to this side of town before?"

"Oh, right," I said sheepishly.

"Anyway, were you serious about learning to surf?"

"Absolutely. I think I could kick your butt if I knew what I was doing."

"I wouldn't go *that* far, but I wouldn't mind seeing you get knocked off the board a few times. Might bring you down to my level."

"Oh, shut up. We're on the same level now. Seeing me get the crap knocked out of myself won't change anything."

"But it'll make me laugh," he said as he grinned at me.

"Sure, it will. What do I need to do, and when do you want to do this? I need time to get a board and stuff."

"Don't worry about the board. You can use my old one that I learned on. As for when, I'm free tomorrow morning until two if you want to start then."

Wow. That was a lot sooner than I'd expected. I wasn't one to turn down a challenge though. "Sounds like a plan to me. What time do you want to start? And where should I meet you on the beach?" I asked.

"Let's meet at eight. There won't be a ton of people around, so you won't have to worry about embarrassing yourself. The beach I surf at is only a few minutes from here."

"Great, I can't wait. Should I bring anything with me?" I asked.

"Nope, just yourself." He gave me a devious smile. "And a bikini."

I felt my cheeks heat, but I refused to look away from him. He was testing me, and I wasn't about to lose this one.

"I think I can handle that."

"I don't doubt it."

We talked about nothing in particular as we finished our food. While we didn't get into anything personal, I felt like I could relate to Jesse a little bit better. The guy was smart, really smart. I could tell just by the way he talked. While he came off as easygoing and even a little wild, I didn't think he was as bad as he seemed. Still, underneath the shaggy hair and tattoos, he was a force to be reckoned with. There was just something about him. Maybe it was the way he carried himself as if to say, "Don't mess with me."

When we were both done, Jesse pulled out his wallet and set a few bills on the table to cover our dinner. I grabbed my purse and followed him out to the parking lot. I stayed a few feet behind him, admiring his ass as he walked. I couldn't help it. I was only human.

The ride back to the school was quiet. As he pulled in next to my car, he turned to me.

"Well, this was fun. Thanks for inviting me," I said.

"You're welcome. I know it wasn't five-star dining, but I like this place."

"Screw five stars. I have to wear a dress when we go to places like that."

He laughed. "I wouldn't mind seeing you in a dress sometime, preferably something short."

I wasn't sure if he was kidding or not, so I just smiled as I opened my door.

"Don't forget. Eight o'clock sharp, or I'll paddle out without you."

I saluted him. "Yes, sir."

He waved as I started my car, and pulled away. I watched him in my rearview mirror until I was out of the parking lot. I was going to have a lot of fun figuring Jesse out.

I groaned as I pulled my car into our garage. My mother's car was inside, which meant she was home. *Why me?* I thought she'd told me that she would be gone until tomorrow, but I'd apparently heard her wrong. I'd had such a good day, and I didn't want to deal with her tonight. She'd just ruin my mood.

I slipped out of my car and walked to the door that led inside the house. Maybe, just maybe, if I were quiet enough, she wouldn't know that I'd made it home. I crept through the house and went up the stairs to my room. Just as I was about to breathe a sigh of relief, I heard my mother's bedroom door open.

"Emma, I see you made it home."

Damn it. "Hi, Mom."

"How was your day?" she asked.

What's up with that? She never asked about my day. "Um, fine. Why?"

"Can't I ask how my daughter's day was?" she huffed.

"Well, yeah, I guess. You just normally don't."

There was no use sugarcoating it. We both knew that she didn't give a damn about how my day went unless it pertained to her.

"Emma! That was very rude of you!"

"Sorry," I grumbled.

"I'm sure you are," she said sarcastically. "I was talking to Todd's mom today. She said the two of you went out last night. How did that go?"

And there it was. She didn't give a damn about my day. She was simply fishing for information about Todd. His parents were one of the highly influential people who she chased after. The two of us together would be like a wet dream to her.

"It was nice," I said.

"Just nice?"

It took every ounce of self-control I had not to run to my room and lock the door. I did not want to talk about Todd with my mother. Now that she knew we'd been out together, she'd never let it go.

"What do you want me to say, Mom? We went out. It was nice."

"I thought you had a crush on that boy. Why aren't you more excited over the fact that you two went on a date?"

"It wasn't a date. We just went out for a little bit. He didn't ask to go out again, so don't get your hopes up for a repeat performance."

"I might not be a teenager anymore, but the last time I checked, a date consisted of two people going out. I'd consider last night a date."

Then, you'll be glad to know I went on another date tonight with someone you wouldn't approve of. I would have loved to say it *to* her, but I knew better. She'd lock me up and never let me leave the house again. She couldn't have her princess going out with the poor boy. She'd freak over the fact that I went to the other side of town, let alone with Jesse.

"I don't consider it a date."

"Well, I think Todd did. That's how his mom took it anyway."

"I have no idea. Maybe you should go ask them if it was or not," I replied, unable to keep the sarcasm from my voice.

"Don't use that tone with me, Emma. I raised you to be polite."

"No, the never-ending flow of nannies raised me to be polite."

Before she could reply, I turned, walked into my room, and slammed the door behind me. I knew I was being a snotty bitch, but I couldn't help it. My mom had no interest in being an actual mother. She simply wanted to use me to help her get in good with the high class folks of Santa Monica. *Well, she could take that notion and shove it right up her ass.* I had no intention of being her puppet.

6
EMMA

I was up and dressed before seven the next morning. I'd spent most of the night tossing and turning. I was too excited at the prospect of spending the morning with Jesse. There was a good chance that I would embarrass myself before the day was over, but I didn't care. I was going to spend time alone with Jesse. I'd take my chances with embarrassing myself.

I'd finally decided to throw caution to the wind and see where things ended up between the two of us. I wasn't even sure if he was interested in me or not, yet I was willing to take a chance that my mother would find out that I was spending time with him. That said a lot about my self-preservation skills…or rather, the lack of them.

I slipped quietly from my room and went down the stairs to the door leading to the garage. Hopefully, my mother was still sleeping and wouldn't catch me to see where I was going. I had every intention of lying if she asked, but I was a horrible liar. I didn't want to tell on myself before I even made it out of the house. If I were going to get locked in my room for eternity, I wanted to at least commit the crime.

Luck was with me as I slipped into the garage and walked to my car. I cringed when I started my car and clicked the button to raise the garage door, but my mother never appeared. I held my breath until I turned the corner, and my house disappeared from view. I'd done it. I did a small happy dance as I drove through town. I was proud of myself for escaping and making it this far. I wasn't too concerned about anyone seeing me on the beach with

Jesse. No one who would rat me out to my mom would be on Jesse's side of town. At least, I hoped not.

I followed the directions Jesse had texted to me the night before as I approached his side of town. Just like he'd said, the part of the beach that he surfed at was only a few minutes away from the restaurant we'd been at last night.

The lot was almost empty when I pulled in. I didn't see Jesse's Jeep anywhere, so I turned off my car and waited with the windows down. Even this early in the morning, the temperature was already starting to rise. I grabbed a hair tie out of my console and pulled my hair up into a messy ponytail, fighting the pieces already matted to my neck with sweat. I couldn't wait to get in the water and cool off.

' I glanced up as a car pulled in beside me. I couldn't hide the smile that broke out across my face when I saw Jesse sitting in the driver's seat of his Jeep. He was out of the car and opening the back before I even realized that he'd moved. I quickly got out of my car and walked back to where he was unloading two boards. He didn't mess around.

"Hi," I said nervously.

"Hey. Can you grab that duffel bag and carry it down to the beach for me? I'll get the boards."

"Sure," I said as I picked up the bag from the back of his car.

I followed him down to the beach. We stopped halfway, and Jesse put both boards down in the sand and took the duffel bag from me.

"Where do we start?" I asked. I had no idea what surfing entailed, but I was anxious to find out.

"First things first. I'm going to show you the basics—how to wax your board, how to put the leg leash on, and things like that. I also borrowed Andy's sister's wet suit for you to use today. You two look like you're about the same size." He unzipped the duffel bag and pulled out what looked like a bar of soap and a leg rope.

"Are we taking a shower or something?" I joked as I stared at the soap.

"Huh? Oh, no." He laughed. "This is board wax, not soap."

"And now I feel like an idiot," I groaned.

"Nah, it's cool. You've never been around this stuff, so it's understandable that you didn't know."

He was trying to make me feel better, and I was fine with that. I hated looking like an idiot.

"Anyway, what do we do first?" I asked.

"I waxed both boards last night, but I'm still going to show you how to do it. You need to keep your board waxed, or you'll slide right off. When you wax it, it makes little bumps that give you traction."

I nodded to show that I was listening.

"There are two different types of wax. The first is the base coat that you put on every few months. I'm not going to show you that because I already got both boards ready. The board I brought for you is called a longboard. It's the easiest thing for you to learn on. I always wax the entire surface of a longboard with the base wax. After I do that, we move on to the top coat. You have to add that wax a lot because it is softer and rubs off easily."

He motioned me forward and held out the wax for me to take. I gripped it tightly as I looked at the board.

"Top coat—got it. So, how do I wax it?"

"With the base coat, you need to put a lot of pressure into it but not so much with the top coat. I always go from one end to the other until you cover it all. Try it." He stepped back to give me room to start waxing.

I ran the wax across the board, unsure of whether or not I was doing it right. "Is this okay?"

"Put just a little more pressure into it, not much though."

I did as he'd said, and I smiled when he nodded in approval. "I think I've got it."

"You do." He took the wax from my hand and threw it on top of the duffel bag. "Just remember, you'll need to do it every few trips in because it wears off."

"Great. What's next?"

"Next is the leg leash. It's easy to do once you do it a few times. Watch me do mine first, and then I'll help you do yours."

I paid close attention to how he tied his, and then I started working on my own. He had to help me once or twice, but I soon figured it out. I felt a sense of pride when I finished.

"Yay! I did it!"

He laughed, and I couldn't help but stare at his dimple. Dear God, I wanted to lean forward and lick it. Forcing myself to look away before I did something stupid, I focused my attention on the board between us.

"What's next?"

"Normally, we'd get in our wet suits and head out, but I want to teach you the basics before we get in the water."

"Okay…" I had no idea how he planned to teach me to surf without water, but I wasn't about to make myself look stupid by asking. I looked out at the water longingly. It was too hot to be this close without going in. "Do you care if I swim for a minute? The sun is about to fry me."

"Sure, go ahead." He watched me closely with an amused look on his face.

"I'll be right back," I said as I stood and shimmied out of my shorts. My shirt went next, and I threw them in the sand beside him. I ran out to the water, and I sighed in relief as I dove in. It felt cool on my overheated skin, and I loved it. I swam just a few feet out and dove under again before stepping back out of the water.

"Feel better?" Jesse asked as I approached him.

"Yes, much. It's too hot out here."

"You won't even notice it once we get out there. Let's get started, so you don't have a heatstroke."

His eyes traveled down my body slowly, and I tried not to fidget or cross my arms over my chest. His mouth said nothing, but his eyes told me everything that I needed to know. There was a heat within them that made me burn inside. I normally felt comfortable in a bikini, but with the way he was staring at me, I felt naked.

"You're so sweet," I said sarcastically, trying to relieve the tension in the air.

"I try. Okay, I'm going to show you where to lie on the board first. It's important to position yourself right, or you'll mess up when you try to stand. If you're too close to the front, the nose will dip under, and if you're too far back, the wave will go right under you. Go ahead and get down on the board."

I crawled on top of the board, feeling like an idiot. "Am I doing it right?"

"You're a little too far back. Scoot up a bit."

I scooted up until he stopped me by placing his hand on my bare back. I jumped a little at the contact, but I said nothing. My skin tingled where he was touching me, and I focused on remembering how to breathe.

"Okay, that's good. Try to remember where you are, so you can stay there once we go out into the water. Next, we need to cover paddling out. It sounds easy, but there are tricks that will help you. When you're paddling out, you need to position yourself so that the nose is about an inch out of the water. When we are out there, you need to walk your board until you're about waist deep and then mount it."

I nodded. "Okay, I'll make sure to remember that."

"Good. Once you're paddling out, you're going to come across small waves. It's easier to dip yourself and your board under them instead of fighting against them. If you don't, you'll wear yourself out before you even make it out far enough to surf. Grip your board here, and push down. It will sink under the water, and you'll follow it. Once you surface, just keep paddling. I'll let you know when we're out far enough. You need to keep your board facing out toward the ocean until you see a wave you want. Once you do, you need to turn your board and start paddling. Remember to keep yourself centered, so you don't dip the nose or let the wave pass under you. When you feel it start to move you, you'll need to stand up, which is what I'm going to teach you now."

"Okay, just show me what to do."

"When you start riding the wave, do a push-up and pull your knees toward your stomach. Make sure to keep your center of balance as you stand up. Put whichever foot feels comfortable in the front, and keep your center of gravity low, or you'll fall flat on your ass. Honestly, you're going to fall off of this board a lot today."

"Great. I can't wait," I joked.

"Learning is half the fun. I promise to have you standing up and surfing by the end of the day."

"I'm holding you to that."

"Please do. I like a challenge."

I looked up to see him a lot closer than I'd realized. His eyes were sparkling with mischief, and I felt my stomach tighten. He was beautiful but even more so up close. I had no idea how I was supposed to ignore that little fact when I was going to spend half the day with him.

"Okay, let's try it a few times. Remember, push up, pull knees, pop up, one foot in front of you, and keep your center of gravity low."

"Got it," I said as I prepared to stand. I did it quickly, feeling proud of myself until he shook his head.

"You stood up too fast. Out there on a wave, you'll lose your balance and fall off. Try it again."

I nodded as I repeated the movements, only slower this time. Again, he shook his head.

"Too slow. The wave will reach the shore before you finish standing up. Try it again."

"You're a slave driver, you know that, right?"

"Shut up, and try it again." He shot me a smug smile.

I did it again, trying not to go too slow or too fast. I nearly did a cartwheel when he nodded his approval.

"That was perfect. Now, do it a few more times."

After several minutes of me popping up off the board, I felt like I had it down. "I think I'm good. Can we get in the water yet?"

"Do you think you're ready?"

"No, but I don't think I'll ever be. Might as well get on with the embarrassing myself part of the day."

"Sounds good to me. I could use a laugh."

I rolled my eyes as we put our leg ropes on, and I stood up. I picked up my board, and it was a lot lighter than I'd expected, but it still felt bulky and awkward in my hands.

Jesse stood up and pulled his shirt over his head. My eyes widened as I took in his tight stomach and broad shoulders. He wasn't ripped, but he was in excellent shape for a seventeen-year-old guy in high school. Living in California, I'd seen a lot of shirtless guys, and I was thoroughly impressed with him to say the least. He grabbed his board, which was a lot smaller might I add, and he started walking to the water. I forced my eyes away from him as I followed.

"Wait!" I called out. "What about our wet suits?"

"We can put them on in a few. I want to make sure you're going to stick with this before we suit up."

"So, you think I'm going to get discouraged and quit?" I asked, offended by his lack of belief in me.

"I think this is a lot harder than you think it is. A lot of newbies give up after being tossed around by the waves a few times."

At least he was being honest. I'd give him that. It still didn't make me feel any better about the fact that he assumed I would just give up if I didn't get it as soon as we started.

"I'll show you. I don't give up that easily," I said stubbornly.

"I hope not. Come on, let's go catch a wave."

I held my head high as we walked down the beach and into the water. I did as he'd said, and I waited until I was waist deep in the water before climbing on. Just like he'd warned, it wasn't as easy to get on the board as I'd expected. He climbed on to his easily, and he waited as I tried to climb on to mine. It took a few tries, but I finally managed to get on the stupid thing.

"Okay, I'm good," I said as I looked up at him.

"You might want to scoot up a little bit. You're too far back."

"Oh shit." I slowly scooted up my board, not wanting to fall off after all my hard work of getting on it.

He'd been right. It felt completely different out here on the water, and I felt more than a little unsure of myself.

"You're good. Let's start paddling."

I watched him closely as he started paddling, and I tried to mimic his moves. I was a lot slower than him, and I knew he was slowing down occasionally to let me catch up with him. I used the technique he'd shown me when we started meeting the smaller waves. I had to admit that the guy knew what he was doing on a surfboard. I was already impressed, and I hadn't even seen him surf yet.

When we were out far enough, he stopped paddling, and he sat up on his board. "This is far enough. We'll wait here until we see a wave we want."

"How do we know which wave is the right one?" I asked.

"You don't want one that's too small or too big. If it's too small, you won't be able to surf on it obviously, and if it's too big, it'll knock you down."

"Why don't you pick one out for me?" I asked as I looked out at the waves making their way closer to us.

"No way. You have to figure it out on your own."

"Fine," I huffed. "That one coming at us now—it's too small, right?"

"I don't know. Is it?"

"You're an ass. Help me!"

"No way. You figure it out."

I sighed as I eyed the wave. "It's too small."

"If you're sure…"

"Oh my god, Jesse! I'm going to kill you!" I growled.

"Fine, you're right. It *is* too small. Good call."

"Was that so hard? Gesh," I grumbled, trying to act annoyed, but I wasn't.

I was enjoying the easy banter between the two of us. Jesse wasn't a big talker, but I could tell that he was more relaxed and open out here than he was at school.

"Are you getting used to our school now?" I asked.

"I guess. It's just school."

"Yeah, but I know it has to be hard to be the new kid."

"Being the new kid isn't a big deal. It's dealing with spoiled brats all day that gets annoying."

"Do you think I'm a spoiled brat?" I asked.

He hesitated for a second. "I think you could be if you wanted to. I *do* think you're spoiled, but you're not a brat. When we met, I assumed that you were, but I was wrong."

That wasn't the answer I'd expected. Honestly, I wasn't sure what his answer would be. "Thanks, I think."

He laughed as another wave approached us, and I gripped my board with my knees and hands. It pushed us back a bit as it slipped under our boards.

"It was a compliment, I promise. You're different from the rest of them."

"How so?"

"I don't know. You're just…you. You aren't stuck-up, and you're easy to talk with. Everyone else gave up on talking to me when they figured out that I didn't want anything to do with them, but not you. You kept talking until I had to talk back."

"Well, I do talk a lot," I joked.

"It's endearing. Kind of."

"Sure it is," I said as I watched another wave approach us.

It was bigger than the last, but I wasn't sure if it was big enough. I studied it closely, chewing on my lip as I debated. If it weren't big enough, I'd fail before I even tried.

"What has you in such deep thought over there?" Jesse asked.

"I'm debating on whether or not that wave is the right one."

"Well? Is it?"

"I don't know. I think so, but I'm not sure."

"There's only one way to find out. Try to surf it."

I knew right then that it was *the one*. If Jesse suggested I try it, I was going to try it.

"Let's do it."

He smiled. "Good. Now, turn your board around and start paddling."

I did as he'd said, and I turned my board so that it was facing the shore. I started paddling as the wave closed the gap between us.

"You're going to feel it start to push you. When it does, keep paddling for a minute, and then stand up. Okay?"

"Okay," I said nervously.

My stomach was in knots over the prospect of trying to stand up on this thing. I was normally pretty graceful, but I felt out of my element out here. The wave was on us before I even realized it was close, and I felt myself sailing forward with my board. It was an incredible feeling. I smiled as I paddled a few more times, and then I prepared myself to stand up. I pushed up and pulled my legs toward my chest, just like Jesse had told me to. I took one last deep breath before standing up, careful to keep my body crouched down low. I wobbled a bit as I put my right foot in front of me, but I didn't fall. *So far, so good.*

"You've got it! Just move with the wave!" Jesse yelled from beside me.

I glanced over to see him standing on his own board, looking completely at ease. I couldn't tear my eyes away from him as he maneuvered his board on the wave, causing the muscles in his stomach and arms to tighten. I was so caught up with watching him that I'd stopped paying attention to what I was doing, and before I knew what was happening, I was being thrown off my board.

I crashed into the water and slipped under the surface. Shocked and confused, I tried to kick my way to the surface, but I wasn't sure which way was up. I hadn't had time to grab a breath before going under, and my lungs were already starting to burn.

Suddenly, I felt myself being pulled up by my arm. My head broke the surface, and I took a deep breath just before a wave crashed over my head. I was pushed back under, but I felt someone holding on to my arm still. I was pulled back up again, but without any waves crashing into me this time. My board was a foot in front of me, and I grabbed it.

"Holy shit, are you okay?" Jesse asked from beside me.

I nodded, unable to speak. I'd spent most of my life out in the ocean, and I'd never once been afraid—until today. The terror I'd felt when I couldn't find the surface was like nothing else I'd ever experienced.

"You scared the crap out of me, Emma."

"Sorry," I said as I held on to my board for dear life.

"What happened?" Jesse asked with concern.

"I don't know. I guess I got distracted."

"By what?"

Oh shit. "Uh, I was watching you and not paying attention."

"Why were you watching me? You always have to pay attention when you're on a board, or you'll fall off."

"You were distracting. Sorry." The words slipped out before I could stop them. I wanted to hit myself over the head when a grin crept across his face.

"Why am I distracting?"

"Are you really going to make me spell it out? You were all wet and shirtless, and I was distracted. Okay? There, I said it."

His grin widened as he listened to me embarrass myself. "So, I'm distracting when I'm shirtless?"

"You know you are, so stop trying to embarrass me more. I just had a near-death experience a minute ago."

He grabbed my board, so he could use it to float as he leaned in closer to me. "And you think that you wearing that bikini isn't distracting for me?"

"I have no idea what you're talking about."

"Stop acting innocent. You know what you look like, and you don't try to hide it. I've been...distracted since you stripped down on the beach, but you don't see me falling off my board because of it."

"I…you…" I stuttered.

Jesse was always blunt, but this was taking it to a whole new level.

He laughed. "I guess we both know that we're distracting each other now. Do you want to try again or take a break?"

"After falling off and you saying all of that, I think I need a break."

"Fine by me. We can hang out on the beach for a few until you're ready to go again."

He helped me back onto my board, his hands lingering on me longer than necessary when he pushed my legs up. I shuddered as he ran his hand down my thigh to my knee. I wasn't used to this game we were playing. Usually, if a guy was interested, he told me. With Jesse, I wasn't sure how to handle the situation. He had just said that he found me attractive, but that didn't mean that he was interested. I felt like I was walking on thin ice. One slip, and I'd come crashing down from the high his words had given me.

We paddled back to the beach, and once we were far enough away from the water, we stuck our boards in the sand. Jesse pulled two beach towels out of his duffel bag and handed me one.

"Is there anything that you don't have stashed away in that thing?" I asked as I spread out my towel and settled down onto it.

"Nope. I carry all kinds of crap in it when I come to the beach." He pulled two bottles of water out of it and gave me one. "Here, I brought us each one."

"Thanks," I said gratefully as I took the bottle and opened it.

Jesse spread out his towel beside me and sat down on it, watching me as I sipped my water.

"What?" I asked.

"What did you think?"

"Of surfing?"

He nodded.

"It was fun…until I fell off, that is."

"I thought you might like it. Just don't let your slipup scare you. You're going to fall off a lot, but you'll get better with practice."

"I'm not giving up, I swear. I just need a few minutes to chill out. It freaked me out when I couldn't find the surface."

"I know what you mean. I did that once when I was younger. Andy was with me though, and he helped me, like I did with you. Just remember to never go surfing by yourself, okay? It's not safe, and I don't want to have to worry about whether you're out here by yourself or not."

"You'd worry about me?" I asked, touched by his thoughtfulness.

"Yeah, I guess I would."

"You know, you can be sweet when you want to be."

He grinned. "Just don't tell anyone that, okay?"

I pretended to zip my lips and throw away the key. "Your secret is safe with me. Who would've thought that Jesse is the caring type?"

"I don't usually care."

"So, why do you care about me?"

He looked unsure. "I don't know, but I do."

We both stayed quiet, reflecting on what he'd just said. For some reason, I cared about Jesse even though I barely knew him. I'd said it a million times before, but there was just something about him that pulled me in. I wanted to know everything about him, every little detail—his likes, his dislikes, what made him tick, his home life, what he wanted to do with his life.

"You said before that you're close to your mom. Will you tell me about her?" I asked.

He raised an eyebrow in surprise. "What do you want to know?"

"I don't care. Anything. What's her name, where does she work, what's she like?"

"Her name is Trish, and she's a waitress. She's the strongest person I know, and I love her for it. She never lets anything get her down. It's just been the two of us for as long as I can remember. My dad disappeared when I was little, and she stepped up to be both mom and dad to me."

"It sounds like you two are close."

"We are. She wants me to meet some asshole named Mark tomorrow for dinner."

"You don't sound happy about that."

"I'm not. We don't need some prick coming into our lives and screwing everything up. We have a system, and it works."

"Maybe he's not as bad as you think. I mean, you've never even met the guy. Give him a chance before you judge him."

"Yeah, I guess," he said doubtfully.

I could tell that he wasn't going to even give this guy a chance. He'd already made up his mind about him.

"What about you? You didn't seem to like your mom when you mentioned her before."

"It's not that I don't like her. It's just that we're two very different people. My parents divorced when I was younger, and my dad tours with his band a lot, so I have to live with her. She'd rather spend all her time trying to climb the social food chain of Santa Monica rather than be a mom to me. I'm just another toy she can use to get in good with them. I befriend their kids, and she uses that to her advantage. It sucks."

"Sounds like she's one of the stuck-up assholes that I was complaining about earlier."

I laughed. "She is. My dad is the total opposite though. He couldn't care less about what people think of him. I never understood how the two of them ended up together. They're so different."

"Sometimes, opposites attract," Jesse said.

I gave him a sly grin. "Like us?"

"I never said that I was attracted to you."

I raised an eyebrow, and he conceded. "Okay, maybe I did."

"You so did."

"You're kind of cute. Don't get all big-headed over it."

"Me? Never."

"Whatever." He laughed. "Want to try the surfing thing again? I promise not to distract you with my shirtless, wet self."

"You're hilarious, you know that?"

"I do. Come on, let's go surf."

I stood and followed him back out into the water with my board tucked under my arm. We spent the rest of the morning catching waves. I fell off on almost every one of them, but I never gave up, and Jesse never laughed at me. He would just tell me what I had done wrong, and then he'd help me back up onto my board.

By the time we finally called it a day, I was exhausted. I carried my board to where our towels were, and I stuck it in the sand.

"I need a nap," I said as I fell to the towel and closed my eyes.

When Jesse didn't reply, I opened my eyes and squealed. He was no more than two inches away from my face.

"What are you doing?"

"Seeing how long it took for you to notice me. I wanted to make you scream like a girl."

"Well, mission accomplished. That wasn't funny."

He still hadn't moved, and my eyes dropped to his lips as he spoke.

"I thought it was hilarious. You need to get up and go home or wherever you're going to go. I don't want to leave you out here on this beach alone, and I need to get to work."

"I can take care of myself," I whispered, my eyes still on his lips.

His eyes turned dark as he noticed what I was watching. "What are you watching?"

"Nothing."

"Do you want to kiss me, Emma?"

"No. Do you want to kiss me?"

"Nope."

"Then, why are you still so close?" I asked, refusing to back down. I wanted to kiss him more than anything, but I wasn't going to be the one who caved.

"I like making you uncomfortable." He leaned in until I could feel his breath on my lips. "Are you uncomfortable right now?"

"No," I lied as I tried to keep my breathing normal. My heart was racing, but I couldn't let him know how much he was getting to me.

"I think you're lying," he whispered.

He leaned in that last centimeter and touched his lips against mine. He didn't kiss me though. He just rested his lips there. Before I could stop myself, I kissed him. It was like I had no say in the matter. One minute, I was staying strong and fighting my impulses, and the next, I had my hand around his neck as I thoroughly kissed him. His lips felt incredible, and I couldn't seem to get enough of them. I moaned as he ran his tongue over my bottom lip. He was going to kill me or at least put me in a lust-induced coma.

He pulled away first, much to my dismay. "I thought you didn't want to kiss me."

"I didn't. You kissed me," I said.

"Wrong. You definitely kissed me." He leaned forward and kissed me lightly. "Now, I kissed you. We're even."

"Not even close. You kissed me twice, and I have yet to kiss you."

He grinned. "Why don't you make it even then?"

My breath caught as I stared at him. Whatever was happening between us, I didn't want it to stop. I knew what we were doing was wrong, but I'd never felt anything so right in my life.

"Maybe later," I said.

"I'm holding you to that. Come on, let's get packed up, so I can go to work, and you can do whatever it is you do on the weekends."

I nodded as I helped him pack up our stuff. I was still in a daze from our kiss, and I could barely pay attention to what was going on around me. I thought I'd told him good-bye once we had loaded his surf stuff in his Jeep, but I wasn't sure. I pulled out of the lot, thinking that I might just be the luckiest girl in Santa Monica.

7
JESSE

I drove to work with the most idiotic smile on my face. I had no idea what had made me kiss Emma, but I didn't regret it in the least. *Okay, maybe I'm lying.* I *did* know what made me do it. Spending the day with her, especially while she was wearing that tiny bikini, had driven me insane, and I'd clearly lost my mind. I'd spent a lot of time kissing girls over the past few years, but kissing Emma had been something else. She'd tasted as sweet as she looked, and I already wanted more.

I kept telling myself to stay away from her, that anything between us could never work out, but I couldn't seem to control myself around her. She was beautiful, and she had a kindness to her that seemed to be rare in this world. Considering the first time we met, being able to say that was a bit of a shock. Instead of being the stuck-up princess I'd expected, she'd blown me away with her warm heart and down-to-earth personality.

I pulled my car into the shop parking lot just as my phone dinged with an incoming text.

> *Emma: I had a lot of fun today. Thank you.*

> *Me: I did, too. We'll have to do it again sometime.*

> *Emma: Tomorrow?*

I smiled at her text. We'd just separated, and she already wanted to hang out again. This was good, really good. Or it could be really bad, depending on how I looked at it.

Me: I can't tomorrow. I have that dinner thing with my mom and asshole.

Emma: Oh, right. Well, if you finish early or something, just text me.

Me: I will. By the way, thanks for kissing me. I'm glad I could brighten your day.

Emma: I did NOT kiss you. You kissed me.

Me: Whatever helps you sleep at night.

Emma: Ohmigod. I give up.

I slipped my phone into my pocket and walked inside the shop with a stupid grin on my face. I was surprised to see Andy's twin sister, Ally, sitting behind the counter. It wasn't unusual for Andy to stop by and hang out while I worked, but Ally rarely came by the shop.

"Hey, what are you doing here?" I asked.

"Waiting for you to show up. I was starting to wonder if you were coming in or not."

I looked up at the clock to see that I still had a few minutes before I was officially working. "I'm not late."

"But you're always earlier than this."

I rolled my eyes. "What's with the interrogation?"

"I saw you on the beach today…with a girl."

Well, shit. I'd been so into watching Emma's every move that I hadn't noticed anyone else around us. "And?"

"Who is she?"

"Does it matter?" I had no idea why Ally cared so much.

"Of course it matters. Do you have a girlfriend that you're not telling us about?"

I laughed. "Is that what this is all about? You think I'm dating someone and keeping it from you and Andy? You're nuts."

"If she's not your girlfriend, then who is she?" Ally asked, her eyes narrowing in suspicion.

"Her name is Emma. She goes to school with me, and she wanted to learn how to surf."

"You're hanging out with one of *them*? I thought you were better than that."

"Oh, give me a break. Emma's nice. She isn't stuck-up, like most of the kids at school."

"Whatever. They're all stuck-up assholes, and you know it."

Ally was one of my favorite people in this world, but she was starting to annoy me. I'd never seen this overprotective side of her, and I didn't like it.

"I'm done with this conversation. Is there another reason you stopped by? Or did you just want to interrogate me?"

"See? You're already acting stuck-up."

I ran my hand down my face in aggravation. Ally needed to leave before I kicked her out. "I need to work. Go."

"Whatever. Just don't forget the little people when you marry the rich princess."

"You say 'whatever' a lot!" I yelled as she walked past me and out the door.

I walked into the employee room and slipped on my work shirt, glad to be rid of her. I loved the girl like a sister, but Emma wasn't her business. Ally had always had a bit of a protective streak with Andy, but now wasn't the time or the place to start acting that way about me.

I spent most of my shift checking in clients and cleaning. I still had an hour to go with nothing to do when Rick yelled for me to come back to where he'd just started setting up with a client.

"You yelled?" I asked as I stuck my head inside the room.

"Yeah, you want to watch?"

"Hell yeah!" I said as I stepped inside the room. I didn't get to come back and watch the guys work very often, and I never turned them down when one of them would ask me.

"Good. Grab a stool, and sit down."

I pulled a stool over next to the guy who was facedown on the table with his shirt off. Rick pulled another stool over and sat down on the opposite side of the guy.

"Jesse, this is Wendell. Wendell, this is Jesse. He works here, and he's hoping to tattoo when he's old enough."

I raised a hand in greeting. "Hey."

"Hey," the guy grumbled.

Okay then. It looked like this guy wasn't up for much conversation.

I got comfortable on my seat as Rick applied the outline, and then he had the guy check it out in the mirror. It was the first good look I'd seen of the guy, and I had to admit that he was scary as fuck. He had a long beard and even longer hair that was tied into a ponytail at the base of his skull. A bandanna covered much of his head. Both of his arms were covered in ink as well as the side of his neck. When he stood next to Rick, he was several inches over Rick's six feet four inches. Between his size and his appearance, he was one scary dude. We never questioned clientele, but I would have bet my paycheck that he was a biker and not the ride-for-fun-on-the-weekends kind of guy. This guy was the hardcore biker-gang type. There were a few of those gangs just north of us, and we saw them from time to time. They always made me nervous, but Rick didn't seem to mind them.

"Look good?" Rick asked.

"Yeah," Wendell said as he settled back onto the table.

It was a cool piece that would take more than one appointment to complete. It was a dragon wrapped around a sword that started at his shoulders and stopped just above his pants line.

I paid close attention as Rick dipped the tip of his gun into the black ink and started the outline. It would take a while to trace it, probably most of this appointment, if not all.

Outlines weren't that hard to do, so I started to get bored as time passed. Wendell never once flinched as the ink went under his skin, even when it was over his spine. I didn't have any tattoos on my back, but I knew a lot of customers would complain of discomfort when they had tattoos in that area. It was the second-worst spot after feet.

Two and a half hours later, the outline was complete. Even without any shading or coloring, it looked amazing. I stood and walked back to the front counter to start closing up as Rick finished with the guy. As soon as he was out the door, I locked it behind him and started shutting off the lights.

"Do you know who that was?" Rick asked.

"Not a clue. Why?"

"That was one of the leaders of the gang a few towns over. He's bad news."

"How do you know?" I asked.

Rick gave me a mysterious smile. "I have my ways. Good night, Jesse."

I had often wondered if Rick was part of some gang, but I never had the guts to ask him. We weren't located in the best part of town, but as far as I knew, there had never been even one break-in. Something told me that had to do with Rick's connections to the gang world. I waved good night as he let me out of the side door before he locked it behind me.

Once I was in my Jeep, I pulled my phone from my pocket to check my messages. I had a few from Andy and one from Emma. She'd sent it while I was watching Rick.

*Emma: Dear Lord, my mother is having some stupid fancy dinner, and
I have to go. Why couldn't you have let me drown? It would've been
kinder.*

Me: That's not funny. Sorry you were stuck at a party all night. :P

She replied back almost immediately.

*Emma: It's not the fun kind of party. I have to pretend I care as these
pompous asshats go over and over their achievements. I'm trying to
think of an excuse to go to bed. I feel a migraine coming on. ;)*

Me: You could always tell them you have a date with a surfer.

Emma: I thought you didn't go on dates.

Me: I don't, but I might make an exception for you.

*Emma: Well…you could always invite me over for dinner tomorrow.
I'll help you deal with your mom's boyfriend.*

I frowned. I refused to think of Mark as my mom's boyfriend. He was
simply some asshole who wanted to visit. I also didn't want Emma to come
to my house. I wasn't ashamed of living in a trailer, but I didn't want to give
her a reason to look down on me.

*Me: As tempting as that is, I can't. We could meet up afterward
though if you want. It'll give me an excuse to leave.*

Emma: Works for me. Want to meet at that burger place again?

Me: Sounds like a plan. Night, Emma.

Emma: Sweet dreams.

Yeah, there was no doubt I would have sweet dreams tonight that would
feature a certain strawberry blonde in them.

My mom knocked softly on my door before opening it. "Jesse, Mark is here."

"Great," I mumbled as I shut off my stereo. *Might as well get this over with.*

I stood and walked down the hallway to the kitchen. Mark and my mom were already sitting at the kitchen table, waiting for me.

Mark stood and held out his hand as I walked to the table. "It's nice to meet you, Jesse."

"Likewise," I lied as I shook his hand and sat down.

I looked him over as he took the seat across from me. He looked out of place in our small trailer. He was wearing a dress shirt with a tie and slacks. I noticed that his shoes were black and polished when I sat down. The guy screamed money, and I instantly disliked him because of it.

"Who wants to say grace?" my mother asked.

I stayed silent. I hated saying grace, but it was something that my mother was adamant about.

"I will," Mark piped up.

"Jesse, bow your head," my mother scolded.

I rolled my eyes as I lowered my head, and Mark started the prayer.

"Heavenly Father, I want to thank you for the blessings we have received, for the food in front of us, for the roof above our head, but most of all, for blessing me with the presence of the beautiful woman beside me. Amen."

I looked up to see my mother blushing. *Give me a break.* This guy was a total suck-up.

"That was wonderful, Mark. Thank you."

"My pleasure," Mark said as he picked up the bowl of salad and used the tongs to put some of it on his plate. "So, your mother tells me that you're enrolled at Hamrick. How do you like it so far?"

"It's fine," I replied, not wanting to discuss my life with this stranger.

"Just fine? People would murder to be enrolled there."

"If they want to be enrolled with a bunch of stuck-up assholes, then it's the place for them. For me, it's boring."

The table went silent. Neither my mother nor Mark knew what to say to that.

"So," my mother said, trying to find something to say, "why don't you tell Jesse what you do, Mark? I'm sure he'd love to hear about it."

"I work as a mine safety inspector. I go into the mines and make sure that everything is up to regulation. I'm usually in West Virginia or Kentucky, but the office brought me out to California for a few months to help them update some of the regulations and train new employees."

"So, you won't be here long?" I asked, hopeful that he would be gone soon so that I didn't have to deal with him.

"I will be here for another month or two, and then I head back to West Virginia."

"I thought people in West Virginia had accents. Why don't you have one?" I asked. I could hear a bit of a twang to his voice, but nothing like they had on TV.

He laughed. "I'm from Northern West Virginia. Our accents aren't as noticeable as people from the Southern part of the state."

"I see. Do you miss home?" I asked, hoping that he did and would decide to go home early.

"I do. I travel a lot, but West Virginia will always be home. I have to admit that this is the farthest I've been away from home, and it's a bit of a shock. It's fall now in West Virginia, and I keep expecting to see the leaves on the trees changing colors."

My mother smiled. "I bet it's beautiful there this time of year."

"It is. You'll have to go there sometime and see it for yourself. We could spend a weekend, just driving around."

"That would be wonderful. I grew up in Kentucky, and I miss seeing the leaves change," my mother said excitedly.

Whoa, wait a minute. Why are they talking about my mom going to West Virginia? It was clear across the country.

"Why would you ever fly all the way over there to look at leaves? Google a few pictures, and call it a day," I grumbled.

"Don't be rude, Jesse."

"What? I'm just saying that it's stupid to go that far away for a weekend. How are you planning on paying for the plane ticket? You have a secret hooker fund that I don't know about?"

"Jesse, enough!" my mother said as she shot daggers at me.

I stayed quiet through the rest of dinner, listening as my mom and Mark told stories about people they worked with. I was bored out of my mind, and I was anxious to meet up with Emma. I'd texted her earlier this morning to tell her to be ready when I texted her tonight. I planned on suddenly remembering that we had a date as an excuse to make a quick escape from Mark.

My mind started to wander back to the beach and Emma, but I snapped back to the real world when Mark mentioned the word *date*. It seemed he was planning on taking my mother someplace fancy the following night.

"Don't you have to work?" I asked my mom.

"I can have Lynette cover for me."

"And lose the money? You know we can't afford to take days off," I replied.

I watched as my mother's face turned pink. I felt bad for embarrassing her, but this guy couldn't walk in here and screw everything up for us. We needed money too bad for my mom to start taking days off.

"I'll figure something out," my mom said.

No, she won't. She'd go out on her date, and our electricity would get shut off or some shit like that.

I turned to look at Mark. "Listen, I'm not trying to be an ass here, but you can't just walk in here and throw everything into chaos. Unlike you, my mom and I can't afford the finer things in life. We have to work constantly to keep this craphole we live in. I don't know what game you're playing with her, but try to remember that as you sweep her off her feet."

"That's enough!" my mother yelled.

She was mad, madder than I'd ever seen her.

"I know that you don't like me, Jesse, but it's not my intention to come in here and then just disappear. I really like your mom, and if you two need money, all you need to do is ask," Mark said calmly.

"No one just hands out money. Try again," I replied.

"If I get to spend more time with your mother, then I'll give you both every dime I have."

I snorted. "Whatever. I'm out of here."

My mother called my name as I grabbed my keys, but I ignored her. I needed to get out of here. I texted Emma and told her to meet me, and then I pulled out of my driveway.

I had to wait a few minutes in Joe's parking lot for her to show up since she had to driver farther than I did. As soon as she pulled in, I hopped out of my Jeep and walked to her door. I opened it and pulled her out. I hugged her as soon as her feet hit the ground.

"Um, hi?" she questioned.

"Don't ask. Let's eat." I'd barely touched my food at home, and I was starving.

"Okay…" she said.

I took her hand and led her into the diner. We sat in the same booth as before. We both stayed silent until after the waitress had come to take our orders.

"I take it the dinner went bad?" she asked.

"Yeah, you could say that. They were talking about leaves and dates and all kinds of bullshit stuff."

"Leaves?"

"Yeah, he wants her to fly to his place in West Virginia, so they can look at the fall leaves or some crap like that. It's complete bullshit. This guy lives thousands of miles away, and he acts like they can have a real relationship. As soon as she falls for him, he's going to pack up and go back home. All he's going to do is hurt her."

"If he wants her to go to West Virginia, maybe he's serious about her. Maybe he wants her to go with him. Did you ever think about that?"

Actually, I hadn't. The thought of her moving all the way across the country for some guy was ridiculous. My mom was smarter than that. I stopped and thought about the way she'd looked at him at dinner. *Maybe she really is that stupid.*

"I don't want to talk about this anymore. How was your party last night?"

She groaned and dropped her head to the table. "It was awful. I could barely fit in the room with all the overly inflated egos in there. At least Todd and Lucy were there with their parents, so I had someone to talk to."

"Todd was there?" I asked.

"Yeah, and it would have been nice if my mom and his mom hadn't tried to play matchmaker all night. And Todd went right along with it. I could have smacked him."

"Do you like him?"

"Todd? Yeah, he's a nice guy. I just wish he'd tell his mom to back off."

"I meant like him as in *like* him. I could have sworn you had a crush on him that first day."

Her face flushed. "I *did* have a crush on him then."

"Did? What changed your mind?"

She picked up her napkin and started shredding it. "You."

"Me? What did I do?"

"You're different, and I don't know. I guess my *like* switched from him to you."

"So, you *like* me?" I teased, but secretly, I was on cloud nine.

"Oh, shut up. I don't need to deal with someone else with an overinflated ego. I have enough of them on my side of town."

"You like me," I sang, causing her to laugh.

"Oh my god. Yes, I like you. Happy?"

"Delirious," I teased as the waitress put our food on the table.

"Why did you kiss me?" she asked as she picked up a fry.

"Why'd you kiss me?"

"Are we back to this again? I didn't kiss you. You kissed me."

"Nope. I put my lips on yours. You did the kissing," I said.

She threw a fry at me. "Fine, I kissed you, but you kissed me the second time."

"True, but we're focusing on the first time."

"Your lips were right there. What did you expect me to do? Lick you?"

"I wouldn't turn you down if you offered."

"Of course you wouldn't. You're a guy."

I just grinned at her as I started eating.

"Stop grinning at me. This isn't funny."

"Actually, it is," I said through a mouthful of food.

"So, we know I *like* you, but you never said if you *like* me."

I looked at her, really looked at her—not at her outside appearance but at the person she was. Contrary to the assumptions I'd made when I first saw her, she wasn't the stuck-up princess that I'd expected. Instead, she was turning out to be one of the sweetest and most down-to-earth people I'd ever met. She didn't care about her parents' money or the fancy parties. She was just a seventeen-year-old girl trying to live a normal life in an unusual situation.

Before this moment, I thought of her in a way that I knew I shouldn't, but it took me until just now, when she'd flat-out asked me, to realize that I actually cared about this girl.

8
EMMA

Apparently, Jesse planned on dragging this out. I waited impatiently as he studied me as if I were a science project coming to life.

"Well, do you?" I asked when I couldn't stand it any longer.

He smiled. "What do you think?"

"If I knew the answer to that, I wouldn't be asking. You're a hard guy to read."

"I have no idea what you're talking about. I'm practically an open book."

I snorted. "Sure you are. Stop avoiding the question."

He leaned back in his chair and looked at me. "I'm not sure what to say to you. I think that if we both felt something, this could go south fast. There are too many people out there who wouldn't like the fact that we were... something more than friends."

"Since when do you care what others think of you?" I countered.

"Oh, I don't. I just don't see you dealing with crap just for me."

"I don't think that we would be able to tell anyone—at least not for a while. I'm seventeen for a little longer, and I have to listen to my mom, or I'm shit out of luck. I don't think my dad would care who I'm with, but he's never around to tell me."

"Neither of us have much of a father figure, do we?" he asked.

"At least I know my dad. Yours kind of just disappeared," I said sadly.

"Don't act so sad about it. As far as I'm concerned, his douchery is a blessing. Would I really have wanted to know a guy who abandoned his family?"

"That's true," I said thoughtfully. "You wouldn't be half the guy you are now if he were around."

"Are you saying I'm a good guy?" he teased.

"I am. Underneath all the tattoos and bad attitude, you're a pretty decent guy."

"Wow. Since we're sharing our feelings and all that warm and fuzzy crap, I guess I'll answer your question."

We'd gotten completely off track, and I hadn't even noticed.

"Here is my vague answer. I think there's something here, but I don't know what it is just yet. Let's just see where this goes, okay?"

That was a fair answer. We were both moving into this too fast, and I didn't think it was a good idea to put a label on whatever we were. I didn't want either of us to feel compelled to make a relationship work if we weren't even sure that we needed to be in one. I wanted to let things go naturally, and take it from there.

"That sounds fair to me," I replied.

"Good. We're both done with our food, so do you want to get out of here? We could hang out at the beach or something."

"Yeah, I'd like that."

I grabbed my purse and threw a few bills on the table to cover our dinner. Jesse didn't look happy about the fact that I had paid for dinner, but I ignored the evil glare he was shooting in my direction as I grabbed his hand and led him from the diner.

"Why don't we take my car, and I'll just drop you off here when we're done?"

He nodded as we walked to my car. "Works for me."

The ride to the beach was the quietest five minutes of my life. Neither of us knew what to say after our little heart-to-heart. We both seemed afraid to say the wrong thing. The silence continued as I parked my car and grabbed two towels out of my trunk.

We walked side-by-side down the beach until I found a spot I was happy with. I handed Jesse his towel, and we put them on the sand next to each other. I felt an awkwardness around us that I wasn't used to, and I didn't like it.

"Okay, this silence sucks. Neither of us should ever be this quiet when we're together," I blurted out.

He laughed. "I like to think of myself as the strong, silent type."

I rolled my eyes. "No one goes for guys like that, regardless of how many romance novels they write about them. At least, I don't. I like someone who actually talks to me."

"You'll never find a guy like that. You'd talk too much for him to get a word in."

I elbowed him as I lay down on my towel. "Shut up, asshat."

He elbowed me back. "Make me."

I knew when I was being challenged, and I *never* backed down from a challenge. Before he knew what I was doing, I sprung off my towel and tackled him to the ground.

I straddled him as I raised my arms in triumph. "I think I just did."

"Are you sure about that?"

"Yes, why?"

In one swift move, he flipped me onto my back. I struggled as he pinned my arms above my head and held my legs down with his own.

"That's why."

"You don't play fair," I grumbled as I continued to struggle.

I was getting nowhere fast. Jesse was a lot stronger than I was.

"And what was fair about you tackling me with no warning?"

"But I'm a girl. I needed the upper hand."

He laughed. "Don't try to play the girl card. It doesn't work with me. Ally used to use it all the time when we were kids, and I learned not to fall for it. She can kick ass, and so can you."

"Who's Ally?" I asked.

"Andy's twin sister. She's like my sister, too. We all grew up together."

"That's cool that you have them. I only had Lucy growing up. Everybody else was always too stuck-up to be any fun."

"Then, I'm glad you had Lucy."

I stopped struggling. He'd won, and we both knew it.

"Okay, you win. Will you let me up?"

He kept one hand on both of mine to hold them in place as he ran his other hand down my arm. I shivered at his touch, and he smiled.

"I kind of like you like this."

"Why's that?" I whispered as he ran his fingertips over my arm.

"You look good underneath me."

I would have thought he was kidding, except a look in his eyes told me he wasn't. There was an emotion in them that was lust mixed with something else I couldn't put my finger on.

"I kind of like it here," I whispered.

He leaned in closer, so his weight was fully on me. It felt good, too good, to have our bodies pressed together like this. I needed him to move before I did something stupid, like kiss him again. There was no way that I would be the one to instigate another kiss.

"That's good to know." He leaned down farther until our lips were almost touching. "I really want to kiss you right now."

"What's stopping you?"

"That little conversation we had earlier. I don't want to kiss you if you don't want me to."

"I never said I didn't want you to kiss me."

I held my breath as he searched my eyes, looking for any doubt or uncertainty. He would find none. I wanted this more than anything in the world. He smiled briefly before his lips touched mine.

When we connected, I saw stars and rainbows and all those other things people in the movies claim to see. Jesse released my arms, and I wrapped them around his neck, pulling him tighter against me, as I deepened the kiss. He ran his tongue along my bottom lip, and I parted them as he slipped his tongue inside.

The sensations running through my body were new to me, and I wasn't sure how to react. Sure, I'd kissed boys before, but those times had been nothing like this. There was an ache between my legs, and I rubbed them together to help ease it. He moaned as my movement caused my lower body to press up into his. *Oh dear God.* I could *feel* him through his pants, and he was hard. That alone caused the ache to become unbearable, and I pushed my pelvis up tighter against him without even realizing what I was doing.

He pulled away, his body coiled tight with tension. "Whoa, we need to stop for a minute."

"I'm sorry. I didn't mean to do that." I took a deep breath, trying to get my control back. My body was humming, and it took everything in me not to pull him back down on top of me.

"I think we got a little out of hand."

"A little?"

"Yeah, a little. Not that I minded, but I don't think you want to get naked on a beach full of people."

I looked around to see that several people surrounded us. No one was paying attention to us, but I was still embarrassed. "Oh my god, I've lost my mind."

"Nah, you just got a little...excited."

I sighed. "New rule—we stay at least ten feet apart in public."

He gave me an evil grin. "What about when we're alone?"

"We'll cross that bridge when we come to it. I think I'd better go home now before that bridge is even within sight."

"Are you scared of me?"

"Truthfully? A little. I'm not scared of *you*, just of what I feel and do when I'm around you."

"I can work with that," he teased as we stood up and grabbed our towels.

"I'm sure you can."

We walked back to my car with several feet between us. I knew I was being silly, but I didn't want to take a chance with him. The things he made me feel weren't normal, and I didn't want to embarrass myself—again.

When I dropped Jesse off by his car, a pretty brunette was standing next to it. I knew instantly that this must be Ally, Andy's twin. Obviously, they couldn't be identical twins, but the resemblance between the two of them was uncanny. She had a slim figure, more soft than toned, unlike mine, but it made her look feminine. Something told me that growing up with Jesse and Andy had made her anything but.

She eyed me suspiciously as I stepped out of the car and followed Jesse to his car. She had nothing to be suspicious of. I just wanted to meet his friend and say hello. I had a feeling that if things kept going in the direction they were with Jesse, then Ally and I would be spending a lot of time together.

"Hey, Ally. What's up?" Jesse asked.

"Your mom sent me to look for you. She said you two got in a fight, and then you wouldn't answer your phone. She was worried."

"I left my phone in the car when we went to the beach. She doesn't need to worry about me. I'm fine."

"You shouldn't make her worry. She was having a full-blown spaz attack."

"I just needed some time to cool off. I'm headed back home now."

"You needed time to cool off, so you called *her*? Did you forget that Andy and I are within walking distance?" Ally sneered as she glanced at me.

It was obvious that she didn't like me already, but I wasn't sure why. I hadn't even said a word to her yet.

"Let it go, Ally," Jesse warned.

"Whatever."

I held out a hand. I was determined not to be bothered by her attitude. "I'm Emma."

"I know who you are. I just don't care."

"Ally, just leave. Now," Jesse growled.

His face had a pink hue to it, and I could tell that he was at his limit. I'd never seen him snap, and I wasn't sure if I wanted to.

"What exactly did I do to make you hate me so much?" I asked.

I'd never met the girl in my life, but she obviously couldn't stand me.

"You haven't done a thing to me yet, rich girl. But let me give you a little warning—you hurt Jesse, and you'd better hope Mommy and Daddy have enough money for a plastic surgeon. You're going to need one after I'm done with you."

I rolled my eyes. "Is that why you don't like me? Because you think I'm going to hurt him? I wouldn't do that to him, so you have nothing to worry about."

"Your kind is all the same. You're selfish and spoiled. You don't give a damn about anyone else, and I thought Jesse knew that but apparently not."

This girl was really starting to piss me off. I never judged anyone based on whether or not they had money or their living situation.

I stepped forward until I was standing inches away from her. "You know what? Screw you. I don't give a damn about what you think. Jesse *knows* what kind of person I am, and that's all that matters. So, you can take your opinions and shove them up your ass."

Ally looked like she was going to claw my eyes out, but Jesse pushed in between us, so she couldn't reach me. I wasn't sure whether I should appreciate the fact that he was trying to protect me or be offended that he thought I needed the protection.

"Okay, why don't we all call it a night before someone loses a limb?" he asked as he looked between the two of us. "Go home, Ally."

"Are you really going to let her talk to me like that?" Ally yelled.

"Go. Home."

She shot me one last glare before turning and getting into her car. She spun her tires as she pulled out of the parking lot.

"Were you trying to get a concussion or what?" Jesse asked as he looked at me with concern.

"What do you mean?

"I love Ally like a sister, but the girl has a mean streak, and she can back it up. I've seen her take down guys my size."

"I can handle myself."

"Not against her. Trust me on this. Just stay away from her, okay?"

"Sure." It wasn't like she went to our school. I could avoid her if I needed to.

"I'm serious."

"I know you are, and I promise not to cross her path any more than I have to."

"Good. I have to say that it was kind of hot that you were willing to get in a girl fight over me."

I rolled my eyes. "Sure it was."

"I'm not kidding."

He stepped closer to me, and I held my breath as he leaned down.

"You're hot when the claws come out."

I opened my mouth to reply, but his lips were on mine before I could say a word. I wasn't complaining though. Kissing Jesse was quickly becoming one of my favorite things to do. He continued to kiss me until I felt breathless. When he finally pulled away, I clung to him to keep from falling.

"Wow. I need to be mean more often."

"Nah, but the occasional outbursts are hot."

I stuck out my tongue. "Gee, thanks. I guess I should probably go home, and I'm sure your mom is waiting for you."

"Joy," he grumbled. "I'll see you tomorrow."

I smiled as I walked to my car. Despite the showdown with Ally, things were looking up.

"Where have you been?" my mother asked as soon as I walked through the door.

"I went out to grab something to eat. Why?"

"You've been gone for hours. You could at least let me know where you are."

"Sorry."

"I'm sure you are. Your dad called while you were out. You need to call him back."

"Okay, I'll go do that right now," I replied.

I'd do just about anything to get away from her suspicious stare. I was horrible at lying, and I wasn't sure how many questions I could answer before I gave myself away.

I walked past her and went up the stairs to my room. I made sure the door was shut before I pulled my phone from my purse and called my dad's number.

"Hey, Emma."

"Hi, Daddy. Mom said you called while I was out."

"Yeah, I did."

"Why didn't you just call my cell phone? You know I try not to stay here anymore than possible."

"Well, I needed to talk to your mother before I talked to you."

That set warning bells off in my head. My mom and dad *never* talked unless they had to.

"What's wrong?"

"Nothing, I promise. It's actually something good."

"Okay…"

"It's been too long since we were together. I asked your mother if you could come out for a weekend, so we could spend time together."

"Seriously? That would be amazing!"

He laughed at the enthusiasm in my voice. "I was hoping you would say that. Your mother said that you have a three-day weekend coming up and that she was fine with you flying over to see me. You can even bring a friend if you want."

Instead of thinking of Lucy like I normally did, my mind went straight to Jesse. I knew my dad would like him and that he would keep him a secret from my mother.

"That sounds great."

"I have to go now, but I'll email you with the details. The label has a private plane you can use to get over here. As soon as I have everything finalized, I'll let you know."

"Thanks. This means a lot to me." And it did.

My dad had been right. It had been far too long since we last saw each other, and I missed him. If I'd had any say in the matter, I would have gone to live with him instead of staying with my mom—even if that meant that I would have to live on a tour bus with a bunch of rock stars and their groupies. I loved my dad *that* much.

"I'll talk to you later, Emma."

"Bye," I said before the call ended.

Things were definitely looking up. Now, all I had to do was get Jesse to agree to go with me.

After listening to my mother yell at me for the better part of an hour, I walked to my room and closed the door behind me. If I had to hear her tell me how rude and immature I was one more time, I was going to throw something. I loved her, but she knew how to lay on the guilt trip pretty heavy.

I was on my bed, staring at the ceiling, when my phone dinged with an incoming text. I grabbed it off the nightstand and unlocked it to see Emma's name flashing across my screen. I smiled as I clicked on the text.

Emma: I want to ask you something...

Me: Go for it...

Emma: Okay. I want you to think this through before you tell me no. My dad is touring in England, and he offered to fly a friend and me out for our three-day weekend. I want you to come with me.

Whoa. I wasn't sure how to reply to something like that. She obviously thought a lot of me since she wanted me to go with her on a trip like this. With an extra day off from school coming up, I'd planned to ask Rick for more hours, but now, I wasn't sure what to do. I needed the extra hours, but I also wanted to get out of this place for a while.

Emma: Your silence is making me nervous.

Me: Sorry, I'm debating. You know I have NO extra cash to pay for tickets or anything like that.

Emma: My dad will fly us out on the label's private plane. All you
need to do is get a passport. I'll cover food while we're there.

This just kept getting better and better. I didn't like the fact that Emma
would be paying for me, but I couldn't pass up a chance like this. I'd never be
able to afford something like this, even in my wildest dreams.

Me: Okay, I'm in. I have to clear it with my mom, but normally, she
doesn't care if I go somewhere.

Emma: Yeah, that's probably a good idea. I'm sure she doesn't care if
you go to the beach, but another country might be a different story.

Me: I'll talk to her tomorrow about it. She's pissed at me right now for
what I said to Mark and because I took off.

Emma: I suggest sucking up for a day or two, and then ask her. Just
use that charm of yours, and she can't say no.

Me: I have charm? :-D

Emma: You're impossible. Night, Jesse. <3

Me: Night.

I smiled at the little heart that she'd put at the end. I knew it was stupid,
but I couldn't help it. It wasn't like I'd ever admit to her that it made me
happy. I still had some guy pride after all.

I didn't know where things between us were going, but I wanted to find
out.

I wasn't sure how I was supposed to act around Emma at school. I knew
that we had to keep our *friendship* quiet from her mother, so I assumed that we
had to act like nothing had changed over the weekend. It sucked, but I

understood why she needed to keep things quiet. She was trying to protect both of us from her mom. I'd never met the woman, and I didn't want to. Emma was the type who liked everyone, and the resentment she had for her mother told me all I needed to know about her.

I pulled into the parking lot and stepped out of my Jeep right as Emma was pulling in. I started walking slowly toward the school, giving her a chance to catch up to me if she wanted to. Sure enough, I heard footsteps behind me a few seconds later. I looked over at her as she caught up to me.

"Hey."

She grinned. "Hey. How was your weekend?"

"Kind of boring."

"Oh, really? Nothing exciting?"

"Nope, just the usual. I took some hot girl to the beach and tried to teach her how to surf, but she was just like all the others. She kept getting distracted by my abs, so she kept falling off the board. It was actually kind of funny just how clumsy she was. She did have one thing going for her though."

"And what was that?"

"She looked way better in a bikini than most girls."

"Well, I'm glad to hear she had that at least."

This teasing was fun. I was always stressed with school or my mom's money situation, and Emma could make all of that disappear with just a smile.

"So, how was your weekend?" I asked.

"It was fun. I met this hot surfer guy, but he ended up being this egomaniac who I couldn't stand. He even kissed me without my permission."

"What a douche bag."

"He was."

I pulled her off the sidewalk to a spot where it wasn't so out in the open. I looked around to make sure no one was watching. When I was sure that we were safe, I leaned in closer and whispered into her ear, "It's too bad that you think he was a douche bag."

"Why is that?" she whispered back.

I ran my tongue along her ear, and she shuddered.

"Because if you liked him, he could do that and so much more."

"What else does he have in mind?" she asked breathlessly.

I stepped back and grinned. "He can get pretty creative when he wants to."

I wasn't one of those guys who was with a different girl every night, but I *did* have experience when it came to sex. I'd been with a handful of girls since I started high school, and I'd learned a lot about girls and what they wanted. I had no idea how experienced Emma was, but I knew that I wanted to find out.

"Emma! What are you doing over there?" a voice shouted from a few feet away.

I stepped away from Emma just as Lucy was walking up to us. Her eyes widened as she noticed me standing there, too.

"Oh, hi, Jesse. I didn't see you there."

"Hey, Lucy," I said casually. *That girl has the worst timing.*

"We were just…talking," Emma said lamely.

She needed to learn to lie better if she planned to keep me as her dirty little secret.

Lucy grinned. "What were you *talking* about? It must have been something good because you're blushing."

"Uh…" Emma started.

"I was asking Emma if she could help me with an assignment Ms. Mason assigned to us," I lied flawlessly.

Lucy studied me carefully. "You know, you're an excellent liar. If Emma wasn't six shades of red, I would have believed you."

I grinned. "Maybe she was blushing because she was nervous around me."

Emma snorted. "Ego much?"

"We'd better get to class." I stepped back onto the sidewalk and started walking toward the school.

Emma and Lucy followed behind me, and I could hear Lucy whispering to Emma.

"When we're alone, you're *so* telling me what just happened."

I rolled my eyes as I made my way through the doors and down the hall to the classroom. There was no way that Emma could lie to Lucy. Hopefully, Lucy could be trusted not to blab to the rest of the school.

I ignored Emma through first period since Lucy kept watching us. I didn't want to make Lucy anymore suspicious than she already was in case Emma was going to try to lie to her.

Emma was forced to ignore me in second period because Todd was keeping her attention on him as he passed note after note to her. I gritted my teeth every time one fell on her desk. I was sitting right beside her, and I couldn't do a damn thing about it.

She wasn't mine to claim—at least, not yet. If something happened between us, she would need to get used to the idea of me protecting what was mine. *Mine? Shit.* I was already thinking that she was mine when she wasn't.

I had no idea what the hell was wrong with me, but this wasn't how I normally acted. People came and went in life, and I refused to form attachments to any of them—with the exception of Ally and Andy. I was safer that way. No one could hurt me if I didn't care. I mean, look at my mom. Even now, years after my dad had left us, I knew she still missed him. There was no way that I would give someone that kind of power over me.

When the bell rang, I grabbed my books, and I all but ran from the room. I did not want to see Emma and Todd talking together. It would bring out jealousy that I didn't even know I had inside me. It was one of those things I was better off not knowing.

I was one of the first people in line for food when I got to the cafeteria. After I paid, I walked to my usual table. Sean and Charles weren't anywhere to be seen, and I was glad. Even though I'd been sitting at this table since my first day, I rarely spoke to either of them. They were nice and all, but we had nothing in common.

My phone vibrated in my pocket, and I pulled it out to see a text from Emma.

Emma: Where'd you run off to so fast?

Me: I was hungry.

Emma: Oh, okay. The way you left class, I thought you were mad at me or something. Do you want to sit at my table? I don't think anyone would mind.

Me: Do you think that's a good idea? I thought you were hiding me.

Emma: I guess you're right. I didn't even think.

I put my phone back in my pocket, not bothering to respond. I was irritated, and I didn't want to yell at her, so it was better if I stayed away. I finished my food before Sean and Charles even showed up.

I dropped off my tray and walked out of the cafeteria, passing right by Emma's table. She was sitting with a few of the other cheerleaders, and of course, Todd was sitting in the seat beside her. She gave me a small smile, but I ignored it. I walked through the hallways, trying to kill time before my next class.

The school was small enough that everyone had lunch at the same time, so the halls were completely empty. I was enjoying that simple little pleasure when I heard footsteps behind me. I had wandered to the opposite side of the school from the cafeteria, so I assumed it was a teacher.

Two hallways later, the footsteps were still behind me. Feeling slightly annoyed with my followers, I turned to see who it was. Todd and two of his friends were at the other end of the hallway.

"You guys need something?" I asked, not bothering to hide my annoyance.

Todd waited until they were closer before answering. "Yeah, actually, I do. I want you to stay the hell away from Emma."

"What are you talking about?"

"I've seen the way you watch her," Todd growled as he stepped closer to me.

His two buddies followed him, and they surrounded me. This wasn't going to end well for any of us. I doubted I would win a fight since I was outnumbered, but I'd be sure to get in a few good hits before they took me down. The Todd I'd seen with Emma was gone, and a raging asshole was standing in front of me. I *knew* there was a reason I didn't like him. He was finally showing his true colors.

"I have no idea what you're talking about," I said casually as I tried to figure out which guy I should hit first if they came at me. I wanted Todd, but that would be the obvious choice. I needed to take out his buddies and go for him last—if I could make it that far. Judging by the size of all three guys, my chances were slim.

"Don't pretend that you don't want her. I can see it every time you two are in the same room. This is your one and only warning, trailer trash. Stay away from Emma. She's mine."

So much for my plan to go for Todd last. As soon as I heard the words *trailer trash*, I saw red. I drew back and threw all my weight into a punch. I hit my target, and I heard a sickening crunch as his nose broke.

He howled in pain as he clutched his face. "You son of a bitch. You're going to pay for that."

One of his friends charged me. The guy was big, but he had no idea how to fight, and I dodged him easily. He turned to charge me again, but before he could, I slammed my fist into his face. I didn't break his nose, but I definitely slowed him down. Before he could recover, I grabbed his head and yanked it down as my knee came up.

When he dropped to the ground, I turned to the other guy. He didn't look as sure of himself as he had just a few minutes ago. He hesitated for a split second before turning and darting down the hallway. *Coward.*

Since the first guy was incapacitated on the ground, that left just Todd and me to settle things. I turned back to him, and he started walking backward down the hall, trying to escape me.

"Where are you going?" I taunted. "I thought I was going to pay."

"You're fucking nuts!" he shouted.

"What is going on here?" a voice screeched from behind me.

I cursed under my breath as Ms. Mason ran toward us. *I am so screwed.* Unlike these assholes, I was here on a scholarship, and they could take that away from me any time they wanted to.

"Ms. Mason! Thank God! My friend and I were walking down the hall, and he just attacked us. He's crazy!" Todd yelled.

"You're fucking lying. Your *two* friends and you tried to corner me. You're just pissed off that you couldn't take me down even though you outnumbered me."

"Enough!" Ms. Mason yelled. "Both of you, follow me to the office now."

We followed her as she hurried through the hallways. The secretary looked up and gasped when she saw us.

"Call an ambulance immediately. James Thrones is knocked out in the English hallway!" Ms. Mason yelled as she stomped past the secretary.

She knocked on the principal's door before throwing it open. "We have a serious problem, Principal Thompson. These two and another student were brawling out in one of the hallways."

Principal Thompson was older, probably in his mid-sixties, but he had an air of authority about him that made him seem younger and even a bit scary. He was around six feet tall with a lean build and a thin mustache that was as white as his hair.

"Son, I think your nose is broken," he said as he looked Todd over.

"I believe it is, sir," Todd said as he grabbed a few tissues off the desk to wipe away the blood.

"I had Lauren call an ambulance for the other boy. He's knocked out cold," Ms. Mason said.

"Todd needs looked at, too. Why don't you take him out so that he can get that taken care of? I'll deal with him later," Principal Thompson said.

Great. That meant that it would be just the two of us to battle it out. Ms. Mason herded Todd out the door. Principal Thompson waited to turn to me until she closed the door behind her.

"Want to tell me what happened?" he asked.

"We got into a fight. There were three of them and one of me. Imagine their shock when I actually won."

"Who started it?"

"They did. I left lunch early, and they waited to approach me until I was on the other side of the school." Maybe if I stayed calm and told the truth, he would believe me. I wasn't holding out much hope though.

"And what was the reason they started this fight with you?"

I hesitated. If I told him it was over Emma, he might call her in or call her mom. I decided to go with the truth, but I'd leave her name out of it.

"It was over a girl. He thought I was interested in the same person as him."

"And who is she?"

"I'd prefer to keep her out of this. He had his facts wrong. I have no interest in her."

He watched me carefully for a moment. "Fair enough. Now, here is my problem. There are two of them—"

"Three. There were three, but one ran when he figured out that his friends weren't doing too well."

"Who was he?"

"I have no idea."

"I see. Well, if Todd and James both say they were the only two involved, there's nothing I can do about the third one. Anyway, here is my problem. There are two of them and one of you, and I'm sure they will have the same story. Do you see where I'm going with this?"

"Two against one, so I'm automatically the bad guy. Why did you even ask me what happened? What I say doesn't matter anyway."

"It always matters, but in this case, it won't be enough. Was there anyone else around?"

I shook my head. "Nope. They waited until we were completely alone."

"This looks bad for you. You're here on a scholarship, and you fought with two private-pay students. Both of those students are on the varsity football team, and they have never been in any kind of trouble."

"Look, I know I'm in trouble. Just tell me what my sentence is," I said, not bothering to hide my anger. I didn't see the point in staying calm when I was going to be persecuted anyway?

He stared at me. "You're telling the truth, aren't you?"

"Yeah, I am."

"I believe you, but it doesn't change anything. Todd's father gives several generous donations a year, and the board will have my head if I don't punish you. I'm going to suspend you for a week."

That wasn't as bad as I'd expected. I'd walked into this room assuming that I would be expelled. I could live with being suspended for a week.

"Thank you," I said.

"I just suspended you. Most students don't thank me for that."

I laughed. "We both know you could have done a lot worse. Will either of them get in trouble?"

He shook his head. "Doubtful. I'll have to talk to the board before I do anything to either of them."

I'd assumed as much, so his words hadn't surprised me. I stood and walked to the door. There was no reason for me to hang around here. Maybe if I were lucky, Rick would give me a few extra hours at the shop since my schedule had just opened up.

"Jesse..." Principal Thompson called as I opened his door.

"Yeah?"

"I grew up in the same park where you live in now. Don't let your roots control where you end up in life."

I was speechless for a minute. *The principal was from my trailer park?* I didn't see that coming.

"Thanks."

I kept my head low as I walked down the hall. There were students everywhere, and they were all giving me the same cold glare. I ignored the whispers as I walked by. I knew they were talking about me, but I really didn't give a fuck. I'd never belonged here, and this just solidified it to everyone. I walked outside and down the sidewalk to the parking lot. I tensed as I heard footsteps approaching rapidly from behind me.

"Jesse!" Emma called.

"Go back inside, Emma."

"What happened? Everyone is saying that you attacked Todd and James. I told them all that they're wrong. You wouldn't do something like that."

"Just go back inside!" I yelled as I turned to face her.

"Kiss my ass! I'm not going anywhere until you tell me what happened."

"Fine. You stay right where you are, but I'm out of here." I walked to my Jeep and got in.

She ran to the passenger door and jumped in beside me. "Oh no, you don't!"

"Emma, just let it go."

"Please talk to me. I want to help," she pleaded.

"Fine. You want to know what happened?"

She nodded.

"Todd and two of his buddies attacked me. I won, but it's my word against theirs. Of course, they're going to lie, so I'm suspended."

"Why would they do something like that?" she asked.

"Apparently, Todd doesn't like the way I watch you."

"*What?*" she shrieked.

"Yep. They attacked me over you."

"Oh my god, I don't even know what to say. You're okay, aren't you?"

"I'm fine."

"I'm so sorry, Jesse. I have no idea why Todd did that."

"Because he wants you."

She looked down at her lap. "I didn't know. I mean, I think I knew he was interested, but I never thought he cared enough to do something like this."

"I don't know how you missed it. I even knew it."

"It doesn't change anything with us."

"Who said there was an *us?*" I asked. I winced at my words. *That was harsh.*

"Do you want there to be an *us?*" she asked.

Do I? I had no clue. I just didn't want to leave this beautiful girl alone. I wasn't even sure if I could. *Didn't I try to ignore her at first?* For some reason, I couldn't, and that worried me. I didn't want to get attached to her.

"Your silence says everything that you aren't," Emma said as she started to open the door to get out.

I leaned over and grabbed her wrist. "I don't know *what* I want. I don't do *this.*"

"What is *this* exactly?" she asked.

"Fuck. I don't know."

"Are you scared of me?"

I shook my head. "No, I'm not scared of you. I just don't get close to people."

"You're afraid to get too close because you don't want me to hurt you. Let me tell you something though—I'm not going to hurt you."

"Maybe not on purpose."

She shook her head. "Nope, not even by accident. For some reason, we're under each other's skins, and I want to find out why. I think we should try this and see where it goes."

"What is *this* exactly?" I mocked her.

"Dating."

"How do you plan on *dating* if we can't even tell anyone about us?"

"I'll figure that out later. I just want to know that when you leave here, you're not going to go to some other girl. I want to stake my claim on you."

What the hell am I supposed to say to that? If I agreed to this, I was sure that we would crash and burn eventually. How could we not when there is so much against us?

"Emma—" I started.

She stopped me by leaning over and kissing me. She always let me take control when we kissed but not this time. Instead, she palmed the back of my head and held my mouth against hers as she slipped her tongue between my lips. When she flicked her tongue against mine, I growled. I'd actually growled. *Fuck it. She's mine.*

I pulled away. "Damn it, Emma."

"What?" she asked innocently.

Innocent my ass. "Fine, you want to stake your claim on me? Go for it, but it works both ways. If I see Todd touch you, I'll break his arm."

She grinned. "Fair enough. I'll deal with Todd, I promise. He won't bother you again."

"We'll see about that," I grumbled.

The guy was an ass, and I knew he wouldn't leave her alone just because she asked.

"I need to go," Jesse hinted as I stared at him.

"Right. Of course. I'll text you later," I said as I stepped out of his Jeep.

He waved as he backed out of the parking spot, and then he drove away.

This was a mess. Jesse was suspended, and it was all my fault. Todd had attacked him over me. I had no idea what Todd had thought he'd gain from that, but it sure as hell had backfired. I was going to kill him the next time I saw him. Although, from what people were saying about the fight, I wasn't sure that anything I would do was going to matter. Jesse had knocked James out, and Todd's nose had been broken. I knew I should feel bad for them, but I didn't. They'd brought this on themselves.

Since we only had one class left for the day, I decided to just skip and go home. Hopefully, my mom wouldn't be there, and if she were, I'd just drive around for a while. I pulled out of the lot without anyone noticing me.

When I arrived home, I was relieved to see that my mom's car wasn't parked outside or in the garage. I parked my car in the garage and walked up to my room.

I powered on my computer to give it time to start up as I changed out of my school clothes and into something more comfortable. After sending Lucy a quick text to let her know that I was "sick" and wouldn't be at cheer practice, I sat down in front of my computer. I checked my Facebook and

Twitter accounts first before signing into my email account. A huge grin
stretched across my face when I saw an email from my dad.

> *Emma,*
>
> *I talked to the label, and they have no problem flying you out. My pilot
> for my personal plane is on vacation this month, or I'd have him do it.*
>
> *Anyway, you know the drill. The plane is at LAX, and your flight is
> scheduled for eight in the morning on Thursday. I know that you'll miss
> a day of school, but I want to have enough time with you. Plus, I'm sure
> you'll be jet-lagged when you arrive, and you'll need a good night's sleep.
> I told them that you would have another passenger with you as well.*
>
> *I have a show that night, but I have a car scheduled to pick you up and
> take you to your hotel room here in London. The room has already been
> paid for, and it is in my name.*
>
> *If you have any questions, call me. I'll see you Friday morning.*
>
> *Love,*
>
> *Dad*

I frowned. With Jesse getting in trouble today at school, I seriously
doubted that his mom would let him come with me. I needed to think of
something fast, or I'd be flying to London on my own. As I sat there, trying
to figure out a way to get him to London, my bedroom door opened, and my
mother walked in.

"Emma, I saw your car in the garage. What are you doing home already?"
she asked.

"I wasn't feeling well, so I left early."

"I completely understand."

I gave her a confused look. "Understand what?"

"Todd's mom called and told me what happened today. I would have left early, too. I'm sure you were upset over that."

I rolled my eyes. "I wasn't upset because Todd got his nose broken. Actually, he deserved it for starting that fight."

"What are you talking about? He didn't start the fight. That horrible scholarship boy did. I told the board that it was a mistake to create that scholarship program, and look, I was right."

"Why was it a mistake? It gave kids who can't afford tuition a chance at a better education. It's the best thing that the school has done in a long time."

"We don't want our children associating with those kids. They don't belong there. Of course, the board still won't listen. They refuse to kick out those kids," she said with a sour look on her face.

"How are we even related?" I asked.

I had no clue how this woman could possibly be my mother. We had nothing in common, and we never saw eye-to-eye on anything.

"Don't get smart with me. I have no idea where you get your opinions from—probably that father of yours. He could never understand why I would get upset when he would sign autographs and such when we were out. We are better than those people."

"Are you even listening to yourself talk? We are not better than anyone. Everyone is equal, regardless of how much money they have."

Flames flashed in her eyes. I'd really pissed her off now.

"You listen to me, Emma. You are *not* to talk to those kids who are part of that scholarship program. If I find out that you're friends with any of them, I'll pull you from the cheer team."

"So what? Do it," I said as I returned her glare. "You might be stuck-up, but I'm not."

I grabbed my keys, and I ran from the room. I could hear her yelling as she followed me through the house, but I had too much of a head start for her to catch up.

I was already in my car and pulling away from the house by the time she made it to the bottom of the driveway. *Screw her.* There was no way that I was going to let her push her ridiculous values on me.

I drove around town aimlessly as I tried to control my temper. My mom already hated Jesse, and she didn't even know his name. *What would she do if she ever found out that I'm not only friends with him, but I've kissed him as well?*

After driving for over an hour, I steered my car toward Jesse's side of town. I had no idea where he lived, but I did know where he worked. Hopefully, he had to work tonight because I needed to be around him right now, and he wasn't answering any of my texts.

I pulled into a space in Rick's parking lot. After making sure that my car was locked, I walked into the shop. There was no one around, so I stood nervously at the counter. A few seconds later, a guy came out of the back.

"Can I help you?" he asked.

"Is Jesse here?"

He eyed me suspiciously. "No. Why?"

This guy was obviously protective of Jesse. It was nice to see someone looking out for him. He always seemed so alone and closed-off from the world.

"I'm his...I'm Emma. I go to school with him, and I needed to talk to him."

"I sent him home early. I'm not sure where he's at."

"Oh."

"I would try his house or maybe the beach. He's usually at one of the two. The kid doesn't get out much."

"Can you tell me where he lives? I've never been there."

He shook his head. "No can do, kiddo. If Jesse hasn't told you where he's at, I'm not about to."

"Please," I pleaded. "I really need to see him. I swear I'm not some weird stalker or anything."

"Do you know what happened to him today?" he asked.

"I do."

"Care to fill me in? I've never seen him so pissed off."

"He got into a fight with two guys over…over me."

He raised an eyebrow. "Jesse doesn't fight over girls."

"Well, he did this time. Please tell me where he is."

He sighed. "If I tell you and he gets pissed—"

"He won't. I swear. If he gets mad, I'll tell him I forced you to tell me."

He laughed. "I'm sure you could force me. All right, listen. When you leave here, go left. In about five miles, start looking for signs for the Santa Monica Trailer Park. His house number is thirty-two."

I could have kissed him. "Thank you so much."

"No problem. Now, get out of here, and go cheer the kid up."

I followed his directions as I went deeper into the poverty part of town. When I pulled into the trailer park, my stomach dropped. While some of the trailers weren't that bad, others looked like they were falling apart. I prayed that Jesse wasn't in one of those as I searched for the one labeled thirty-two. When I saw it, I let out a sigh of relief. His house wasn't the nicest, but it also wasn't one of the ones falling apart.

I parked my car beside his Jeep and stepped out. Gravel crunched under my feet as I walked up the driveway. His trailer had a small porch with several hanging baskets. I stepped up onto the porch and knocked on the door. No one came, so I knocked again, louder this time. A few seconds later, the door opened, and there stood Jesse, shirtless and barefoot, wearing only a pair of shorts.

"Emma? What are you doing here?" he asked, his voice thick with sleep.

"I'm sorry to bother you. I just wanted to check on you. Plus, I got into another fight with my mom. I needed to get away."

"How did you even find me?" he asked in horror.

I had no idea why he was so upset that I had shown up on his doorstep. "Um, the guy at the tattoo place gave me directions. Can I come in?"

"I don't think that's such a good idea."

My heart squeezed painfully in my chest. *He must have someone in there with him.* That had to be why he was so upset that I'd just randomly shown up.

"I didn't mean to interrupt anything. I'll leave now." I turned to walk back down the steps as tears stung my eyes. *Why did we even have that conversation in his car if he planned on doing this to me?* It had only been a few hours, and he'd already betrayed me.

"What? Wait, Emma. It's not what you think!"

He grabbed me and pulled my body up against his. I tried to shove him away, but he held me in place.

"Stop struggling, and let me explain."

"I don't want to hear it, Jesse. Just let me go."

"Not with you thinking that I have a girl in here."

He pulled us both inside his house. He actually picked me up enough, so my feet weren't touching the ground as he walked down a narrow hallway and stopped in front of a door.

"This is my room. There's no one in here."

He released me, and I turned to look at him.

"If there's no one here, why didn't you want me to come in?"

He walked past me into his room and sat down on his bed. "I didn't want you to know where I lived, period."

"But why?"

"Because I live in a fucking trailer while I'm sure you're in a damn mansion. I don't want you to look down on me."

"Are you crazy? I'd never look down on you. I thought you knew that by now." I walked into the room and over to where he was sitting on the bed. I stopped when I was standing between his legs. "I don't care where you live."

He looked away from me. "Sure you don't."

"I don't." I grabbed his chin and pulled his face up to look at me. "All I care about is you."

I leaned down and kissed him. It was a gentle kiss, and I hoped it showed my sincerity. I didn't care that he lived in a trailer. I wouldn't care if he lived in a tent.

"What was that for?" he asked when I pulled away.

"No reason at all. I just wanted to."

"Come here," he said as he leaned back on his elbows.

"I can't get any closer," I teased.

"I bet you can."

He sat up and grabbed me. I squealed as he pulled me down onto the bed with him. I straddled him as he grinned up at me.

"I told you we could get you closer."

"I guess you were right." I leaned down and brushed his hair from his eyes.

"I'm always right."

"Mmhmm, sure you are."

He reached up and ran his hand across my cheek. I was positioned just right on top of him, so I could tell that he was aroused. I'd never been in this position with a guy before, and I was nervous. I didn't come here for *that*, and I wasn't sure what he was expecting from me.

"Why are you so nervous?" he asked. "Your entire body is rigid."

"I'm not nervous," I lied.

"Bull. What's wrong?"

I sighed. *This is going to be awkward.* "I'm not sure what you expect from me when we're together like this."

"Are you talking about sex?" he asked.

"Yeah."

"Look, I don't expect anything from you. I also don't think we need to have sex if you can't even say the word to me."

My face turned bright red. I was so embarrassed by all of this, and he was not helping.

"No way," he said.

"What?" I asked.

"You're a virgin."

He'd said it as a statement, not a question. He already knew, and there was no sense in trying to deny it.

"I am."

He smiled as he pulled me down and kissed me. "That's so cute."

"How is that cute? I feel like an idiot right now."

"It's a nice change."

If that wasn't a mood killer, I didn't know what was. "So, after that comment, I think it's safe to say that you're not."

"No, I'm not. Does that bother you?" he asked.

"I don't know. Yes."

"Why?"

He was enjoying this far too much.

"Because I have no experience when it comes to that stuff, and you do."

"I could teach you if you want." He winked, actually winked, at me.

"I'm sure you could," I grumbled. *I'm so out of my league with him.*

He rolled me off of him and pinned me to the bed with his body. "It's pretty simple once you get into it."

"I'm sure it is."

"No, seriously. Just watch."

"Jesse—"

He silenced me with a kiss. "Just watch."

He kissed a trail from my lips to my ear. I sucked in a breath as he probed his tongue into my ear. Before now, if someone had told me that it was hot to do that, I would have laughed. But when Jesse was doing it…*dear God*. It was the most erotic thing I'd ever felt.

"It's all about the kissing…and where you kiss." He bit down on my earlobe. "And biting."

His lips slipped farther down as he kissed and licked his way to my collarbone. My body was coiled tight in anticipation of where I'd feel his lips next.

"And it's about touch. You have to explore until you find those certain spots that make the person go wild."

His hands roamed down my sides and slipped to the bottom of my tank top. He raised it up until the hem was sitting just under my bra. My body jumped as his fingers skimmed across my stomach. His lips followed soon after, and I moaned as my body came alive. Everywhere he touched, it was like my skin was on fire.

His hands traveled down to my hips. He rubbed small circles across them as he pulled my shorts down just a bit. My body was humming, and that ache between my legs was back. I didn't care what he did at this point. I was enjoying it all too much.

His lips slowly ascended the length of my body. He kissed between my breasts, just close enough to them to drive me nuts, and then he finally trailed his lips up to my neck.

"See what I mean?"

"What was the question?" I asked.

I looked up to see him smiling at me.

"I think that's enough for one night. Next time, I'll teach you the basics of undressing."

I sat up and did something I never thought I'd do. I pulled off my tank top. I could see the shock on his face. He hadn't expected me to do something like that.

"I think I have the basics down."

"What are you doing?" he asked as he stared at my chest.

I thanked the heavens above that I'd worn my favorite Victoria's Secret bra today that made my boobs look awesome. From the way Jesse was staring at them, I could tell that he agreed.

"Showing you that I need the advanced class for undressing. I have the basics down."

"You should put your shirt back on," he said as he looked up at my face.

"Why? Is it bothering you?" I knew that it was. I could feel the hard length of him pressed against my hip.

"Nope."

"Are you sure?" I asked.

"Yep." His eyes were back on my chest.

I took a deep breath as I reached around behind me and undid the snaps on my bra. He sucked in a breath as it fell away from my body.

"Jesus, Emma. What are you trying to prove?"

"You said it wasn't bothering you, so I don't see what the issue is."

"I'm a guy, and I have a really hot half-naked girl in my bed. I'm about to bust the seam of my shorts."

"How is that my problem?" I teased.

It was nice to be on this side of the conversation for once. I felt completely awkward and embarrassed by doing this, but I wasn't about to tell him that.

He pushed me down until I was flat on my back again. "It's definitely your problem."

The fire in his eyes told me he wasn't kidding. By teasing him, maybe I'd bitten off more than I could chew.

"Jesse—"

"Oh no. Don't *Jesse* me after you did this…" He grabbed my hand and ran it across his length. "To me."

His mouth was on mine then, and I lost all my reservations about the position I was now in. The sensation of his bare chest rubbing against mine made the ache between my legs almost unbearable. I pushed my body up tighter against him as I wrapped my legs around his waist. His hardness was right where I was aching, and I ground my hips against him to get some relief. Instead of soothing, the movement only made it worse.

Jesse pulled his lips from mine. "Don't do that, or I really won't be able to stop."

"I can't help it. I feel like I'm going to explode."

"You will if you keep that up. Have you ever had an orgasm before?"

I shook my head. "No."

"Why don't we take care of that?"

His voice was deeper, and I knew he was trying to control himself.

"I'm not ready to have sex," I told him honestly. I wanted to—*god, I want to*—but I couldn't. I had no idea how I would find the willpower to make him stop, but I had to. I didn't want him to think I was easy.

"You don't have to have sex to have an orgasm. I bet I can make you come without even taking off your shorts."

"How?" I asked.

"You'll find out. I promise I won't push you for sex, but I need something, or I'm going to go insane. Is that okay?"

I nodded. "I trust you."

"Good."

With that, he went to work. He wasted no time with the small kisses from earlier. Instead, he lowered his head and ran his tongue across both my nipples. My body came up off the bed as a moan escaped my mouth.

"Keep making those sounds. They're a total turn-on," he said just before he pulled my nipple into his mouth and sucked on it.

The ache between my legs was completely unbearable now. I tried to grind my hips against his, but he'd angled his body, so I couldn't. With a mind all their own, my fingers slid down between my legs, and I pressed where I was aching. I made small circling motions as I pushed down, feeling a tiny amount of relief from the ache.

"Fuck. Are you playing with yourself?" Jesse asked after he released my nipple with a *pop*.

"No, I just couldn't stand the ache. I had to do something."

"Your hand is between your fucking legs. You're playing with yourself."

"Is that bad?" I asked. I had no idea what I was doing.

"No, it's fucking hot. I wish we could take off your shorts, but we can't. If you're completely naked, I won't be able to stop."

I pulled my hand away, feeling vulnerable and stupid. "I didn't do it on purpose. I'm sorry if it made things harder for you. I wasn't trying to tease you by doing that."

"It's hot, Emma. I'd love to see you completely naked and doing that. I want you to promise me something."

"What?"

"I want to watch you do that one day. Promise me that I can watch."

My face couldn't possibly turn any redder. "Are you serious?"

"Yeah, I am." He leaned down and flicked his tongue across my nipple. "Promise me?"

"I...I don't know," I whispered as electricity shot through my body.

He ran his tongue from one nipple to the other and then down my stomach. "Promise me."

"Jesse..."

"Fine, I guess I'll have to convince you." He reached between my legs, and his thumb rubbed that one spot through my shorts.

My hips bucked. "Oh my god."

His lips covered my nipple, and he sucked on it as his thumb continued to circle. I spread my legs wider as I grabbed his hair with both of my hands.

"Oh my god. Okay, okay. I promise."

Instead of stopping, he sucked harder, and softly bit down as his thumb pressed harder. I lost control of my body as my hips thrust up, and I held his head tightly against my chest. I screamed as my body exploded around me. I'd never experienced anything like it, and I clung to him until I finally drifted back to reality.

He lifted his head to grin at me. "Too bad we didn't put money on that bet. I just gave you your first orgasm. I accept cash and checks."

"Wow. I can't handle your smart-ass comments at the moment."

"I told you I could do it."

He was far too excited over this for a guy who still hadn't gotten off.

"What about you?" I asked.

"What about me?"

"You didn't...you know."

"You're so innocent."

"You do realize you just said that to the girl who's currently lying half-naked in your bed, right?"

"I do. You're innocent, and I like it. I feel like I'm corrupting you."

"You are," I said as I pushed him off of me.

When he was flat on his back, I climbed on top of him. I was still sensitive down there, and I shuddered when I felt him pressing against me.

"What are you doing?"

"I'm not going to leave you hanging after that."

"You don't have to—"

"I know. I want to."

I leaned down and kissed his lips first. Then, I repeated what he'd done to me. I kissed his neck and bit his earlobe before moving down to his nipples. When I ran my tongue over them, he shuddered. I considered that a good sign, so I took my time with each one, biting and licking until he was moaning. I licked a trail down his stomach, but I stopped when I got to his shorts. I had no idea what I was doing, and I wasn't about to try my luck with licking down there just yet. *Baby steps.*

I sat up and scooted back, so I could pull his shorts down slowly, inch by inch. When they were far enough down, I took a deep breath and grabbed his shaft. This was my first up-close-and-personal with a guy, but he seemed kind of big. I had no idea how *that* was supposed to fit inside me. I ran my hand along it carefully, afraid to hurt him. I knew guys were sensitive there, and I didn't want to cause him any pain.

"You sure about this?" he asked.

"I am. Just tell me what to do. I have no idea what I'm doing."

He smiled. "You don't have to be that gentle. I'm not going to break."

I did as he said and tightened my grip on his shaft as he groaned again.

"Squeeze as you go."

I squeezed lightly, and he made a sound that instantly turned me on again. I continued running my hand up and down his shaft, squeezing occasionally just so he'd make that sound again. From the way he was responding, I seemed to be doing it right. Feeling braver, I leaned down and ran my tongue across the head.

His body arched off the bed. "Holy fuck!"

I smiled as I repeated the action, and he balled his hands into fists.

"Emma, you need to move. Now."

"Why?" I asked, immediately thinking that I'd gone too far.

"Because I'm about to come, and I don't want it to go all over you."

I laughed as I sat up. "What a gentleman."

"I try. You might want to move your hand."

"It's fine," I said as I started stroking him faster.

His body twitched as he came all over my hand. I wasn't grossed out, like I'd thought I would be. Instead, I was turned-on again at the sight of him coming like that. I felt a sense of pride from being the one who had made him do it.

"There's a bathroom right across the hall," he said.

I stood up and walked to the bathroom. After washing my hands, I soaked a washcloth with water and walked back to the bedroom. I sat down on the bed, and I was careful as I started wiping him since I knew he had to still be sensitive.

"I've never seen another girl quite like you."

I glanced over my shoulder to see him watching me walk back into the bathroom to throw the washcloth into the hamper.

"What do you mean by that?"

"You're just…you. Come over here."

I walked to the bed, and he pulled me down beside him. I snuggled into his chest as he wrapped his arms around me.

"This is nice."

He kissed the top of my head. "It is."

I couldn't remember the last time I'd felt this safe or this content. I'd just given him a piece of myself that I'd never shared with anyone else, and I felt closer to him because of it. *I could get used to this.*

Sometime later, I woke up to Jesse calling my name. I groaned as I tried to find the covers to pull over my head.

"Emma, wake up."

"No," I grumbled.

He laughed as he started tickling my ribs. "You have to. My mom will be home soon, and if she walks in on us like this…"

"Oh crap." I definitely needed to get up. I didn't want to meet his mom for the first time while I was half-naked in her son's bed.

"Yeah, crap. You need to get dressed. Here are your clothes."

He shoved my tank top and bra into my hands as I sat up. I slipped on my clothes and followed him out into the rest of his house. He held my hand to lead me through the dark surrounding us. It was a lot later than I'd realized.

He continued to hold my hand until we were standing beside my car. I suddenly felt awkward and unsure of myself again. The contentment I'd felt while he held me in his arms was now gone.

"So…I guess I'll see you later?" It came out as a question, showing just how unsure I felt about our situation now.

He laughed as he leaned down, and then he kissed my forehead. "You will, just not in school."

"I'll stop by tomorrow with your assignments."

"You don't have to do that."

"Maybe I want to."

"You're just using that as an excuse to come over again."

"And if I am? Does that bother you?"

"Nope. I'll see you tomorrow night. I have to work tomorrow though, so I won't be home until around nine thirty."

"That's fine. My mom leaves tomorrow morning for San Francisco. She'll be gone most of the week. Thank God. I don't think I can handle any more of her right now."

"What did you two fight about earlier? You said you were upset."

I wasn't about to tell him that it was over him and Todd. He didn't need to feel guilty. "Just stupid stuff. She was on one of her usual rants."

"At least you're rid of her for a few days."

"Yeah. I should probably go before she starts calling my friends to see if I'm with them."

"Night, Emma."

He leaned down and kissed me. It held none of the passion from earlier, but it was sweet and innocent. I loved it.

"Night."

11
JESSE

I waited until Emma's taillights disappeared before I walked back inside. As soon as I made it back to my room, I crashed down onto my bed and stared up at the ceiling. Tonight had been unexpected to say the least. I'd never planned on bringing Emma to my house, but she hadn't seemed to mind the fact that I lived in a trailer park. I should have known she would be okay with it, but I had obviously underestimated her again. I sounded like a lovesick sap, but the girl could do no wrong in my eyes.

Her innocence had thrown me at first. I had assumed that she was pretty naive when it came to sex, but I hadn't expected her to be so inexperienced with *everything*. She was a very pretty girl, and I'd assumed that she'd at least experimented a little before she met me.

The fact that she had trusted me with some of her firsts told me just how much trust she had in me. That meant a hell of a lot to me. I had no idea what I'd done to end up with someone like her, but I wasn't complaining.

Holding her in my arms as she slept had been a completely life-changing experience. She had looked so peaceful as she snuggled tightly into my arms. While she slept, she'd mumbled something about being safe, but I didn't want to tell her that. The fact that she considered me a safe haven was…mind-blowing to me.

When she'd thought I had another girl in my house, the moment I'd seen the tears in her eyes caused me to throw my reservations about having a relationship with her right out the window. I knew she wouldn't leave me. She'd been truly hurt when she thought I had betrayed her. Surely, if she'd been bothered that much by it, then she wouldn't just randomly walk away from me. I realized we still had a lot to deal with that would keep us apart, but I knew we would figure it out. It was official. I was in a relationship that I actually cared about for the first time in my life.

I sat up as I heard my mom's car pulling into the space where Emma's car had occupied just a few minutes ago. I knew she would be mad when I told her that I'd been suspended, but I was too high from my night with Emma to care. My mom knew that I didn't usually get into trouble. Hopefully, that would be enough to keep her from grounding me. I still needed to ask her about the trip with Emma, but I wasn't sure how. I just knew that tonight wouldn't be a good night to do it.

My mom came through the door just as I entered the living room.

"Hi, honey. How was school?"

"Yeah, about that—"

"Jesse, what did you do?" she asked when she saw my expression.

"I didn't do anything. A couple of the rich kids attacked me. I actually won, but a teacher walked in at the end. I'm suspended for a week."

"Jesse, what on earth am I going to do with you? You're lucky that they didn't kick you out permanently."

"Trust me, I know, but I swear I didn't start it. I was just defending myself."

"Did you at least hurt them enough, so they won't bother you again?"

"I did. I broke the one guy's nose, and then I knocked out his friend."

"Dear Lord!"

I grinned. "Sorry, but they were asking for it. Don't worry though. Emma is going to bring my work to me, so I don't fall behind."

Her head snapped up, and I cursed as I realized what I'd just said.

"Who's Emma?"

"Uh…she's my, uh…" I started, unsure of what to call Emma. *Friend?*
Girlfriend? The girl I'd given her first orgasm to?

"Jesse, are you keeping something from me? Do you have a girlfriend?"

"No…well, maybe. I don't know what to classify her as."

"I want to hear all about her! I'm so excited that you finally found
someone who caught your attention."

"What do you want to know?" I asked. I knew I might as well get this
over with, or she'd never leave me alone.

"Anything you want to tell me. What does she like to do? How did you
meet?"

"She's a cheerleader, and I met her in class. Actually, that's a lie. Do you
remember taking me to the rich people's park when I was little? There was a
little girl who told me I didn't belong there?"

"Vaguely. I think you were really upset, but that was a long time ago.
Why do you ask?"

"Because she's that little girl. I thought she'd be a horrible, spoiled brat,
but she's not. She's so kind and innocent."

"Oh my. Did you ask her if she remembered that day?"

"No. I doubt if she'd even remember it."

"That's true. I'm glad you've finally found someone. I have to admit that
I'm surprised you like her when all you do is complain about school and the
students there."

"Yeah, me, too. She drives a car that costs more than our trailer, but she
doesn't care about stuff like that. She doesn't look down on me like a lot of
them do."

"She sounds wonderful. When do I get to meet her?"

"I have no idea. She's bringing my school stuff over tomorrow after I get
off work, but I think you have to work."

"What time will she be here?"

"Around nine thirty. Why?"

"Because I'll make sure to be here. I want to meet her."

I groaned. "Is that really necessary?"

"Of course it is. I want to meet the girl who has finally snagged my son."

"I'm going to bed now. You're crazy."

"Night, sweetie. I'm still mad at you for getting kicked out."

"Sure you are." I walked into my room and closed the door.

I knew I'd sleep good tonight with Emma's perfume covering my bed.

I was bored out of my mind. To kill time, I'd slept in until almost noon, and after I made myself something to eat, I'd spent the rest of my afternoon staring at the TV. I had no idea who came up with these stupid reality shows, but they needed to be tested for drugs. *Who cares about a trio of rich sisters who are famous for no reason? Definitely not me.* I turned off the TV and threw the remote down beside me on the couch. I still had an hour to kill before I had to be at work, and I had nothing to do.

I debated on cleaning the kitchen for my mom, but I wasn't that bored yet. Instead, I pulled my phone out of my pocket and texted Emma.

> *Me: I'm bored.*

I didn't expect a reply until later, but she responded almost instantly.

> *Emma: What do you want me to do about it?*

> *Me: You could always sneak out of school and come visit me. I could give you a few more lessons, like last night. ;)*

> *Emma: I'm sure you could. And thanks by the way. Lucy just asked me why my face was so red.*

> *Me: Ha-ha. I'll see you tonight.*

Emma: Okay! <3

I put my phone back in my pocket and grabbed my keys off the stand. I figured Rick wouldn't care if I came in a little bit early. It wasn't like he would pay me for it anyway.

I took my time driving to the shop as I tried to kill time. I even sat out in the parking lot with my radio blaring Devour the Day's latest song, "Good Man." When the song finally ended, I walked into the shop. I loved my job, but we'd been so slow lately that I dreaded going in. Time passed by so slowly when I had nothing to do.

I changed my shirt, and then I walked to the back where Rick and one of the guys, Tony, were working on a couple of clients. I liked working with all of the guys, but Tony was my favorite. He was only a few years older than me, and we had a lot in common. He was married and had a two-year-old, but he still managed to come out and party with Andy and me from time to time.

The client he was working with had her eyes closed tightly as he worked on a piece located on her foot. It was a flash piece that we had in one of the books out front, but he'd added a few extras to the standard vine and flower design. The main part of the vine spelled out the name Jane before it branched off to where the flowers grew.

I loved doing that on my designs. It was such a cool feeling to take a tattoo that had been used hundreds of times and put my own spin on it to make it something special.

The girl looked young, barely over eighteen, but she didn't complain like a lot of clients would. Instead of yelling about the pain, she simply kept her eyes closed and gritted her teeth as he finished up the outside of the tattoo. When he used blood inking for the shading, I actually saw tears forming in her eyes. That shit hurt because he had to mix her blood with the ink. I'd watched grown men howl in pain when an artist did that to them.

"Okay, you're done," Tony said as he shut off his gun.

The girl opened her eyes and looked down at her foot. "Oh my god."

"Do you like it?" he asked.

"Are you kidding me? I love it! Thank you so much!"

"Anytime. Let me give you our aftercare instruction sheet. If you have any questions, just give me a call."

"I will. Thank you!"

She watched him place a bandage over her new tattoo. As soon as he was finished, he handed her our instruction sheet and walked her to the front door of the shop.

I followed them and took a seat on my stool behind the counter. Tony pulled another one up next to me and sat down.

"Have fun at school today?" he teased.

He knew I hated going to Hamrick, and he was constantly on my case about it.

"I got kicked out for a week."

He started laughing. "I should've known. What did you do?"

I shrugged. "Fought a few assholes."

"Did you at least win?"

"I did."

He patted me on the back. "Why the hell did you get into a fight? I thought you were the one who kept his nose clean while Andy started brawls just for the hell of it."

"They called me trailer trash and threatened me."

"Whoa. What the hell?"

"Yeah. Three of them cornered me. They didn't realize that being trailer trash has a few perks. For example, I can apparently beat the shit out of two spoiled assholes at once while sending the other one running."

"That place has to be hell." Tony shook his head. "I have no idea why your mom wants you to go there. Fuck college. I know for a fact that Rick would hire you on here while you do your apprenticeship. You're like a second son to him."

"She wants *better* for me. She just doesn't understand that I want *this*, not some fucking college degree and a desk job."

"Did you tell her that?"

"How can I? She thinks she's doing what's best for me. If I told her I was okay with this life, it'd break her. She's spent her whole life trying to make up for the way my dad left us."

"You're a good guy, Jesse. You'll figure it out."

"I hope so."

"Besides those ass-wipes, how is school going?"

I thought of Emma and smiled. She'd made that place bearable. Actually, I kind of missed school today because I couldn't see her. "It's not too bad."

"Why are you grinning like you just got laid? Oh shit, are you screwing one of the Barbie dolls at that school?"

"I'm not screwing her, but—"

"But what? If you're not screwing her, why the hell are you smiling like an idiot?"

"I don't know. She's just…different. She doesn't look at me like I'm trash. She looks at me like I'm a whole new world she can't wait to explore."

"If you start spouting off poetry, I'm going to throw up. You have it bad."

"Says the guy who is married and has a kid."

"Okay, you've got me there. I just never saw you as the kind of guy who wanted a relationship. Besides Andy and Ally, you keep to yourself a lot. I mean, you hang out with all of us, but you're not into it like the rest of our group."

"I don't know. I just don't get close to people."

"Because of your dad?" Tony asked.

I wasn't sure where all this heart-to-heart bullshit was coming from, but it was starting to make me uncomfortable. "Are you trying to get a psychology degree or what? I feel like I should be lying on a couch while you take notes."

"And he deflects. Smooth move."

A customer walked in, effectively ending his interrogation. I checked the guy in while Tony went back to set up for him. The guy was a regular, and this was his third and final session with Tony. They'd been working on a sleeve piece for him. It was a dragon that started at his shoulder and wrapped around his arm. The head of the dragon stopped on top of his hand. I wasn't big on dragon tattoos, but this one was sick.

Tony took him back to get started, so I decided to clean up the place before we had any more customers. The schedule book said that we had only one more client tonight, so it was sure to be another slow one. I finished cleaning up and sat back down in my stool to wait for the rest of my shift to go by.

Rick left around seven, leaving me alone with Tony for the rest of the night. The last appointment came and went not long after, so we spent the rest of the night playing cards on the counter. He had taken the hint, and he didn't ask about Emma again.

Tonight was dragging by especially slow. It was probably due to the fact that I was waiting to meet Emma after work. I seriously hoped that my mom wouldn't make it home on time. I knew that made me an ass, but I wasn't sure how I felt about the two of them meeting. Emma and I had jumped into this all of a sudden, and it felt like things would be different, more real, if she met my mom.

When the shop finally closed, I flew home. I almost beat my head on the steering wheel when I saw both Emma's and my mom's cars sitting in the driveway. *So much for hoping that Mom wouldn't be here.* Emma was still in her car when I parked in the yard beside her. At least, she hadn't decided to go in and meet my mom on her own.

She was out of her car before I even shut off my Jeep. She surprised me by opening my door and leaning in to kiss me. She hadn't been shy about it either. It was like she'd actually missed me during the day, and she was trying to make up for it with a single kiss.

I slid my tongue between her teeth as she crushed her lips against me. The moan that escaped her had me adjusting my pants.

"Hi," she said as she pulled away.

"Hi." I stepped out of my Jeep and pulled her into my arms. "That was a nice hello."

"I missed you today. School was boring without you."

"I'm sure it was."

She elbowed me as I threw my arm around her, and we started walking toward my house.

"It was. Although, you were a hot topic today."

"Why's that?"

"Everyone was talking about the fight. Half of the school is either terrified or in awe of you while the other half hates you."

"Let me guess. The half that hates me are all part of your circle of friends."

She looked away. "Yeah, they are."

"It's a good thing you're keeping me your dirty little secret then," I teased, but it bothered me. *What chance do we have of making this work when everyone she knows hates me?*

"You're hilarious," she grumbled as I held the door open for her.

As soon as we walked inside, we were bombarded with the smell of food cooking. I'd recognize my mom's famous chicken casserole anywhere. She'd really gone all out to meet Emma.

"Oh, wow. Something smells good," Emma said as I closed the door behind her.

My mom stuck her head out of the kitchen, and she smiled when she saw Emma. "Just in time! I'm just taking dinner out of the oven."

"You guys eat dinner at nine thirty?" Emma asked.

"Well, I usually work late shifts, so Jesse has to fend for himself."

"Oh, I see," Emma said politely.

"Mom, this is Emma. Emma, this is my mom," I said as I gestured between them. *This is so weird.*

"It's nice to meet you, Ms. Daniels."

My mom wiped her hands on her apron as she walked out of the kitchen. "It's nice to meet you, Emma. Please call me Trish."

"I can do that." Emma smiled at my mom. She was bouncing her weight from foot to foot as we all stood in the entryway, staring at each other.

"Why don't we all head into the kitchen to eat?" my mom asked.

"Sounds like a plan," I said.

I placed my hand on the small of Emma's back as I steered her into the kitchen. It didn't go unnoticed by my mother. I watched her try to hide a grin when we walked past.

Emma and my mom sat across from each other at the table while I was in the middle. Emma was trying to hide her nervousness, but she kept fidgeting in her chair. I supposed I should have warned her that my mom might be home, but I never thought about it. My mom was rarely home, and I hadn't expected her to actually be here.

My mother made me say grace tonight. I knew there weren't a lot of families who said it anymore, and I didn't want Emma to think we were strange. She didn't seem to mind though as she bowed her head right along with us. Everyone was quiet afterward as we filled our plates with food.

It was starting to feel awkward, and then my mom finally spoke up. "Has my son been behaving himself in school?"

Emma glanced at me and smiled. "He has with the exception of yesterday. He's actually pretty quiet."

"He always has been. Even when he was little, he'd keep to himself rather than play with the other kids."

"He's a hard nut to crack, but I think I finally managed to get him to like me."

"I'm glad. You just take care of my baby, okay?"

"Mom, really?" I asked as I rolled my eyes.

"Yes, really."

Emma laughed. "I will. You have nothing to worry about."

"I'm glad to hear that. So, what do you like to do in your spare time? My son kept quiet about you until last night, so I know nothing about you."

"I'm pretty boring. I don't do much besides school and cheerleading. Jesse has been *trying* to teach me to surf. Keyword there is *trying*. I'm not very good at it."

"It takes time. I don't know how many times Jesse had come home bruised and discouraged before he finally got the hang of it. Don't let him give you a hard time, or I'll bring out baby pictures, so we can laugh at him together."

"I have no words for where this conversation is going," I groaned before I started shoveling food into my mouth. I needed to get Emma away from my mom fast.

"Oh! I'd love to see those sometime. I might even make copies and pass them around at school." Emma stuck her tongue out at me.

"I like this girl, Jesse. You need to bring her around more often."

"So that the two of you can embarrass me? No, thanks."

"Oh, hush. We're bonding," Emma said as she squeezed my knee under the table.

"So, what do your parents do?" my mom asked.

"Well, my dad is part of the band, Seducing Seductresses, and my mom is a retired model. They've been divorced since I was little, so I don't get to see my dad that often."

"I'm sorry to hear that. At least you have your mom around though."

Emma snorted. "I wouldn't go that far. She's not much of a mom."

"That stinks. I had a rocky relationship with my mom when I was a teenager. Hopefully, you two can learn to get along," my mom said.

"I doubt that. She isn't worried about being a mom."

"Well, you're welcome here anytime. I mean it. Even if Jesse is in one of his moods, I'll let you hide out here."

"That's very kind of you. Thank you."

"Of course. I swear that I'm not one of those mean moms who make the girlfriends miserable."

Emma laughed. "I'm glad. I could use a nice mom once in a while. Speaking of nice moms, I have a question for you. I'm not sure if Jesse told you or not, but my dad is flying me over to London to see him this weekend. He told me that I could bring a friend, and I was hoping that I could bring Jesse with me."

"To London?" my mom asked as her eyes widened.

"Yeah, it's only for the weekend, and we won't be on our own either. We'll be in the same hotel as my dad, so you don't have to worry about us getting in trouble." Emma looked at my mom hopefully.

She was pleading with her eyes, and my mom had to say *yes* to that look. *Hell, I'd give the girl anything if she gave me that look.*

"London. Wow. I don't know. It's so far."

"Oh, come on. You'll be working all weekend anyway. You won't even miss me," I said.

"What about a passport? You don't have one, and those take weeks."

She had a good point. I looked at Emma, hoping that she could help us out.

"It does take weeks unless you're the daughter of a rock star who has a friend that can expedite the process. I brought the forms with me. If you fill them out tonight, we should have it by Thursday."

My mother's mouth dropped open even farther. "Wow, I'm not even sure what to say to that. I guess you can go, Jesse. *But*, and this is a big but, you have to call me as soon as you land and at least once a day for every day you're there."

"I'll make sure that he does," Emma said. She was grinning from ear to ear. "This means so much to me. Thank you!"

"You're welcome. Just make sure that you're both careful."

Emma and my mom kept a steady flow of conversation as we ate. With the two of them together, I never had the chance to get a word in. I hadn't been sure how the two of them would get along, but it was obvious that they already liked each other.

We finished dinner, and Emma tried to help my mom do the dishes, but she shooed Emma away. "Go help my son with his homework. I think I can handle a few plates."

"If you're sure…" Emma seemed unsure of whether or not to leave.

"I am. Now, go." She glanced over at me. "And leave the door open, Jesse."

I rolled my eyes. I wasn't fifteen. If I wanted to have sex with Emma in my room, I would. I wouldn't care if the door were open or not. "I'll try to remember to keep it open."

12
EMMA

I grabbed my bag full of books and followed Jesse back to his room. I was nervous about being in there alone with him when his mother was only a couple of rooms away. He did leave his door open, which I was thankful for. His mom seemed really nice, and I didn't want her to hate me.

"So, what all did you bring me?" he asked as he sat down on the bed.

"A little bit of everything. I wasn't sure about all the classes you're taking, but I got the work from the classes we have together and the ones that I know you are taking."

"I'm sure they thought you were nuts."

"Nah, your teachers like you. Ms. Mason was even cool with me taking your work, and someone said she was the one who caught you guys fighting."

"Well, that's good to know, I guess."

I pulled a notebook out of the bag and handed it to him. "All of your assignments are in there. These are my books. I need your locker combination, so I can borrow yours. I never even thought to ask you for it."

He smiled as I pulled the books out of the bag and set them on the worn-out table where he had scattered other books.

"Thanks."

"No problem. Also, Ms. Mason had us partner up for a project. Since I'd told her that I needed your homework before class started, she put us together. It's a paper on any war of our choice, but it's not due until the end of the month."

"That's fine. I can do research while you write it if you want. I'm good at looking up stuff, but I can never put it down right on paper."

I smiled. "Well, I hate researching, so that sounds perfect. I have your passport paperwork with me, so we just need to fill it out and get a picture of you. I'll scan it and email it all to my dad's friend when I get home."

He shook his head. "You're something else."

I wasn't sure what he'd meant by that. "Why?"

"You just blow over the fact that your dad is a famous rock star and that you have all these friends in high places."

I laughed. "I don't mean to. I just don't think anything of it because it's what I've always known."

"What do you want to do with your life when you're older?" he asked, looking serious.

"I don't know. I do know that I don't want to be part of the life that my mom and dad have. I want my kids to grow up with a normal life."

"You realize that you won't have the money and everything else that comes with the life you live now, don't you?"

"I do. I don't care if I won't have a new car or a big house. I just want a family who really cares about each other and sticks together."

He was staring at me like I'd lost my mind. "You have no idea what you're saying."

"Yeah, I do. I hate the kind of life that my mother lives now. You think that I'm going to look down on you for the life you live, but I don't. I'm jealous. I can only dream of a mom like yours."

He pulled me down beside him and kissed me. "You're nothing like I expected."

"I'll take that as a compliment."

"It is."

I smiled as I pulled away and started digging through my bag for the passport information. "Let's get started on this."

We spent the next few minutes filling out the papers. When the paperwork was done, I pulled my camera from my bag and motioned for him to stand against the far wall. "Go stand there, so I can take your picture."

He did as I'd said, and I snapped a few pictures. When I had what I needed, I stepped closer and started taking more pictures.

"What are you doing?" he asked.

"Nothing."

"Sure you aren't. Quit taking my picture," he teased.

"You're very photogenic."

"I'm sure I am." He moved away from the wall and pulled me tight against his chest. "Let me see the camera."

I handed him the camera. There was no way I could tell him *no* when his body was tight against mine. I wrapped my arms around him as I closed my eyes. "This feels nice."

When I heard the camera click, I opened my eyes back up. "I thought we were done with pictures."

"You're done taking pictures of me. Now, it's my turn." He held the camera away from us. "Now, smile."

I grinned up at the camera as he took a few pictures of us together. I had no idea what to do with this side of him. It was a nice change from the guy who had always kept me at an arm's length. I was quickly learning that there were several different layers to my Jesse, and he kept getting better as I peeled each one away.

"There. Now, we're done with pictures."

He handed the camera back to me. I took it from him and started looking through the pictures that he had snapped of us. It warmed my heart to see the two of us together, happy and smiling. I hadn't felt this free in a long time.

There was just something about him that brought out the best in me, and I often wondered if I did the same with him.

"We look good together even though we're just so different from each other," I said.

"How so?"

I ran my hand across the bright ink designs running down his arm. "You look so wild with these while I look so plain and boring. I wish I had a tattoo."

"You will never be plain or boring, and I could do a tattoo for you if you want. I mean, I would have to do it after hours at the shop since I'm not legally an artist, but I'm still good. I've done most of my own and Andy's. You just can't tell anyone, or Rick could get in some serious trouble."

"Really? That would be so cool! I'd just have to figure out where to put it, so I could hide it from my mom. And, of course, I wouldn't tell anyone."

"I can think of a few places." He stared down at my chest.

"Um, no. I'm not getting a tattoo on my boob."

"Just a suggestion. Think about what you want and where you want me to put it, and I'll draw something up."

"I know what I want. I just don't know where."

"Tell me. The suspense is killing me."

"I want the word *freedom* somewhere. I'm so sick of always being trapped by my mom."

"Pull down your shorts a little bit."

"Excuse me?" I asked. *That wasn't random or anything.*

"Pull your shorts down a little bit. I want to see something."

"I'm sure you do. I'm not pulling down my shorts with your mom in the other room."

"I'm not going to molest you. I want to see if I could make it fit without it looking like shit."

"Okay…" I pulled my shorts down a bit, feeling super awkward as I did so.

"That isn't far enough. Here, let me," Jesse said as he pulled them farther down.

I tried to yank them back up, but he grabbed my hands to stop me.

"Relax. I just want to look."

I fidgeted as he inspected the area just below my hip bone.

"Hurry up," I said.

He ran his finger across my hip bone, and I shivered at the touch.

"I can put it right here, and no one will ever see it unless you want someone to."

"What about when I wear a bikini? I mean, we live in California after all."

"I'll put it so that it's hidden, even when you're wearing almost nothing."

"When do you want to do it?" I asked, feeling excited.

"I can do it now if you want. Rick gave me the key and alarm code for the store last summer."

"Seriously?"

"Yep. You want to?"

"Sure." I pulled my shorts back up. "I'll drive us over."

"Works for me. Let's go."

Jesse stopped to let his mom know that we were leaving. She gave him a disapproving look, but she said nothing. I all but ran to my car in excitement. I'd always wanted a tattoo, but I never thought I'd ever have the guts to get one. Being with Jesse was changing me. I wasn't afraid to do what I wanted in life anymore. As long as he stayed by my side, I could handle anything.

"Where are you going?" a female voice called from behind us.

We turned to see Ally and Andy walking toward us.

"Shit," Jesse grumbled under his breath.

I prepared myself for Ally's attitude when they stopped beside us. She was already sneering at me, but I refused to let her bother me.

"Hey, guys," I said.

"Where are you going?" Ally asked again.

"Out. Why?" Jesse asked shortly.

"Maybe we want to come," Ally said.

"I don't remember inviting you," Jesse shot back.

"What's with the fucking attitude? Are you too good for us now that you have a rich bitch to occupy your time?" Ally snarled.

"Whoa, cool it, both of you," Andy said as Jesse took a step toward Ally. "What is up with you guys? You never fight."

Ally pointed at Jesse. "Ask him. I don't have a problem."

"Bullshit. You attacked Emma the other day for no reason, and you just called her a bitch. You need to take a step back or else."

"You wouldn't hit me. I'm a girl," she taunted.

"No, I wouldn't. But I also know I can tie your ass up without you being able to get loose. I've done it before."

Ally rolled her eyes. "Whatever. It's not my fault that you have no taste in women."

"Excuse me? I'm standing right here," I said.

"And your point is?" she asked.

"Ally, enough. Get the stick out of your ass. If Jesse likes Emma, then I have no problem with her," Andy said as he glared at his sister.

"You're both idiots then. I'm out of here." Ally turned and walked back toward the direction where they'd come from.

"Sorry about that. She isn't usually that hostile," Andy apologized to me.

"It's fine. I don't care what she thinks," I replied.

"So, where *are* you two going?"

"I'm taking Emma to the shop for a tattoo."

"No way. The rich girl is getting inked?"

"Yeah, I am." I stuck my tongue out at Andy. I knew he was kidding, but I was tired of being referred to as the *rich girl.*

"I was going to see if you wanted to go to a party down on the beach, but you're obviously busy. We're having another one tomorrow night if you want to come. You, too, Emma."

Jesse turned to me. "You want to?"

"Sure, sounds good to me."

"Awesome. I'll see you guys later," Andy said.

"Later," Jesse said.

I unlocked my car, and we got in.

"She really doesn't like me, does she?" I asked as I started driving toward the shop.

"No, but I'm not sure why. Just give her time. She'll come around."

"I hope so. I don't want to put you in the middle or make you feel like you have to choose. I know she's your friend."

"Don't worry about it. I'll handle Ally and her claws."

"Thanks."

I reached across the console and put my hand on his. He turned his hand over and threaded our fingers together. I squeezed, enjoying the feel of my hand in his. His hand was so much bigger than mine, and I felt safe with even that small touch. We spent the rest of the drive in silence, enjoying the feel of each other.

"You ready?" Jesse asked when I pulled into the shop's lot.

"As I'll ever be. Is it going to hurt?"

"A little, but it's not bad, I promise."

"I trust you." And I did.

For reasons unknown to me, in such a short time, this boy had wormed his way into my life like no one else ever had. For the thousandth time, I wondered if I'd lost my mind when it came to Jesse. His presence in my life had completely thrown my world off course.

"Come on, let's get you inked."

We got out of the car, and he held my hand again, leading me to the front door. After unlocking the door and disarming the alarm, he took me to one of the back rooms. I glanced nervously at the table in the center of the small room. I'd been thrilled on the way here, but now, I was terrified.

"I'm nervous," I said.

"Don't be. You said you trusted me, so prove it. Lie down on the table, and get comfortable while I get everything ready."

I did as he'd said, and then I watched him as he started prepping for my tattoo.

"Do you have any kind of script in mind?" he asked as he placed a small cup on a rolling cart and filled it with black ink.

"Not really. Something girlie, I guess."

He smiled. "Let me do a few, and see what you think."

"What? You're going to freehand them? Don't you use a computer to print them out?"

"Some do, but I prefer to freehand them if I can." He grabbed a piece of paper and pen. "Give me a second."

I watched silently as he started running the pen across the paper. I'd never seen him in such deep concentration.

"Here are a few different ways I can do it. You choose which one you want."

He put the pen down and handed the sheet of paper to me. I was surprised by how precise he was on each different way he'd written *freedom*. If I hadn't seen him write them down, I would have sworn that he'd printed them off of a computer.

"Damn, you are good." I grinned at him.

"I hear that a lot. Which one do you like?"

"The third one," I said as I handed the paper back to him.

It was a flowing cursive script. There were loops coming out of the *F* and *M* that wrapped around the rest of the tattoo. It was amazing how he could do something like that in just a few seconds.

"Lie back on the table, and I'll draw it on. I'll let you look before I start tattooing, I promise."

I settled back and rested my head on the cushioned part of the table. Jesse stood beside me and started slowly lowering my shorts again. When I raised my hips off the table to make it easier for him, he smiled.

"You're making this too easy."

"Shut up. I was trying to help."

"I don't mind when you help me take off your clothes."

"I'm sure you don't."

"Are you sure you want it here? Once I start, there's no going back."

"Where else could you put it where I can hide it?"

"You already turned down my first suggestion, so that leaves your ass."

"Yeah, I think I'll pass. Hip, it is."

"Works for me. Now, stay still while I draw it on."

I didn't move a muscle as he started drawing the letters on my skin. He pulled back a few seconds later and grabbed a mirror off the cart holding his gun and the ink.

"Check it out."

I angled the mirror, so I could see the design. It looked exactly as it had on the paper. "Looks good to me."

"Okay, let's get started. Just remember to breathe. A lot of first-timers forget that, and it's kind of important."

I laughed. "I'll keep that in mind."

"Good. Also, don't move around a bunch. I don't want you to yell at me if I mess it up because you moved."

"It'll be fine. Let's do this."

He picked up the gun, powered it on, and dipped the tip in the cup of ink. I balled my fists as he placed the gun over me, an inch from my skin.

"Stop teasing, and get it over with." I squeezed my eyes closed.

The next thing I knew, the gun shut off, and his lips were on mine. I gasped in shock as he sucked my bottom lip into his mouth. His hands held my face in place as he continued to kiss me until my body felt like jelly.

"What was that for?" I gasped out as he pulled away.

"You were tense. I wanted to relax you."

"Mission accomplished."

He smiled. "Then, let's get back to work."

He picked up the gun again and powered it on. I kept my body relaxed as he lowered it to my skin. There was a small stinging feeling, but it wasn't as bad as I'd expected. He worked carefully on each letter with his arm resting on my thigh. His breath tickled my skin as he leaned in closer, and a shiver ran through my body. I was in a blissful hell with him this close to me.

"You doing okay?" he asked.

"I'm fine," I whispered.

He nodded as he continued to work. "We're almost done."

He'd been right. Just a few seconds later, he powered off the gun and used some kind of solution on a paper towel to wipe off the excess ink.

"Stand up, and look."

He held out a hand, and I took it as I stood up. There was a mirror beside the table, and I stood in front of it to inspect my tattoo. It was simple and elegant. I loved it.

"It's beautiful. Thank you."

"You're welcome. I'm glad you let me do it."

"I told you I trusted you."

He walked up behind me and wrapped his arms around my stomach, careful not to touch the tattoo. I rested my head back against his chest as I looked at us together in the mirror. There was a happiness to Jesse that hadn't been there when I first met him. It made me happy as well to know that I was the reason for that.

"Come home with me tonight," I blurted out.

"What?" he asked as I watched him raise a brow in the mirror.

"Come home with me. My mom isn't home, so it'll be okay."

"I don't know, Emma."

"Please. I just want to spend the night together."

I wasn't sure what she was asking when she'd said she wanted me to come home with her. I didn't want her to think that my mind was only on one thing, but she was pressed up tightly against me, and I was sure she could *feel* exactly what I was thinking about.

"If you're sure…"

"I am. I'm not asking for anything. I just want to fall asleep with you beside me."

I smiled. This girl was going to be the death of me. "I think I can handle that. Let's get something over your tattoo first."

After I applied the bandage and cleaned up the room, I locked up and followed her to her car. She chatted as she drove, but I was barely paying attention. The farther we drove, the nicer the houses were that we passed. I wasn't sure what to expect when we arrived at her house, but I knew it was going to blow me away.

"Why are you being so quiet?" she asked.

"I'm not."

"Yes, you are. Tell me."

"I don't know how I'm going to feel when I see where you live."

"You're an idiot. A house is just a house."

"Try saying that from my position."

She slammed on the brakes and brought the car to a dead stop right in the middle of the road. I grabbed the dash as I flew forward.

"What the hell was that for?"

"You listen to me, Jesse Daniels! I don't give a shit about where you live. I've told you that a million times, and you still don't believe me. *When* are you going to realize that I'm telling the truth?"

"Okay, okay. I believe you. Jesus."

"You better," she growled as she started driving again.

We pulled up to her house a few minutes later. *Damn.* It was bigger than I'd expected. It was dark out, so I couldn't see much, and I was secretly glad. I didn't need to feel worse about the differences in our situations.

"This is it."

"Wow," I said as she parked in a garage connected to the house. Correction—it wasn't a house. It was a mansion. I really hated my life right about now.

"Come on, I need to get your passport stuff sent in."

I followed her through a door that led inside the house. She flipped on a few lamps as she went so that we could see. The grandeur of the place completely amazed me. Her living room alone was bigger than my entire house. It, along with the rest of the house that I'd seen so far, had polished hardwood floors. The couch and the matching love seat were both a bright white that I would be afraid to sit on in fear of getting them dirty. Surprisingly, there was no TV in the room.

"Where's your TV?" I asked as I followed her out of the room and up a set of steps.

"That's the sitting room, so it doesn't have one. The room beside it does though," she said.

"Fuck me," I said under my breath.

After we made it to the top of the stairs, we walked down a hallway.

She stopped at the door at the end of the hall. "This is my room."

I walked into the room behind her, and then I stopped in my tracks. Her room was almost as large as the first one we'd passed through downstairs. She had a massive California king–size bed against the far wall. There was a computer desk to the left of the door that was piled high with books and notebooks as well as a laptop and printer. A massive mirror was hanging on the wall between her bed and a dresser. Other than that, the room was noticeably empty. There were no pictures or knickknacks to be seen anywhere. I'd been in enough girls' rooms to know that this wasn't normal.

"Where are your pictures and stuff? I've never seen a room so bare in my life."

She shrugged. "I don't know. I just never put up anything."

"It's like you don't even live here."

"Most of the time, it feels like I don't. Sure, I go to sleep in this bed most nights, but I don't consider this home."

"And where do you consider home?"

"I haven't figured that out just yet, but I will someday."

"You're so strange. As soon as I think I have you figured out, you do or say something that completely blows my mind."

"I like to keep it interesting."

"Trust me, you do."

"Make yourself at home while I send this stuff in for your passport."

"Sounds good to me." I walked over to her bed and fell down onto it. It was like I was lying on a cloud. I wasn't sure that I would be able to sleep in my own bed ever again after spending the night in this one.

I watched as she scanned the forms into her computer. After she scanned them and uploaded a picture, she sent the email out to whoever her contact was. She wasn't paying any attention to me, and I took full advantage of that to watch her. *Jesus, she has a body to kill.* When we weren't in school, she constantly wore those tiny little shorts of hers and a tank top, showing just enough skin to drive me wild. I wanted her so fucking bad. Apparently, my body agreed because I had to adjust myself to hide how turned-on I was just by lying on her bed and watching her.

I needed a shower, preferably one that was on the cold side. I didn't want her to think that I was only after one thing. *I'm not, honest.* I just couldn't help how I responded to her.

"You mind if I take a shower while you finish up?" I asked.

"Of course not! The bathroom is the door next to my room. There should be towels and everything in there."

"Great. Thanks." I stood and walked to the door, trying to angle my body away from where she could see what was happening downstairs. *Damn it, I need that shower now. Sleeping next to her tonight is going to be hell.*

"You know what? There's no guy stuff in there, but I *think* my mom had the maids put some stuff in the guest shower downstairs. I'll go check and see."

She passed me as I walked into the bathroom.

It was huge, just like every other room in this house. I found a towel and hung it on the holder next to the shower. The shower was surrounded completely by frosted glass, and I slid the door open carefully, afraid to break something. I fiddled with the controls to get the water running, cursing the fact that she didn't have a shower with knobs, like normal people. When I finally managed to get the water on and to the right temperature, I slipped out of my clothes and stepped into the shower. Despite the cold temperature I'd set it on, the water felt like heaven as it fell across my skin.

"Jesse? I found some shampoo and body wash for you," Emma called from the bathroom door.

"Great. Thanks."

I could see her outline through the glass as she approached the shower.

"Um, how do you want to do this?"

I snickered. She was so damn nervous about shampoo. "However you want to do it."

"I really hate you sometimes."

"No, you don't. You think I'm awesome." I cracked the shower door enough to get my hand through. "Just hand them to me."

She slipped two small bottles into my hand and retreated back to the bathroom door. "There. I don't have any clothes for you to wear, so you'll have to put yours back on. Sorry."

"It's cool. I like to sleep naked anyway."

"I'm going to strangle you with my bare hands."

I laughed as I heard the door open and then close again. She was so easy to embarrass. I finished my shower and pulled the shorts I'd been wearing back on. I put both of the bottles Emma had given me on the sink, so we wouldn't forget to put them back from wherever they had come from. We didn't need one little slipup to screw Emma over with her mom.

Emma was closing the door to her closet just as I walked back into the room.

"That was fast," she said.

"I shower fast."

"I can see that. I'll be back in a few."

My eyes followed her ass as she walked out of the room. I was so screwed. I was pretty sure that after spending the entire night in the bed with her, I would physically combust by the time morning rolled around.

I lay down on her bed to wait while she showered. *How long does it take for a girl to shower?* She'd been in there twice as long as I had, and she still wasn't back. I was about to get up to go check on her when she walked back into the room.

"I thought I was going to have to do a search and rescue mission to find you. How long does it take you to shower?" I asked as I turned my head to look at her.

Fuck! She had traded her shorts for a pair of those boy shorts underwear, and instead of a tank top, she had on a spaghetti strap shirt. *No bra.* Her nipples were showing clearly through the tight material, and I couldn't bring myself to look away. There was no way I would survive this night with my sanity still intact. As soon as she'd come into the room, the effects of my cold shower disappeared, and I was ready to go yet again.

"I like to take long showers. It's the one time of the day where I can just relax." She walked to the side of the bed that I wasn't occupying and sat down on the edge. "You're okay with this?"

"Yeah, I'll be fine." I fake yawned. "I'm beat, so I'll probably pass out soon."

"Okay. Cool," she said nervously.

I waited for her to lie down next to me, but she remained where she was.

"Are you going to lie down or not?" I asked.

"Yeah."

She still didn't move. I would have laughed if I weren't putting all of my energy into not tackling her.

"Oh, for God's sake," I grumbled as I reached over and grabbed her arm. I tugged, and she fell down on the bed beside me. "There. That wasn't so hard."

"I'm sorry. I must look like an idiot right now. It's just that I've never had a guy in my bed before. I feel like a moron for asking you to stay with me."

I laughed. "It's kind of cute how nervous you are when it's just us. You're never like this in public. You're always so collected in everything you do."

She shrugged. "You make me nervous."

"Why's that?"

"Because you're not like anyone else that I've ever met. You don't give a damn about what others think. You just do what you want. And you're kind of cute, too."

"Kind of?" I teased.

"If I said I thought you were hot, your head would swell to twice its normal size."

"Which one?"

"Ugh! I give up."

I laughed. "I'm just teasing. Let's go to sleep and forget all the awkward shit."

"Easy for you to say. I'm sure you do this all the time."

"Actually, I don't."

"You mean you've never slept in a bed with a girl before?" she asked skeptically.

Do I lie or tell the truth? I didn't want to hurt her, but I also didn't want to lie to her.

"I've been in a bed with a girl, but I've never spent the night there."

"Oh."

"Come on, let's go to sleep." I was done with this talking crap, especially where it was going now. I pulled her tight against me and threw the blankets over us. My arm wrapped around her waist as she snuggled in beside me. "See, this is nothing to get all excited over."

"Then, what's poking me? A flashlight?"

I busted out laughing. "It is. Now, go to sleep."

I held her tight as her breathing evened out. Lying here next to her was physically painful, but somehow, I managed. The last thought I had before falling asleep was how well we fit together.

I was having the best dream ever. Or at least, I thought it was a dream. When I opened my eyes to see Emma lying next to me, I realized that it hadn't been a dream at all. *Shit.* I had Emma pulled tight against me with my hand between her legs. How the fuck did I manage that in my sleep? I started to pull my hand away, but the motion caused her to moan in her sleep as she clamped her legs shut around my hand. Fire shot through my veins as she wiggled against my hand and moaned again.

If she woke up now, there was no way that she'd believe me if I told her that I hadn't done this on purpose. I stayed completely still as I tried to figure out a way to get my hand out from between her legs without waking her up. I tried to pull my hand away again, but she clamped down harder and moaned. *Jesus.* If my hand didn't wake her up, then my aching dick pressed against her ass would.

"Mmm, Jesse," she moaned in her sleep.

I closed my eyes as I dropped my head back onto the pillow and groaned. She was apparently dreaming about me, too. That was all it took to set me off. I couldn't help it. I started stroking her through her underwear.

She moaned again as her breath hitched. "God, yes."

She relaxed her legs for a split second, but it was enough for me to better angle my hand until I was right over her clit. I started stroking it slowly, loving the way her body responded to me in her sleep.

"What are you doing?" she whispered.

"In my defense, I tried to be the good guy."

She turned her head to look at me with sleep-filled eyes. "What are you talking about?"

"I tried to move away, but you wouldn't let me."

She gave me a sleepy grin. "Well, it was a nice way to wake up."

"Go back to sleep, and I'll wake you up in an even better way."

She laughed. "What do you have in mind?"

I pulled my hand from between her legs and rolled her until she was on her back. I leaned over and kissed her. My tongue slipped between her lips as my hands started exploring her body.

"Let me show you."

Gone was the shy and nervous girl from last night. In her place was a girl who had fire in her eyes as she nodded, giving me permission to do what I wanted. I had no clue how far that permission extended, but I was going to go as far as she'd let me.

I kissed a trail from her ear to her neck and then across her collarbone. Her nipples were hard as they pushed against the thin material of her night shirt. Unable to stop myself, I leaned down and bit one of them through her shirt. I loved rough sex, but I didn't want to tell her that just yet. She was new to all of this, and I didn't want to scare her. She moaned as my teeth clamped onto her nipple. I made sure not to bite too hard. There was a fine line between pleasure-inducing pain and straight pain. I released it almost instantly and flicked my tongue across it.

"Can I take off your shirt?" I asked, praying that she'd say yes. I had to go slow with her, or she'd freak out.

"Yes."

I barely heard her whispered reply. I tugged the shirt up and over her head. I threw it on the floor next to the bed before turning my attention back to her. *God, she's beautiful.* I kissed her softly on the mouth before cupping both breasts and rubbing my thumbs across them. She closed her eyes and moaned as I leaned back down and took first one and then the other into my mouth again. Instead of biting, I sucked on them. Her hips bucked as I rolled each one around with my tongue.

I released her nipple. "Do you like that?"

She only nodded.

I ran my hand between her breasts, close enough to torture her, and then I moved down her stomach to the top of her underwear. Her boy shorts were a pale gray, and I could see just how turned-on she was by how soaked they were already. I slipped my thumbs under the waistband and started slowly pulling them down her legs.

She tensed for a split second. "Jesse…"

"Shh, I won't do anything that you don't want me to do, but I want to see you, all of you."

She shuddered as I slipped them off her ankles and threw them on the floor with her shirt. I didn't touch her as I stared down at her now fully naked body. Knowing that I was the only person who had ever seen her like this made me feel possessive. She was mine, and I wanted to keep it that way.

I reached between her legs and flicked her clit gently. She nearly came up off the bed as she cried out. I settled down in front of her as I pushed her knees apart.

"Is this okay?" I asked.

"Yes, just…"

"Just what?"

"Please touch me again."

She didn't have to tell me twice. I slipped my hand between her legs again and parted her with my fingers as my thumb started rubbing. My fingers were soaked instantly, and I nearly came right then and there. I pulled my hand away, knowing that I was about to lose control.

"Why did you stop?" She groaned.

Her legs were still spread wide open, screaming at me to take her. Normally, I never asked a girl if it was okay. If they were in a bed with me, I knew it was fine. With her, I couldn't be sure.

"Emma, I have to stop."

She propped herself up on her elbow. "What? Why? Did I do something wrong?"

The innocence in her statement made me groan. "You didn't do anything wrong. I just...I can't go halfway with you again. I want inside you, and I don't think you're ready for that."

Her eyes widened. "Oh."

"Yeah, oh. I want you so bad, and I'm not going to be able to control myself if we keep going."

She studied me carefully. "You really care about me, don't you?"

"What kind of question is that?"

"You do. If you didn't, you wouldn't waste your time on me if you thought you'd get nothing out of it."

I leaned down and scooped up her clothes off the floor. "Here, put these back on."

She took them from me and did something I hadn't expected. She threw them as hard as she could against the far wall. She sat up on her knees, so she was mere inches away from me. "I trust you."

I had no idea what she'd meant by that. Maybe she'd meant that she trusted me to control myself, but I didn't. "I don't."

She smiled as she wrapped her arms around my neck and pulled our bodies tight against each other. We were both on our knees, and her heat was tight against the crotch of my shorts. I was in the best possible hell right now.

"You don't have to trust yourself because I trust you not to hurt me. I want you, Jesse. I want my first time to be with you."

"Are you sure?" I asked, still unsure of what to do. I didn't want her to regret this later.

"I'm sure. You just have to be patient with me."

"I can do that." I smiled at her.

She leaned back and pulled me with her as her back hit the bed.

"You trust me completely?" I asked one more time. I didn't want her to stop me once I started.

"Completely."

That was all I needed to hear. I held her hands above her head as I kissed her, working my way down her body. I ran my tongue down her stomach, heading to the place I wanted most. I pushed her legs apart and ran my tongue across her clit. The sound she made had me repeat the action. I did it over and over, tasting her as I went. *Fuck, she's sweet.* Innocence poured out of her, and I savored every bit of it.

I sat up and replaced my tongue with my fingers. They slipped farther back until they were probing her entrance. I slipped one finger inside, feeling just how tight she was. *This is going to hurt like hell for both of us.*

I slowly pushed another finger in, trying to loosen up her body a bit more. I looked up to watch her as I did so to make sure that I wasn't hurting her, but she didn't seem to be in pain. Instead, her head was thrown back in ecstasy. I wanted to make her come before we actually had sex. That way, she wouldn't be as tight. I continued to push two fingers in and out as my other hand reached up and tweaked one of her nipples.

"Oh my god, Jesse. I can't take anymore."

"Shh, just let go."

I ran my hand down her stomach to play with her clit again. As soon as I touched it, her body exploded. She cried out as she fisted the covers. Her internal muscles tightened around my fingers, and I damn near lost it again. I had no idea how I was going to be able to go slow when I pushed inside her. I was barely hanging on by a thread now.

I stood as she quieted down, and I slipped off my shorts. I grabbed my wallet and pulled out a condom from inside. I turned back to her to see her staring at me with her mouth agape. The heat in her eyes was mixed with fear.

"Hey, we don't have to do this, Emma. I mean it."

"No, I want to. I'm just afraid that it's going to hurt."

"It will. I won't lie to you. But I promise to be gentle."

She nodded. "I trust you."

I ripped open the package and put on the condom before walking back to the bed. I lay on top of her and started kissing her. I wanted her to relax, or this would never work. The kiss worked as I felt her body relax beneath me.

"Are you ready?" I whispered.

"Yes."

She wrapped her arms around my neck, and I positioned myself at her entrance.

"I'm going to go slow and give you time to adjust. If it starts to hurt, tell me, and I'll stop."

"Okay."

I pushed in only an inch or two and stopped, giving her time to adjust. I started thrusting my hips slowly, barely moving, as I slipped in just a bit farther. *God, she feels good.* I had to stop when I'd made it a little farther in. Between her heat and the tightness, I was ready to blow.

"You still doing okay?" I asked.

"Yeah. It hurts a little bit."

"It will. I'm going as slow as I can."

"I know."

I started thrusting again, still barely moving, as I wedged myself deeper in. I knew I couldn't go any farther like this.

"Baby, I'm going to finish going in. This is the part where it hurts. You just have to relax for me, okay?"

"I'm ready."

I was impressed at how relaxed she was keeping her body. I took a deep breath before thrusting fully into her. She cried out, and I felt like a bastard as tears sprung to her eyes.

"I'm sorry."

"It's okay. Just give me a minute." She whimpered.

I held completely still as we waited together for the pain to pass. I didn't want to cause her any more pain than I'd already had.

"I think I'm okay now. Just go slow for a minute, please," she said.

"Okay."

I leaned down and kissed her as I started moving my hips slowly. She was still tight, almost tight enough to cause me pain. I worked slowly, stretching her so that both of us were comfortable.

I worked her that way until I couldn't handle it anymore. I *needed* to go faster. Instincts took over as I started thrusting harder and deeper, fighting my own body for control. She moaned as she wrapped her legs around my waist, allowing me to go deeper. I still held back, afraid that I would hurt her.

"Jesse, faster. I need it faster."

I groaned as I started thrusting faster. I couldn't keep this up much longer, but I didn't want to come without her.

"I can't hold back, baby. I have to go harder."

"I'm okay. Go ahead."

I let go, allowing pure instinct to take over, as I thrust hard and fast into her, over and over. She clung to me as she squeezed her legs tighter around me. Sweat dripped off of my nose and onto her, running down her cheek. Our bodies were both covered in sweat as we worked together. She screamed out my name as she came, and I let go. I gave one final thrust deep inside her as I came. Her muscles squeezed me until I wanted to scream in both pleasure and agony.

This girl was going to be the death of me.

I kept my weight on my elbows as my head dropped to her shoulder. I was exhausted, but I didn't want to crush her.

"Are you okay?" she asked.

I raised my head to look at her. "I think that's supposed to be my line."

She smiled. "Whoops, sorry."

"I'm fine. That was fun." I pulled out and rolled to my side.

"It was. Thank you for being so gentle with me. I know that had to be hard for you."

"Not at all. I didn't want to hurt you. I feel like an asshole for hurting you as much as I did."

"You were as easy as you could be."

I kissed her nose before I stood up. "I'll be right back."

"Where are you going?" she asked.

"I need to clean up."

I walked to the bathroom and threw the condom away. I made sure to wrap it in toilet paper, so no one would notice it. I grabbed a washcloth and wet it with warm water before returning to her room. She was still on the bed in the exact same spot that I'd left her in. Her eyes were closed, but she opened them as I nudged her legs apart and started wiping away the small amount of blood that was there.

"Thank you," she whispered.

I threw the washcloth in the hamper in her room before lying down on the bed beside her. "No thanks needed."

"I think I'm falling for you," she said as she laid her head on my chest.

"I kind of figured that after you let me do *that* to you a few minutes ago."

She propped herself up on her elbow and smacked my bare chest with her free hand. "That's not what I meant. The deeper I get in with you, the harder I fall. I think I'm falling in love with you."

For once in my life, I was speechless. I had no idea how to respond to that. *Do I care a lot about her? Damn straight. But do I love her? I have no idea.* The thought of loving someone scared me.

"You don't have to say it back or anything. I just wanted you to know," she said quietly.

"I'm not sure what to say. I've never even considered the possibility of loving someone. I care a lot about you, but I'm not sure I'm ready to say that to you."

"I understand. If you ever do feel that way, please don't hide it from me. I promise that I won't ever hurt you."

I kissed her forehead. "I know. I can't say *I love you* yet, but I can tell you that you're the closest I've ever let myself get to someone."

"That means a lot, especially coming from someone like you."

We were both silent as I held her close. I had no idea what was happening, but I did know that things were changing. I could see it happening right before my eyes. And for a split second, I wasn't scared of it.

Sometime later, I woke up to the sound of my phone ringing. Emma was still sound asleep beside me. I slid my arm out from under her and climbed from the bed. My phone was on the dresser, and I grabbed it just as it stopped ringing. I unlocked it to see three missed calls from my mom and one from Andy. I had several unread text messages, too—most of them from my mom and one from Andy, reminding me about the party tonight.

After sending him a quick reply to let him know that Emma and I were still planning on being there, I opened the ones from my mom. They had all been sent within the last two hours. I glanced at the time and cursed. It was almost noon, and Emma wasn't at school.

Mom: Call me.

Another one had been sent only a few minutes after the first.

Mom: I need to talk to you about something. Please call me.

There were several others like this. The last one had been sent minutes ago.

Mom: Jesse, I'm getting worried. Please call me. I need to talk to you.

I hit Reply and sent her a text to let her know that I'd be home soon. I hated to leave Emma, but it was obvious that something was up with my mom. I slipped back into my shirt and shorts before walking back to the bed.

I shook Emma gently. "Emma, wake up."

She moaned as she opened her eyes to look up at me. "What time is it?"

"It's noon. You missed school."

"Shit!" she shouted as she sat up.

"There's no point in going in now."

"I know. I can't believe we fell back asleep."

"I can. We wore each other out."

Her cheeks turned pink in embarrassment. "True."

"My mom keeps calling. I need to head home."

"Let me get dressed, and I'll drive you back." She stood and started throwing on her clothes.

After driving across town back to my house, she parked out front and waited for me to get out.

"Don't forget that we are supposed to meet Andy tonight for his party." I leaned over and kissed her.

"I won't. I'll meet you back here in a few hours."

"Later, babe." I got out and walked to my front door.

My mom was sitting in the chair closest to the door when I walked in. From the look on her face, I knew whatever she had to say wasn't going to be pleasant. I didn't want to deal with any bullshit after the night and morning I'd just shared with Emma. I wanted to be happy even if it was just for a little while.

"I got your texts. What's wrong?" I asked.

"Nothing. I have some good news actually. But first, where were you last night?"

"I stayed with Emma."

She looked at me disapprovingly. "Are you two having sex?"

"Does it matter?"

"Of course it matters! You're my son, and I don't want you to get into a bad situation."

"Bad situation?"

"You could get her pregnant, Jesse! How would you handle school, a job, a girlfriend, *and* a baby?"

"Oh, for fuck's sake! I'm not going to get her pregnant!"

"You don't know that. I like Emma. I really do. But you are both so young, and you have your whole lives ahead of you."

"I'm done with this. If I'm having sex, it's my choice."

My mother took a deep breath. "Look, I don't want to fight. I just want you to be careful."

"I always am. Now, let's move on to what you wanted to talk to me about."

"This isn't over, just so you know."

"Whatever. Spill."

"Well, I wanted to talk to you about Mark."

"Let's not, and pretend we did. I *was* in a good mood until I came home. Let's not ruin the rest of my day."

"Stop acting like an immature brat. You're just proving my point from earlier. You're not ready for the responsibility of a baby. You have a lot of growing up to do, Jesse, even if you don't realize it."

"Fine. Point made. Tell me about Mark."

She smiled that lovesick smile I'd seen on her face when he came over for dinner. This was going to get ugly fast.

"Mark has to leave sooner than expected."

I raised an eyebrow. "Why are you smiling if he's leaving?"

"Well…Mark and I have been talking. He wants us to move to West Virginia with him."

"That was sweet of him. I still don't get why you're smiling." Sarcasm filled my voice.

"I want to go, Jesse."

I froze, just completely froze. There was no way that I'd heard that right. "Whoa, back up. I don't think I heard you right."

She had to be kidding. There was no way that she could uproot our entire lives over a man she'd only known a few weeks.

"You did. It just feels…right. I don't know how to explain it."

I felt the same way whenever I tried to figure out my feelings about Emma. I couldn't explain them. They were just there. But my mom couldn't possibly feel the same way about Mark. She just couldn't. As immature as she made me out to be, we'd supported each other just fine over the past few years. I didn't want things to change.

"You can't just leave everything for this guy. You have a life here."

"I have a crappy job as a waitress, and we live in a trailer in one of the worst parts of town. The only thing I have here that matters is you, and you'll come with me."

"I'm not leaving California."

"You don't have a choice, Jesse. You're not eighteen yet, and I am still your guardian."

"I'll be eighteen soon. If you force me to go with you, I'll just come back the minute I'm legally an adult. You can't stop me," I said stubbornly. There was no way that she was going to force me to move clear across the country.

"Please don't act like this. Just consider it, honey. I think it would be good for both of us."

"It would be good for both of us? No, it would be good for you. I'd be leaving everything behind—Andy, Ally, the shop, surfing, and Emma."

My mom was quiet as she chewed on her lip. She knew I was right. I couldn't understand how she would expect me to give up everything just because she wanted to follow this guy wherever he went. My mom was usually a lot more levelheaded than this.

"I know it will be hard, but you'll make new friends."

"No, I won't. I'm not giving everything up. If you want to go, then go. But don't expect me to follow you."

I felt like a dirty bastard as her eyes filled with tears, but I held my ground.

"I don't know what you want me to do. I want to go with him, but I want you to come with me."

"If you want to go, then go. But I won't go with you."

"Will you at least consider it?"

"No, I won't. I'm not leaving Emma."

"Would you still feel the same way if you weren't with Emma?"

"Yeah, I would. I wouldn't leave Andy and Ally either."

She rested her chin on her hands. "Jesse, I don't know what you want me to say. If you stay here, you'll be responsible for the bills and the rent. How do you plan to make enough money for all of that and go to school?"

I had no idea. Maybe I could get another job for the days when I didn't work at the shop. "I'll figure something out. I always do."

"You're seventeen, Jesse. You shouldn't have to figure anything out."

"I'm done with this conversation. I'm not going with you, and nothing you say will change my mind."

I turned and walked right back out the front door. *Screw this. If she wants to give up everything for some asshole she barely knows, then more power to her.*

But aren't you choosing Emma over your mom when you barely know her? a voice said in the back of my head, but I ignored it.

What I had with Emma was completely different from what my mom had with Mark. *But then again, how would I know that?* I'd refused to be around Mark since we had dinner that one night.

I shook my head. I didn't want to think about this shit right now. So, I
didn't.

I grabbed my board and spent the rest of the afternoon at the beach by
myself. As always, surfing helped to clear my head. I focused only on the
board underneath me and the waves I was trying to catch.

I had no idea what time it was when I finally climbed out of the water,
but I knew I needed to get back to the house to meet up with Emma for
Andy's party. I hadn't seen Andy all day, but I knew where we always partied.
It was a few miles down the beach in a spot only the locals knew about. I had
to climb a ridge and a few decently sized rocks to even reach the place. Most
of the locals knew about it, but they stayed away because of the effort it took
to get there. We'd used it for years and had never had any issues.

I floored it all the way back home, hoping to get there before Emma did.
She'd beat me though. Her car was sitting in the driveway when I pulled in.
At least my mom had already left for work. I didn't want her to tell Emma
about the move. Emma would feel like my decision was based on her, and I
didn't want her to feel any guilt. I knew I had to tell her what was happening
eventually, but tonight wasn't the night.

Tonight was all about having fun and introducing her to everyone else I'd
grown up with. I knew she'd be nervous, but I wasn't worried. *Once they get to
know her, they'd love her as much as I do.*

I froze in mid-step as I realized what I'd just thought. I'd thought I loved
her. I didn't though. At least, I didn't think I did. Love was a scary concept to
me, and I didn't want to even think about it.

"Jesse? You okay?" Emma called from beside her car.

"What? Yeah, I'm good. I just need to change before we head out."

"Okay, that's fine. Do I look okay?"

I grinned as I inspected her. She was wearing a bright pink bikini under an almost completely see-through cover. The colors coupled with the dark tan of her skin were striking. Suddenly, I didn't want to go to this party. I wanted to take her to my room and keep her there all night.

"You look fine."

"Just fine? I brought a few different bikinis in case you thought this didn't look good. I just want to fit in."

"You'll never fit in. You'll always be the one who stands out from the crowd."

Her frown turned to a smile at my words. "You're so sweet."

"Don't tell anyone that, especially at the party tonight. I have a badass reputation to uphold."

"I don't know how you got that reputation. You're definitely not a badass."

"I don't have to be when my best friend is Andy. He gets in enough trouble for the both of us. I've always been guilty by association."

She laughed. "Well, I don't think you're a badass, and I never have. Occasionally, you can be intimidating though."

"Is that so?" I asked as I stepped closer to her.

She automatically took a step back and bumped into her car. I placed a hand on each side of her, blocking her in between the car and me.

"You're not intimidating me right now."

"Are you sure about that?" I whispered as I leaned down to brush my lips against her ear.

She shivered. "I'm sure."

"I think you're lying."

I pulled back to look down into her eyes. There was lust in them but no intimidation.

"Maybe I am, but maybe I'm not."

I grinned as I stepped away from her and started walking to the house. She was definitely holding her own when it came to me. That was good. I didn't like timid girls. She followed as I walked inside, and I continued back to my room. As soon as I was inside, I slipped out of my swim trunks and started searching through my dresser for a dry pair.

"Jesse!"

I turned around to see her blushing furiously as she stared down at the floor. "What?"

"You're…you're naked!"

"And?"

"People don't just randomly walk around naked."

"Don't tell me you're embarrassed," I said as I lifted an eyebrow.

Her cheeks were still pink. "A little bit. Give me some kind of warning next time or something."

I couldn't help myself. I had to torture her. I closed the dresser drawer. She continued to stare at the floor as I walked across the room until I was standing directly in front of her.

"Why are you embarrassed? You've already seen me naked."

"I don't know. I'm not used to this sort of thing."

I laughed. "What? Being naked?"

"Yeah. Until this morning, I'd never seen someone the way I saw you."

I liked that—a lot. I had been her first, and no one could ever take that away from us.

"Is that so? Well, maybe I should walk around like this more often."

She raised her eyes to meet mine. "You're just playing with me. That's mean."

I grabbed her hand to yank her tight against me. I felt my dick respond the second that her body touched mine. The cover she wore was thin enough that it felt like nothing was between us.

"Does it feel like I'm playing to you?"

Her breath hitched as I slid our hands between our bodies.

I placed her hand on my shaft. "Does it?"

She shook her head. "No."

"I didn't think so. You'd better get used to seeing me naked because if I have any say in it, you'll be seeing me that way a lot."

"I never know what to say when you tell me something like that."

She squeezed her hand around me, and I bit back a moan.

"You're not supposed to *say* anything." I gave her a mischievous grin.

"We need to leave, or we'll be late," she whispered.

"Who cares? I'd rather stay here with you."

"Would you really? Even if all we did was just cuddle?"

"I really would. Besides, cuddling often leads to other things," I said as I ran a finger down her collarbone. "Are you sore from this morning?"

"A little bit, but it's not unbearable or anything like that."

"Good."

"What are you doing?" she squealed as I picked her up and carried her to my bed.

"We're going to be late."

I felt breathless as Jesse threw me down on the bed and pounced on top of me. His body covered mine completely. There wasn't an inch of me that wasn't touching him. I could feel my pulse pounding away as he looked down at me. *Dear God.* The look in his eyes made me shiver. He wanted me. No, he wanted to eat me alive.

"This cover thing needs to go, or I'm going to rip it off of you."

He tugged on the thin material, pushing it up over my hips. I sat up to allow him to pull it over my head, and then he threw it onto the floor. He ran his hands down my body from my ribs to my thighs.

"You're so fucking beautiful, Emma."

I pulled his head down and kissed him deeply. I had no clue what I was doing, but I wanted him closer. He responded to my kiss as he thrust his tongue into my mouth. His scent surrounded me as I ran my nails down his back. He smelled like the ocean mixed with another scent that was entirely Jesse. *God, I'm falling hard for him.*

He rolled us until I was on top of him. "I had all the fun this morning. It's your turn now."

I bit my lip as I stared down at him. This was all so new to me, and I was afraid that I would do something wrong. I leaned down and started peppering his face and neck with kisses before slowly moving down to his chest. I ran my tongue across his nipple, and he groaned.

"Do you like that?" I asked.

"I like anything you do."

I smiled as I ran my tongue over his other nipple. I started kissing a trail down his stomach. When his phone started ringing, I froze, and he groaned.

"Ignore it," he mumbled.

I started kissing lower and lower, moving down his body. I placed my hand on his shaft, and I began stroking. The phone stopped ringing, but then it started right back up again.

I sat up and moved off of him. "You better get that."

"Whoever it is better be dying." He stood up and grabbed his phone off the dresser. "What?"

I winced at the malice in his voice.

"We'll be down later. I'm busy right now."

I watched as he listened to whoever it was on the phone. He frowned. "Don't be an ass, Ally. I'll be down later."

I could hear Ally yelling at him through the phone. This wasn't going to end well.

"Oh, for fuck's sake! Fine. We'll be there in a few. Bye!" He ended the call and tossed his phone back down onto the dresser. "Change of plans. We're going to the party now."

"Why?"

"Because Ally brought a guy with her, and Andy is flipping out. According to her, I'm the only one who can control him."

He grabbed a rubber band off his dresser and pulled his hair back from his face. It was the first time I'd ever seen him pull it back, and I was surprised by how much more attractive he was without his blond curls surrounding his face. He was hot with them, but they made him look kind of innocent. With his hair tied back and no shirt on to hide his tattoos, he looked lethal.

"Dear God," I muttered under my breath.

He looked up. "What?"

"You look dangerous when you pull your hair back. It makes me want to jump on you and do dirty things." My face flushed with heat. *What possessed me to say that?*

He was in the process of pulling on a pair of trunks, but he stopped. "That's the hottest thing I've ever heard. I'm going to kill Ally for calling."

I grinned. "We always have after the party."

"I'm holding you to that. Let's make sure that we get you to school on time tomorrow though."

"Good plan."

This time, we took his Jeep instead of my car. We turned down a dirt path that I would have missed if I were driving. We followed it for a few minutes until we came to a clearing where several cars were already parked.

"We have to walk the rest of the way."

I raised an eyebrow, but I said nothing as we got out and started up a foot trail. We walked for several minutes until we came to another clearing surrounded by huge boulders.

"Where do we go from here?"

"Up."

"You've got to be kidding me." There was no way I was going to be able to climb these rocks.

"There's a trick to it. Come on, I'll help you."

I was still skeptical as I took his hand and followed him to one of the smaller rocks. He scooped me up and set me on top of it. I waited as he climbed up beside me. When I turned to look behind me, I saw the beach. There were tons of people already on it. I had no clue how they'd found this place. It was that well-hidden.

"How do you guys manage to get out of here when you're drunk?" I asked.

"We don't. We usually stay on the beach all night."

He jumped off the rock and held his arms up to help me down. I jumped into them, never once worrying about him dropping me. I trusted him with everything in me. He held my hand as we walked down the beach to where everyone was hanging out. There was a large group of people shouting and cheering close to where someone had built a fire.

"Oh shit," Jesse growled as we approached.

He dropped my hand, and then he pushed through the crowd, right into the middle of whatever was happening. I pushed through, too, but I wasn't as big or as strong as he was, so it took me longer. When I finally made it through the crowd, I saw Jesse holding Andy back as Andy was trying to break free. Ally was crouched down next to some guy who was lying in the sand, holding his nose.

"Andy, you're a fucking asshole!" Ally shouted.

"He was kissing you!" Andy shouted back as he again tried to break Jesse's grip.

"So what? I'm not a baby!" Ally shouted back.

"You're my sister!"

"Both of you, chill the fuck out!" Jesse yelled.

"I will not chill the fuck out! Andy just hit him for no reason!" Ally yelled at Jesse. "If you would have shown up sooner, none of this would have happened."

"Don't even try to blame me for this shit! It's between you and Andy!" Jesse shouted back.

He was pissed. There was no question about it. I'd seen him mad before, but this was taking it to a whole new level. If looks could kill, Ally would be dead in the sand.

When her gaze found mine, she screamed, "Bullshit! You've always been part of our family until you met her. Now, you couldn't care less! You're too worried about getting your dick in her to care about who really matters."

The crowd was silent as their eyes traveled between Ally, Jesse, and me. I wanted to crawl back over the rocks and go home. I had hoped to make a good impression on his friends, but I didn't see that happening now after Ally's little show.

"Shut the fuck up, or I swear to God—" Jesse yelled.

Ally cut him off. "Or you'll what? Hit a girl? We both know you won't."

"Ally, shut up!" Andy shouted. He'd stopped struggling in Jesse's arms, but he still looked ready to kill.

When the guy on the ground slowly stood up, all eyes went to him. I was thankful for the distraction as Ally helped him.

"You're all fucking nuts! I'm out of here!" the guy said as he started walking down the beach.

Ally shot all three of us another glare before she started chasing the guy. The crowd stayed silent while Jesse let go of Andy. They were both still pissed as they turned to face everyone.

"Move it along, or I'll beat someone else's ass!" Andy yelled.

The crowd disappeared almost instantly. No one wanted to test Andy's threat.

Jesse walked over to me and wrapped his arms around me. "You okay?"

"Fine. That was…awkward. Ally really doesn't like me."

"Ally needs to get over herself," Jesse growled. "I'll take care of her later."

I hoped that I wasn't anywhere near them when that conversation took place. Both of them had a temper, and I knew it wouldn't end well.

"Just don't fight with her over me. I don't want to get between you guys."

"You won't. Ally needs to accept the fact that you're not going anywhere."

Andy appeared out of nowhere with three beers in his hands. "I need to get drunk."

Jesse laughed as he took two of them, and then he passed one to me. "Why the hell did you punch the guy?"

"He had his tongue down my sister's throat. He's lucky that his head is still attached to his body."

Jesse shook his head as he pulled me down to sit on the sand with him. "She's not a baby, Andy. You have to let her go sometime. It's not like you don't go out and screw girls all the time."

My eyes widened at how casually Jesse had said that.

He noticed my expression and frowned. "Andy screws girls all the time, not me."

Andy laughed as he opened his beer and sat down next to Jesse. "Don't worry, Emma. Jesse is the good guy. Me, on the other hand…I like sex."

"I'll keep that in mind," I mumbled. I opened my beer and sipped it.

"Be sure to do that. If you two ever need any help, I'll be glad to offer my assistance."

"Dude. Shut up."

Andy laughed. "What? I just want her to know she has options out there besides you."

I grinned as I leaned across Jesse. He was going to kill me for what I was about to do.

"Is that so?" I asked in what I hoped was a flirty voice.

He grinned as he leaned closer. "It is. Give me five minutes, and I'll make you forget all about Jesse."

This guy was a total flirt.

I reached out and ran my hand across his arm. "I'll have to keep that in mind."

"You do that. And I'm sure Jesse would be up for a threesome if you wanted to take us both on."

I stood up and walked to stand in front of Andy. I crouched down in front of him, trying not to bust out laughing. "You know what I'd like to do with you right now?"

"What?" he asked with a cocky smirk.

I stood up and tipped my beer so that it flowed over him. "That."

"What the hell?" Andy shouted as Jesse fell back into the sand laughing.

"That is the best thing I've seen all day," Jesse said.

I raised an eyebrow.

"Actually, the second best with you being naked as the first."

"Good save." I laughed.

Andy looked back and forth between both of us as beer ran down the side of his face. "You're both crazy, but I have to admit that I like Emma a little better now."

"I didn't know I needed your approval, but I'm glad I have it." I stuck my tongue out at him.

"Fuck you, both. I'm going to go swim to get the beer off of me."

"Have fun!" I called after him as he ran down the beach to the water.

"You had me worried there for a minute," Jesse said as he reached up and then pulled me into his lap.

"That was fun."

"It was. Don't do it again." He rolled me into the sand and pinned me with his body. "Maybe I should worry about you and Andy being alone together."

"No way. I only want you."

He ran his nose across mine before kissing me hard on the lips. "Glad to hear it. Come on, I'll introduce you to the ones I know."

We spent the rest of the evening going from group to group. I couldn't help but smile each time Jesse introduced me as his girlfriend. He was staking his claim on me.

It was close to midnight when he finally decided that we should head home. After all, I had to be in school the next day. Jesse went to find Andy while I waited next to the rocks.

One minute, I was standing there, waiting for him, and the next, I was knocked down to the ground. I shrieked as a body pinned me against the ground.

"Shut up!" a voice growled out as a hand clamped over my mouth.

Ally. I was so screwed.

I tried to push her off of me, but it was no use. For as tiny as she was, she was strong.

"You think you're so badass, walking around with Jesse like you own him. Well, I've got news for you. He's *mine*, and you need to stay the fuck away from him."

"Emma! Where are you?" Jesse called from close-by.

Thank God.

Ally cursed under her breath. "You tell him about this, and I'll beat the ever-loving shit out of you. Remember what I said—he's mine."

She was gone as silently as she'd appeared. I was still lying on the ground in shock when Jesse walked up to me.

"There you are. Why are you on the ground?" he asked as he helped me up.

"Uh, I tried to climb the rock, and I fell off. It knocked the wind out of me."

"Just wait for me next time. Come on, let's get you home."

I was silent as we climbed over the rocks and made our way back to his car. The silence continued as he drove us back to his house.

"Hey, you okay?" he asked when he pulled into his driveway.

"I'm fine. Just tired."

"Oh, okay. Do you want me to take you home, so you don't have to drive? I don't want you to fall asleep."

"No, I'll be fine. I'll see you tomorrow after school."

"I can come home with you if you want."

He grinned suggestively, but sex was the last thing on my mind right now.

"I'm really tired, so I'm just going to go home and go to bed. I'll call you tomorrow though."

He seemed disappointed, but he only nodded. "That's fine. Just text me when you get home."

"I will." I kissed him good night and drove home.

My mind was still reeling from my encounter with Ally when I parked my car inside the garage. Now, I understood why she had been so hostile toward me. She wanted Jesse for herself. I had to admit that it was kind of shocking. *Didn't Jesse just pull Andy off a guy because he was kissing Ally?* Besides, Jesse had never mentioned anything romantic between them. I was sure that he wouldn't be with me if there were anything going on. I could tell that he thought a lot of her, and he would never hurt her like that.

Maybe he doesn't know, a voice whispered inside my head.

That had to be it. *But should I tell him? What if he secretly feels the same way, and that's all it takes to push him to her?* I didn't want to lose him. *Then again, do I really have him if I'm worried that he'll run to Ally?*

By the time I made it up to my room, my head was throbbing. After a quick shower, I collapsed onto my bed. I tossed and turned, but sleep wouldn't come. All I could think about was Ally and Jesse. I knew I had to tell him, but I just didn't know how.

16
JESSE

The rest of the week flew by, and before I knew it, we were on our way to the airport. I'd never flown before, and I was nervous as fuck. Emma found this little fact hilarious, but me, not so much. We were flying via private plane from LAX to London with one short stop in New York City to fuel the plane back up. Just thinking about it turned my stomach.

My passport had arrived at her house yesterday morning, cutting it way too close in my opinion. She hadn't been concerned though. She said her dad's contact had never failed them yet.

My mom had hugged me tightly this morning when Emma pulled up to drive us to the airport. We hadn't discussed her move to West Virginia since that first day she'd brought it up, and I didn't want to. I knew I couldn't avoid it forever, but for now, that was exactly what I wanted to do.

After checking in and boarding the plane, Emma relaxed in her seat as I fidgeted nervously. She giggled as she watched my knuckles turn white when we taxied down the runway and took off. After a few minutes, the seatbelt light went off, and we were free to move around the cabin.

I had to admit that the setup was pretty kick-ass. There were no more than ten seats on the plane, but that was only so there was enough room for a full-size couch and television in the back. A stewardess told us to let her know if we needed anything. It was an eleven-hour flight total, and she informed us that they would serve us both lunch and dinner. I wasn't sure that I would ever survive flying in a regular plane after the way I was treated on this one.

The stop in New York went off without a hitch, and we were quickly back in the air. Our lunch came soon after, and we ate in silence. Emma had been quiet since the night we went to the beach party, and I wasn't sure why. I had asked on more than one occasion, but she always said she was just tired. I knew something was up. I just wasn't sure how to get her to tell me what it was.

My mind drifted back to that night.

After Emma had suddenly wanted to go home by herself, I walked straight to Ally and Andy's house. I sat on their porch and waited for Ally to come home, so I could let her have it for the way she'd treated Emma on the beach.

After nearly an hour, headlights appeared down the street. She didn't see me until she was out of her car and walking to their house.

"We need to talk," I said as I stood up.

"I have nothing to say to you."

"I don't appreciate what you did to Emma."

She froze in mid-step. "What are you talking about?"

"The way you treated her on the beach in front of everyone. She never said anything, but I could tell that she was upset. You had no right to do that."

To my surprise, her body relaxed, and she continued past me to her front door. "All I did was tell the truth."

"That's bullshit, and we both know it," I said angrily as I placed my hand on her screen door, effectively blocking her from escaping.

"No, it's not. It's the truth. You've changed since you started hanging out with her."

"No, I haven't."

"You have. You used to spend all your spare time with Andy or me. Now? If I see you twice a week, it's a miracle."

"Look, I know I've been a bit distracted lately, but it's not because of Emma."

"Bull. Shit. You're blind when it comes to her, and you don't even realize it."

"Ally, I want you to leave her alone, and I mean it."

"I've left her alone, except for when you bring her around me. As far as I'm concerned, when she's on my turf, she's fair game."

"Why are you doing this to her? I thought you were my friend."

"I am your friend," she spit out.

"Then, why can't you respect me enough to trust me to decide who I want to be with?"

"You're so much better than she is. I just don't understand why you can't see that. Is it because she has money? Or because she is kind of pretty? Or maybe because she has that whole damsel-in-distress thing going on? Help me understand your reasoning."

"You don't have to understand what it is about her. As my friend, you should simply be happy for me and respect my decisions."

"I can't respect your decisions when it comes to her. She'll break you one day, Jesse. And when she does, I'll be the one here to help you pick up the pieces."

I was getting nowhere fast, and I knew it. I had always admired Ally for her refusal to back down, but right now, it was more annoying than anything. I had no clue how to get through to her.

"Look, let's make a deal. I'll try to keep Emma away from you as much as I can, but when I do bring her around you, you'll play nice, or you'll just ignore her. Can you do that?"

She looked at me as she debated on whether or not to agree to my deal. "I don't want to see her ever."

"I can't promise that. She's a part of my life now."

She sighed as she leaned against the door. "Fine. I'll try to ignore her when you bring her around, but you have to try to keep her away from me most of the time."

"I can agree to that," I said as I smiled.

"I don't want to lose you over some sk—"

I raised an eyebrow, and she stopped mid-sentence.

"Fine. I don't want to lose you over some girl. Happy?"

"Delirious."

"Yay," she said sarcastically as she waved her hands in the air. "Now, leave me alone. My bed is calling my name."

"Night, kid," I said as I walked off her porch.

"Stop calling me that!" she shouted.

I ignored her. She was my kid sister as far as I was concerned, and there was no way that I was going to change her nickname after all these years.

I slept on and off with Emma next to me as we flew over the Atlantic. As we were landing in London, I woke up with her head on my shoulder. I shook her gently to wake her up. She groaned as she opened her eyes.

"We're here," I said as I felt the plane coming to a stop.

"What time is it?" she asked as the stewardess was walking by.

"Just after midnight, London time."

"So, we basically just spent an entire day on a plane," I said.

"I guess so. I'm exhausted. I just want to get off of this thing and check into our hotel."

"Me, too," I said as I stood and pulled her up with me.

The stewardess wished us a good evening as we exited the plane.

Despite the late hour, a car was waiting outside of the airport for us. The driver loaded our bags into the back before driving us to The Connaught. My mouth dropped open as we pulled up in front of the building. It was massive with lights shining everywhere. A doorman helped the driver unload our bags while Emma and I walked to the front desk to check-in.

The place was as spectacular inside as it was outside. The floors were a black marble. The entire lobby was made out of dark wood with white trim. Two carpeted staircases led to the upstairs floors. I sincerely hoped that they had an elevator or that we were on a lower floor. This place was several stories high, and I didn't want to drag our luggage all the way to the top floor.

"Can I help you?" a man in a tailored suit asked from behind the counter.

"Yes, we need to check-in. My father left a room under his name here for me."

I waited as she provided her father's name. As soon as she'd said it, the man's eyes widened, and his mouth dropped open.

"Of course, Miss Preston. We were told that you might be arriving late. Your father reserved the Grosvenor Suite for you and your guest. Jace will show you to your room and help with your bags. If you need anything, please don't hesitate to ask."

"Thank you," Emma said politely as she took the two key cards from him.

We followed a man who I assumed was Jace as he led us down the hall to a line of elevators. We were silent as we rode the elevator up to the floor where our suite was located. *Jesus, we don't have a room. We have a suite.* I didn't care if Emma took me to every continent on the planet. I would *never* get used to this.

He led us to our room, and he waited as Emma unlocked the door and held it open for him. He remained silent as he unloaded our luggage from a cart and placed them in front of a massive bed. Emma slipped a bill into his hand just before she closed the door behind him.

I took a minute just to look around the room. I had only stayed in a few hotels before, and they had been nothing like this. I had expected a bedroom and a bathroom, but this was so much more. It had a living room, complete with a couch, chairs, and television. Our bed was positioned next to a massive window that took up the entire wall. We were high enough that I could see London for miles below us. It was beautiful.

"Alone at last," Emma said as she dropped face-first onto the bed.

"I'm exhausted," I groaned as I sat down beside her.

I started rubbing small circles across her back. Her muscles were tight, and I tried to get her to relax as I continued to rub.

"Why are you so tense?" I asked.

"I'm not," she lied.

"Emma, you are."

"I don't know. It must be from sitting on the plane all day."

"Yeah, that must be it," I said skeptically.

I still had no idea what was on her mind, but I was hoping that she would tell me now that we were away from everyone.

"You know that you can talk to me about anything, right?" I asked.

She rolled over and smiled. "I know."

"Good. I just wanted to make sure you knew that."

I leaned down to kiss her, but she sat up and scooted away from me.

"I need a shower. Traveling makes me feel icky."

"A shower sounds good." I grinned, hoping she would invite me to go with her. "Do you need any help? I'll be glad to offer my assistance if you do."

She laughed. "Sure, why not? But you're only washing me."

"I can behave."

"We'll see." She unzipped one of her bags to pull out her toiletries and a pair of pajamas.

I did the same and followed her into the bathroom. She slipped out of the sweatpants and T-shirt that she'd worn on the plane and threw them down on the floor. She reached behind her to unclasp her bra, but I put my hands over hers.

"I've got it," I murmured.

"Thanks," she whispered.

I unsnapped it and pushed the straps down her arms until it fell to the floor in front of her. She shimmied out of her boy shorts, and I took off my shoes and peeled off my shirt and pants. My boxers went next, and then we were both fully naked, inches away from each other. When I ran my fingertips across her shoulders, she shivered.

"I thought you were going to behave."

I grinned as I let my hands fall to my sides. "Sorry. I forgot."

"Sure you did." She stepped forward and turned on the water.

As she walked into the mist, I followed.

"I'll wash you, and then you can wash me," I told her as I grabbed a washcloth and her body wash.

"I don't think that classifies as behaving."

"Sure it does. I'm just going to wash you."

She remained silent as I wet the washcloth and squirted her body wash onto it. I started by running it across her neck before slowly making my way down to her nipples. Her breath hitched as I made circling motions around them. I ran the cloth between her breasts and then down her stomach. Just before I reached her hips, I came back up and started washing the top of her back. Again, I slowly made my way down until I was running the cloth across her bottom. She was trying to keep her breathing steady, but I could see how much effort she was putting into it. I ran the cloth across her arms before rinsing it out and setting it down.

"Done already?" she asked.

"Nope. I just wanted to wash your hair before I finished."

I grabbed her shampoo and poured some of it into my hands. I started running my hands through her hair until I was satisfied. She held her head under the spray to wash the shampoo out as I picked the cloth back up.

"Almost done," I told her.

I ran the cloth across her hips quickly before putting it between her legs. She grabbed the rail as I rubbed her clit with the cloth.

"This isn't behaving," she moaned.

I grinned as I suddenly pulled the cloth away. "Sure it is. I'm done already. Now, it's your turn."

She gave me a wicked smile as she grabbed my shampoo and started massaging it through my hair. I closed my eyes and relaxed as her fingers massaged my scalp.

"Rinse your hair," she ordered.

I did as she'd said. As soon as I finished, she grabbed a new washcloth and started washing me. She used the same teasing method that I'd done to her. She started at my neck and worked her way down my chest. She took her time as she circled my nipples and then further down. I expected her to stop when she reached my hips, but she didn't. Instead, she dropped the cloth and used her hands to wash my shaft. I moaned as she slowly stroked me.

"Now, who isn't behaving?" I groaned.

"I never said that I'd behave."

She had a point. Before I realized what she was doing, she dropped to her knees and ran her tongue over my shaft. My hips jerked, and I grabbed the shower wall. I looked down to see her staring up at me with such an innocent expression. She opened her mouth and sucked me deep inside until I was almost touching the back of her throat. I knew for a fact that she'd never done this, but if I hadn't, I would have sworn that she had. She somehow knew what she was doing.

"Fuck!" I groaned as she started sucking on me.

It felt like there was fire running through my veins as she rotated between sucking and rolling her tongue over my head. She released me when I grabbed her and pulled her up to me. I shut off the water before picking her up and taking her to our bed, both of us still soaking wet.

I threw her down on the bed and walked to the bag I'd grabbed my toiletries from a few minutes earlier. I'd stashed a box of condoms in there, and I pulled one out. I ripped open the package and rolled on the condom.

Seconds later, I was on top of her, thrusting deep. When she cried out, I froze. She was still so tight, and I was afraid that I'd hurt her.

"Shit! Are you okay, Emma? I didn't mean to be so rough."

"I'm fine. Just…just don't stop."

"I can do that. I'm not going to hold back, but if it hurts, tell me, and we'll slow down."

"Okay."

I started thrusting again, deep and hard. I'd held back our first time, but I couldn't this time. I needed this. I needed to feel her tightness squeezing my dick as I pounded into her over and over. I kept up our frantic rhythm, and I felt her explode around me. She cried out as her orgasm rocked through her, but I never once slowed. I was going to make sure that she never forgot this. I wanted to explode inside her, but I refused to. I wanted to make this last.

She screamed as I continued to thrust into her, prolonging her orgasm. I stopped only long enough to flip her onto her stomach before I entered her again from behind.

"Oh god! Jesse!"

"That's it. Scream my name," I said as I pounded into her.

I stared down at her ass and to where I was pounding into her over and over again. The sight alone almost undid me. She was somewhere between screaming my name and just plain screaming when I felt her tighten around me again. I shouted out her name as I exploded and filled the condom. I continued to pump my hips until the last orgasm left my body. She collapsed down onto the bed with me still inside her. I rested my body against her, holding up part of my weight with my arms.

"You okay? I didn't hurt you, did I?"

"No, but I've never felt anything like that. It felt like my entire body was exploding around me."

"Glad I could help you out," I teased as I pulled out.

I walked to the bathroom to throw the condom away and clean up. When I came back into the bedroom, she had rolled over onto her back.

"Jesse?" She asked, her voice timid.

"Yeah?"

"I really like it when you take me from behind."

Shit. My dick instantly started to get hard again. I grabbed another condom on my way back to the bed. "Let's try it again."

I groaned as I heard someone knocking on our hotel room door. Emma was snuggled up tight against me, and she whimpered in her sleep. I sat up and started hunting for a pair of shorts. The pounding started to get louder as I finally found my shorts and slipped them on. I had no idea who the hell wanted to see us so bad, but someone was on my shit list permanently.

I hobbled more than walked as I made my way to the door. My body was sore after spending most of last night having sex. I enjoyed teaching Emma new positions while I explored her body. We'd finally fallen asleep only a few hours before.

I threw the door open to see some guy standing in front of it. He had to be at least six foot five inches, and he was built like a tank. The whole speech I had planned for whoever was at the door died on my lips when I saw him. This guy could rip me in two without even trying.

"Who the hell are you?" the guy asked.

His voice sounded like thunder, and I took a step back.

"Um, Jesse?"

"Where's my Emma?"

"Your Emma? Oh shit."

My brain started functioning again and I finally realized who he was. Seducing Seductresses wasn't one of my favorite bands, but I remembered seeing a photo of them before. The man standing before me had definitely been in it.

"Yeah, shit is right. Where's my baby girl?"

I am so fucked. I couldn't let him in this room with his daughter asleep and completely naked in bed.

"She's sleeping. The flight wore her out, so I'd let her sleep if I were you. I can let her know you stopped by though."

"I'm sure it was the trip that wore her out. Move aside."

"I—"

"Move, or I will make you move."

I stepped aside to let him pass. I groaned as I closed the door and followed him back into the suite. *This isn't going to end well.*

"Emma Bellokavich Preston! Wake your ass up!" her dad shouted when he reached the bedroom.

I walked in seconds after he did to see Emma's eyes spring open as she scrambled to pull the covers around her.

"Daddy!" she shrieked.

"Don't *Daddy* me! You're in so much shit! Who is this tattooed asshole?"

"Hey!" I grumbled. "You have tattoos, too."

He shot me a look that could kill before turning his attention back to Emma.

"I, uh…he's my boyfriend. Jesse, this is my dad, Alexander Preston."

"I gathered that," I said.

"When I told you that you could bring someone with you, I meant Lucy or another girl, *not* your boyfriend."

"Let me explain! This isn't as bad as it looks!"

Her dad pointed to the garbage can that was filled with empty condom wrappers. "Please do. I'd love to hear this."

"It's as bad as it looks," I said.

We were busted, and I knew it. There was no point in Emma trying to lie. She'd only dig our graves deeper in the process.

"At least you're honest," he growled.

"Look, I know it looks bad. But it's not."

He raised an eyebrow, but he said nothing as he waited for me to continue.

"I care a lot about your daughter. I wouldn't be here if I didn't. I'm not an asshole who is just screwing her for the hell of it."

"Jesse! Shut up!" Emma shouted.

"No, I'm going to tell him the truth." I turned back to her dad. "She means a lot to me."

He stared at me for a minute before he said anything. "I'm not happy about this, but I appreciate the fact that you had the guts to be honest with me."

"Thanks...I think," I said.

He looked at Emma. "As for you, does your mother know about this?"

"No! And you can't tell her. Please, Daddy. She'll never let me see him again."

"I'm not who she wants for Emma, but I'm sure you've figured that out already," I added.

"I figured as much. Andria was always set in her ways."

"And she's a stuck-up bitch," Emma said from the bed.

"Watch it, missy. You don't speak like that in front of me."

"Sorry, but it's true. We both know it. Look, can you leave for a minute, so I can get dressed?"

He sighed. "Yeah, that's probably a good idea. Jesse, I think it would be in your best interest to follow me out of the room."

"Yes, sir," I said.

I followed him from the room and closed the door behind me. I hoped that Emma was hurrying because spending any alone time with her dad was not something I wanted to do after what he'd just walked in on. I considered myself lucky to be alive at this point.

He walked into the living room and sat down on the couch. "Have a seat. I think we need to talk."

I sat.

"Obviously, I'm pissed at the situation that I found my little girl in a few minutes ago. I think any dad would be."

"I understand. I'm sure I ruined any chance of you liking me."

"I wouldn't say that. You didn't lie to me when I asked, so you have a few bonus points for that. Something tells me that things are serious between the two of you if she brought you clear to London with her."

"It is. I would never dream of hurting her."

"That's good to know. I don't know how much Emma's told you about our family, but things are…complicated. Her mother and I are civil with each other but only for Emma's sake. I haven't been around much for Emma because of that, and I live with that guilt every day. I love my daughter, but I haven't been a very good father to her. Instead, I left her with a woman I despise. I've always been afraid of what Emma might become under Andria's control, but Emma has proven me wrong time and time again. My little girl is a good person. How, I'll never know."

"She really is. I don't think I've ever met someone who cares about people the way she does," I said.

He smiled. "I'm very proud of her. She means the world to me, and I don't want her to get hurt. Consider this your warning—if you hurt her, I'll hunt you down and make you wish you'd never met her."

I winced. "I understand. I promise that I won't hurt her. I'm not good with people. I never have been, but for some reason, I opened up to Emma. I can't explain it."

"Do you think you love her?" he asked.

The question caught me off-guard. I was still trying to figure that out myself. I knew I felt something strong for her, but I wasn't sure that it was love. After all, we'd only known each other a few weeks.

"I don't know. I care a lot about her, but I don't know if I love her. I don't want to move too fast by throwing that out there unless I mean it."

"That's the best answer you could have given me. You're both young, too young, to be in love. I know what it's like to be seventeen and feel like you're on top of the world. It will take a few years and a few times of getting fucked over to knock you both down a few pegs. But if you do eventually realize you love her, hold on to her."

"I will. I have no intentions of letting her go."

"Good because you have a lot to face. The biggest problem will be her mother. While I have no problem with Emma dating someone who isn't rich, her mother has always been about the money."

"I've noticed," I grumbled.

"You're going to have a hell of a fight on your hands when she finds out about you two. I'll back you up, but there isn't much I can do since I'm not around that often."

"I know we'll have to face her eventually. I'm just hoping it's later rather than sooner."

"You seem like a good kid, Jesse. I hope things work out."

"Me, too."

"What are you two talking about?" Emma asked from the doorway.

"I was just explaining to Jesse about my days in a biker gang before I joined the band…and all the ways I've killed men."

Emma rolled her eyes. "He's lying. Daddy wouldn't hurt a fly."

"That's what you think," he said as he grinned.

"Jesse, if you don't mind, I'm going to steal Emma away for the day. I have a show tonight at Royal Albert Hall, so I want to spend a few hours with her by ourselves."

"Of course. I'll just hang out here or walk around outside for a while."

"Are you sure?" Emma asked. "I hate to leave you after you came all this way with me."

"I'm a big boy. I can entertain myself for a few hours. Go have fun. Bond. Tell your dad how awesome I am."

They both laughed as they walked to the door.

"Just call my cell if you need anything!" Emma said over her shoulder.

"I will."

I sat on the couch for a few minutes, debating on what to do. I could stay here and sleep for a few hours, or I could go out and explore the streets of London. The chances of me ever visiting London again were slim to none, so I decided to explore.

After eating the food I had ordered from room service, I got dressed and walked downstairs. The doorman held the door open to let me pass. Once I was on the streets, I started wandering.

I had no destination in mind. I just wanted to explore. I walked down Carlos Place until I hit Grosvenor Square. There was some kind of park there—Grosvenor Square Gardens according to the sign—and I wandered into it. Santa Monica had nothing on the scenery here. While I loved the ocean, there was just something about the landscape here that drew me in. I was amazed at just how large the trees were that surrounded me as I walked down the stone path. It was incredible to see trees this big right in the middle of London.

I finally made it back to the street and continued to explore. I had a thing for architecture, and I couldn't help but be amazed by the obvious age of some of the buildings here. I hoped that Emma and I would have time to explore part of London together before we had to leave.

I continued to wander through the street until I found myself back at The Connaught. I glanced down at my phone to realize that I'd be walking for hours.

I made my way back up to the room and turned on the television to wait for Emma to get back. She didn't disappoint me. After only an hour or so, I heard her key unlocking the door.

"Hey, did you have fun?" I asked as I watched her put her key card on the dresser.

She started pulling off her shoes. "I had a blast. Dad and I went to this cute little cafe to eat, and then we spent the rest of the day going to places he likes to visit every time he comes to London. I wish you could have come with us."

"I'm glad you had fun. And I didn't need to go. You and your dad needed some time alone together."

"True, but I still missed you." She walked over to the bed and kissed me.

"I missed you, too."

"So, what did you do all day? Please tell me that you didn't hide out in our room, or I'm going to feel even worse."

"I didn't. I went out and explored. It was kind of cool actually. Thank you for bringing me along."

"Of course. I wouldn't want anyone else with me."

"I'm glad to hear it. I'm going to go shower and head to bed. I'm exhausted."

"Me, too," Emma said before she yawned.

I grabbed a pair of shorts and walked into the bathroom to shower. After a quick shower, I went back into the bedroom to see Emma had passed out on the bed. I smiled as I watched her roll over in her sleep. She looked so peaceful. I hated to wake her up, but she was lying across the bed, and there was no way I could go to sleep. I picked her up gently, hoping that she wouldn't wake up.

"What are you doing?" she mumbled.

"Shh, I'm just moving you. Go back to sleep."

"Okay."

I laid her down and settled next to her. As soon as we were both under the covers, she curled up against me and rested her head on my chest.

"Night, Emma," I whispered, and I kissed her hair.

"Love you, Jesse," she mumbled in her sleep.

I squeezed my eyes shut. *Jesus, she loves me.* I stared down at her sleeping figure as I thought about her words, thinking that I loved her, too. I just didn't think I'd ever be able to say it.

I'd been awake for just over an hour. Emma was still on my chest, sound asleep. She was so damn beautiful to look at that it actually hurt. *How the hell did I manage to end up with this beautiful girl?*

She stirred in her sleep as her eyes slowly opened.

"Morning," I whispered into her hair.

"Morning," she replied as she stretched. "Can we just stay like this for the rest of the day? You're kind of comfortable."

"Fine by me."

She smiled as she rested her head back on my chest. Her fingers started tracing the tattoos covering my left arm. "I've never really taken the time to look at your tattoos. I thought it was just one big tattoo, but it's not. It's a bunch of smaller ones."

"It is."

"What do they mean?" she asked.

"A lot of different things. Most of them are reminders of things in my life that I don't want to forget. Others are just designs that I drew and liked enough to tattoo permanently on myself."

"Did you do them all yourself?"

"Most of them. The ones that I couldn't reach I had my friend from the shop do. Tony is wicked talented."

"That's incredible."

"You told me you loved me last night in your sleep," I blurted out.

Her body tensed up at my words. Finally, she said, "It's because I do. I know we're young, and there are so many things fighting against us, but I don't care. I know what I feel, Jesse. I love you."

"You know when I saw you that first day of school in the parking lot?"

She nodded. "Of course."

"That wasn't the first time we met."

She raised her head to look at me. "I'm pretty sure it was. I think I'd remember meeting you before then."

"It was a long time ago, but I never forgot you. You were the first person who ever told me I wasn't good enough."

"What on earth are you talking about? I would never say that to you."

"You were too little to realize what you were saying, but I never forgot your face or your words. We were just little. My mom took me to the nice park on your side of town to play for the day, and you were there with your mom. You were playing in the sandbox, and I wanted to play with you. Even at six years old, I was drawn to you. You were the prettiest girl I'd ever seen. Instead of playing with me, you told me that I was trash, and I didn't belong at your park. You ran off after that, but I never forgot what you said. That's why I was so distant with you when we met. I expected you to be a stuck-up bitch, but you weren't. Instead, I found out that you are one of the kindest people I've ever known. I love you, Emma, even if I shouldn't. I've battled with myself over this time and time again, but I can't deny it any longer."

A tear slipped down her cheek, and I reached up to wipe it away.

"I'm so sorry, Jesse. I was only a child, and I had no idea what I was saying."

"It's okay. You taught me that I needed to be strong to survive this world, and I owe you for that."

"I made you bitter toward the world."

"No, you didn't. You were just the first of many to look down on me. Despite how we met, you've shown me that it's okay to care about someone, to love someone, because there are people who come into your life who deserve to be loved. They are the ones worth taking a chance on, hoping you don't end up broken."

She grabbed my face and kissed me. "I love you, Jesse. I'll never leave you. There's something between us that ties us together."

"I like being tied to you. Just promise not to shatter me."

"I won't."

What came after that wasn't sex. It was so much more. Where words failed, our bodies showed just how much we loved each other. Sex was nice, but it was nothing compared to this. We were one.

We spent the rest of the weekend exploring London and spending time with my dad and his bandmates. I'd grown up around those guys, and they felt more like family to me than my own mother did. When it was time to leave, I cried. I wasn't ready to leave my dad or the pure bliss that I'd found in London.

After our talk on Saturday morning, I felt closer to Jesse than ever. This boy had my heart, and I loved it. There was no one else in the world who could ever compare to him. Every look, every touch between us seemed to mean so much more. He loved me, and I loved him. For those few short days, life was perfect.

The trip back to California was uneventful. As the hours passed, a sense of foreboding came over me. Everything had changed, but at the same time, things were still the same.

Tomorrow, Jesse would be allowed back in school where everyone hated him for what he'd done to Todd. I frowned as I thought of the fight I'd had with Todd when I finally had a chance to corner him and let him know just what I thought of him. He'd claimed that he was only trying to protect me because he cared, but I wasn't buying it. He was as obsessed with status as my mother was, and I wanted nothing to do with it. I had told him to stay away from me, and so far, he had. I just hoped that it would last.

On the car ride back to his house, Jesse dropped a bomb on me. "My mom is moving to West Virginia with Mark, and she wants me to go with her."

I had no idea what to say to that. I sat silently as I waited for him to continue.

"You can stop trying to break the steering wheel in two. I'm not going," he said.

I glanced over at him. "What do you mean? You can't stay here by yourself. Where would you live?"

"I can and will stay here by myself. I'll still be in my shitty trailer. Money will be tight, but I'll manage if I can find a second job."

"How do you plan on working two jobs and going to school? You'll wear yourself out."

"It's only for two years. Then, hopefully, Rick will let me pick up more hours."

"Why are you staying? Be honest."

He paused before answering. "Honestly? Because of you. I just found you, and I won't leave you behind. Besides, Santa Monica is my home. I'm not going to give up everything."

"But your mom will be thousands of miles away."

"I know, and it sucks, but it's her choice. I won't hold her back."

"When is she leaving?" I asked.

"Soon," he said shortly.

I knew that he was done talking about the move, so I let it go. The rest of the drive to his house was completely silent. Both of us were lost in our thoughts. I couldn't believe that he was willing to stay here and work two jobs just so that he could be with me. I didn't want him to leave, but I also didn't want him to pick me over his mom. I was afraid that he would resent me for it later.

I dropped him off and headed to my house. The house was empty as I carried my bags up to my room. I sent my mom and my dad both a text to let them know that I'd made it home safely. My dad was the only one who responded—no surprise there. I spent the rest of my day washing laundry, still thinking about Jesse and his mom. I didn't want either of them to hate me for Jesse's decision to stay, but I didn't want him to leave either.

School was just as I'd expected the next day and the rest of the week. Everyone was either terrified of Jesse or hated him. I hated that I had to keep silent as the whispers followed him through the halls, but I couldn't take a chance on if people found out we were together and someone let it slip to my mom.

We only had a few weeks until my eighteenth birthday. After that, I wouldn't have to hide Jesse from the world. I would be a legal adult, and I knew my dad would pay for me to stay someplace. I wouldn't be trapped under my mother's roof.

I was just hoping that Jesse would wait that long. I could see the resentment in his eyes when we would pass each other in the hallway, and I couldn't say a word to him because my friends surrounded me. I'd texted him a few times to see if I could come over after school, but he always claimed that he had to work.

The next week was the same.

And the next.

Things were beyond tense when we were together, which wasn't often. I tried to talk to Jesse about it, but he refused. I just kept telling him to give me a few weeks until I could move out, and then I'd announce it to the world.

Lucy knew what was going on, but she had no way to help me either. She knew I was hurt by the coldness Jesse was showing toward me, and she would try to cheer me up, but it was useless.

Every day, I felt like Jesse and I were being pulled further and further apart. I'd finally had enough of it one night, so I texted Jesse to tell him that he was coming to my house whether he liked it or not since my mom had a dinner she had to go to. It took him forever to reply, but he finally texted me back and agreed to let me pick him up at his house.

I didn't care how long it took. I was going to make him see how much I loved him and just how hard it was to stay away from him while everyone bashed him at school. I would make things right between us. I had to. There was no way that I could deal with losing him.

I was nervous as I drove to Jesse's. It felt like London had never happened and that we were hanging precariously at the edge of a cliff. One slip, and everything that we'd accomplished together would fall.

I was surprised to see that Jesse's mom was home. I knew she worked the night shift, so it was unusual for her to be home this early in the evening.

"Hey, Emma," she said when she answered the door.

"Hey. Is Jesse here?"

"Yeah, he's in his room. Please ignore the mess. I'm trying to get everything packed and ready to go. Mark and I leave tomorrow."

"Already? Jesse told me you were leaving, but I didn't realize it was this soon."

"He won't talk about it, so I'm not surprised that he hasn't mentioned it."

"He really hasn't talked to me period lately. It's my fault though."

"Well, go fix it. He'll need you around more once I'm gone. I don't want him to be alone."

"He won't. I'll make sure of that," I said as I walked back to his room. I could hear music blaring from inside the room, so I didn't bother knocking. He wouldn't hear me anyway.

He was lying on his bed when I walked in. He noticed me and turned off the music.

"Hey," I said nervously.

"Hey."

"Can we talk? I mean, we *are* going to talk whether you want to or not. I just wasn't sure if you wanted to talk here or at my house."

"We can talk wherever you want."

"Okay...I guess I'll start. Why have you been ignoring me?"

"I think you have it wrong. It's you who's been ignoring me."

"You and I both know why I can't be with you at school. But every time I try to meet up with you, you shoot me down. Why?"

"Maybe I'm sick of being your little secret. Maybe you need to see what it's like."

"Jesse, I'm sorry that I've hurt you. I just don't know how to fix this."

"Neither do I." He sighed. "Look, it's not just you who I'm pissed off at. My mom has been driving me nuts while she's been packing for the last two weeks. She will be gone tomorrow, and I'm trying to accept that I'll be alone."

"But you're not alone. You have me. Just hold on for a few more weeks until I turn eighteen. Once I do, I'll scream that I'm with you from the roof at school. My mom can kiss my ass because I won't have to live with her anymore. I'll be an adult, and I know my dad will let me stay at his place here or pay the rent for an apartment."

He studied me. "You won't hide me anymore?"

"No. I've never wanted to hide you, but if anyone found out now, my mom would lock me in my room, and she'd find some way to have you kicked out of my school. We just have to wait until I can leave."

"It was always there in the back of my mind that you were ashamed of me."

"I could never be ashamed of you. Never."

He pulled me down, so I was sitting next to him on the bed.

"I sound like a needy girl, but that makes me kind of happy. I thought we had things figured out when we were in London, but then everything went to shit as soon as we got back."

"I know, and it's my fault. I promise to fix this."

"All right, I believe you." He leaned over and kissed me.

"Let's go to my house to hang out. My mom has a dinner thing, so she won't be back until tomorrow. She always prowls those parties for some poor unsuspecting guy to sink her claws into."

He laughed. "Poor bastard. I can't wait until I get to meet her. After she hears what I have to say, she'll love me even more."

"It's impossible for anyone to *not* love you. Well, except for her. I mean, you met my dad when he caught me naked in bed, and he still liked you. That's charisma right there."

"I'm lucky that he didn't break my neck. Your dad is one scary motherducker."

I raised an eyebrow. "Motherducker? Really?"

"Well, I didn't want to call your dad a motherfucker, so I tamed it down."

I shook my head. "Only you."

He held my hand as we walked out of his room and down the hall to where his mom was taping boxes. Her eyes lit up when she noticed our linked hands.

"I see you two worked things out," she said happily.

"We're working on it," I told her truthfully.

While we had made amends for right now, I knew things would still be uneasy between us until I could prove to him that I wasn't ashamed.

"I'm glad to hear it. I told Emma that she's in charge of taking care of you once I leave. You know I'm going to worry about you constantly."

"I'll be fine. We both know that I can take care of myself."

"You know, I was just telling Jesse that I'm going to see if my dad will rent a place for me until I finish high school. Jesse could always move in with me instead of killing himself by working two jobs."

"While I appreciate the thought, I don't think that's a good idea. I don't approve of you two living together."

"I'd make sure that it was a two-bedroom apartment," I added.

"And I'm sure you two would sleep in your own beds. I'm not stupid," she said as she grinned.

Jesse shrugged. "It's not a bad idea as long as her dad lets me help with the rent."

"Jesse—"

"It's no different from me staying here by myself. You'll be gone, and you won't know how often Emma stays the night."

This was getting awkward fast. It was embarrassing how he was basically telling her that we were having sex, and there was nothing she could do about it.

"Anyway, I'm ready if you are," I said, hoping that he would stop talking.

"Let's go. I'll see you later, Mom."

"Bye, Jesse. Be good."

"Always am."

"Why do I even bother?" she mumbled under her breath.

"I have no idea," Jesse called as we walked out the door.

"You should be nicer to her. She is your mom, and she's just trying to look out for you."

"I know, but I'm kind of pissed at her for really leaving with this guy."

"She'll be thousands of miles away soon. You shouldn't stay mad at her. You need to take this time and cherish it. I'd kill to have a mom like yours."

"I'll kiss and make up with her before she leaves tomorrow. I promise."

"Good. Now, let's go. I haven't been alone with you for weeks. I *need* some alone time."

"Naked alone time?" he asked hopefully.

"Definitely naked."

"Let's go."

Emma straddled me as she ran her hand down my bare chest. She'd practically carried me up the stairs and to her room as soon as we'd made it to her house.

"I'm so glad that we're finally alone. I've been waiting forever for this," she said.

"For what?"

"This." She undid the last of the buttons on my shirt and kissed a trail from my belly button to my neck.

I moved my head to the side to give her better access. Things had been so tense between us lately, and I planned to enjoy every second of this. I felt my dick jump as she ran her tongue behind my ear.

"You're killing me here," I mumbled as I closed my eyes and relaxed.

"My apologies. I'll stop."

She started to get off of me, but I caught her around her hips and held her in place.

"Oh no. You're staying right where you are."

"I thought I was bothering you," she teased.

"You are but in a good way. I like it when you bother me like this."

She smiled as she leaned down and kissed me on the lips. I slipped my hands into her shirt and skimmed my fingers down her back. She shuddered, and it was officially on. My hands slipped around to her stomach and slowly made their way to her breasts. I kneaded them through her bra, and she bit her lip as a small moan escaped her.

"Now, you're killing me," she whispered.

I pulled her shirt over her head and flipped her onto her back. "Good."

She ran her hands through my hair as I started kissing her neck, heading down and down until I reached her breasts. Her breath came in short gasps when I pulled the cup of her bra down and ran my tongue over her nipple.

I needed to unbutton my shorts, or I was going to bust my damn zipper. I reached between us and unbuttoned them, sighing in relief. I pulled my hand away, making sure to brush her sensitive spot as I went. She jumped and dug her fingernails into my shoulders.

She'd opened her window when we came in, and we both froze as we heard a car door slam below us.

"Oh my god, my mom can't be home yet," she squealed as she pushed me off of her and ran to the window. "Shit! It is her! We have to hide you!"

I dropped my head onto her comforter and groaned. Her mother had the worst timing ever. "Where do you plan to hide me exactly?"

Her eyes searched the room frantically. "There—in my closet. Hurry!"

"You've got to be kidding me. I'm not hiding in your closet!"

"Please, Jesse! I can't let her catch you here. She'll never let me see you again."

"Fine," I growled.

I was pissed, really pissed. Not only did I have the worst case of blue balls on record, but I also had to hide in a cramped space for God knew how long. I stood and buttoned my pants back up as I walked to her closet and opened the door. *Holy shit.* I'd expected a regular closet, but Emma's was bigger than my room at home.

She shoved me inside just as we heard a knock on the door, and I searched for someplace to hide in case her mom decided to search in here. I didn't think she would, but Emma was the most transparent person on the planet, and I was sure her mom would know something was up. I noticed a small gap between where her clothing was hanging and a dresser next to the door. Figuring it was the safest spot, I walked over and crouched in my makeshift hiding spot. I could hear Emma and her mother talking, but the words were a bit muffled. I strained my ears, trying to hear what was being said. I caught the end of the sentence as her mom spoke.

"…you so nervous?"

"I'm not," Emma said.

From in here, I could even tell that there was a nervous edge to her voice. *I need to teach her how to lie better.*

"Todd here?"

"No!"

"If he is, I don't care."

"I swear, he isn't."

I held my breath as the doorknob turned. *Shit.* If her mom caught me in here, we were done.

The door opened, and I could hear the panic in Emma's voice as she spoke.

"Seriously, do you not trust me? Todd is not in there!"

The door was wide open now, but her mother didn't come inside. I breathed a sigh of relief as her voice came from farther inside Emma's room.

"Of course I trust you. I know you're not going to hide someone in your room. I'm sorry. I just thought you were trying to hide something."

"Well, I'm not."

"Okay. I talked to Todd's mom again today, and she said he told her that you were upset with him. I thought you two might be together by now."

I was so sick of her mother's obsession with Todd. As far as I was concerned, the guy was an ass. She'd just stated flat-out that she was okay with him being in her daughter's room, but I knew I'd never have the same offer. Just because his family had money, he was automatically the golden boy while I was the nasty kid from across town.

"No, we're not together, and we're not going to be. Todd is an ass."

"I don't understand why you won't give the boy a chance. Is there someone else who you're interested in?"

"Of course not. I'm not interested in Todd or any of the other trust fund guys at school."

"And why not?"

"I don't know. Does it matter?" Emma asked.

This was a train wreck that I couldn't tear my ears away from.

"Of course it matters! You need to learn your place in life, Emma."

"Are you even listening to yourself? Maybe I don't want to take my place with all of those people who you try to force on me. Maybe I want to choose my own life."

"I'm not even arguing with you about this. I don't know what's gotten into you lately, but it stops now. Get your act together, or you're grounded."

With that, her mom slammed the door behind her as she left. I stayed where I was just in case she was still in the room. I didn't want to get Emma in any more trouble than she already was.

"You can come out now," Emma said as she stepped into the closet.

I stood and walked out of my hiding spot.

"I assume you heard all of that?"

"Kind of hard not to," I replied.

She went back into her bedroom and sat down on the bed. I followed, but I didn't sit on the bed with her. I was so pissed with the entire situation. All the emotions I'd been feeling these last few weeks bubbled up to the surface, and I couldn't ignore them any longer.

"I don't even know what to say. I will never understand her," she said.

"I'm not sure what there is to understand. She'll never accept me, and we both know it. I'm so tired of hiding us from everyone in your world. It's like you're ashamed of me."

Her head snapped up to stare at me. "Are you kidding me? Of course I'm not ashamed of you! I want to shout that you are mine from the rooftops, but I can't. If anyone found out, she'd force us apart."

"You're almost eighteen. What can she really do about it? You won't have to stay here anymore soon."

"You want me to move out of my mom's house right now? Where would I go? I'd have nothing, Jesse, and my dad can't help me until I turn eighteen."

"You could stay with me until your dad gets you a place to stay."

"I can't just give up my entire life!"

"Of course you can't. I don't know what I was thinking, asking you to come to the trailer park with me after living this kind of life."

"It's not even about that, and you know it."

"It will always be about that. Even if we were together ten years from now, I'd never be able to provide this kind of life for you. Never," I said as I realized it was the truth. I would never be able to take care of her the way she'd come to expect. She'd have to lose everything to be with me. "I'm so tired of this game we're playing, Emma. I just…I can't do it anymore."

"What are you saying?" she whispered as tears filled her eyes. "Are you breaking up with me?"

"I don't know what I'm doing. We both knew that we came from different worlds when we started this, but we ignored it. Well, I can't ignore it anymore."

"Jesse, please…"

"I have to go." I walked to her bedroom door. Getting out of here without her mom seeing me was going to be tricky.

"I drove you here. At least, let me take you home," she pleaded.

I shook my head. I needed to be far away from her. "I'll call Andy or something. I'll see you later."

"Will you?"

"Will I, what?"

"See me later?"

I opened my mouth to say *yes*, but I closed it. *Will I?* I had no idea at this point.

"Bye, Emma."

I slipped silently into the hallway and crept to the stairs. I could hear her mom talking on her phone in her room when I passed it, and I begged the powers above to keep her on that phone until I could get out of the house. I moved silently as I walked down the stairs and to the front door. It creaked just a bit when I opened it, and I froze, but no one appeared at the top of the stairs to see what had caused the noise.

When I reached the end of the driveway, I breathed a sigh of relief. I'd made it out without anyone catching me. I pulled my phone from my pocket and dialed Andy.

"Hello?"

"Andy, it's Jesse. Can you come get me?" I asked.

"Sure, where are you?"

"I just left Emma's."

"Okay…I'll be there in a few."

"Good. And call the guys. I need to blow off some steam."

"Fuck yeah! I'll message them and tell them to meet us down at the beach."

I disconnected the call and sat down on the curb to wait for Andy to show up.

I tipped back my beer to get the last few drops out of the bottle.

When Andy said he'd message the guys, what he had really meant was that he'd message half his school. Soon after we'd arrived at the beach, car after car had pulled in until the lot was full.

We were a good four hours into this party, and it showed no signs of slowing down. I'd already had too much to drink, but I didn't care. I just wanted to forget about my stupid fight with Emma and relax for a while. Things were always so complicated with her, and quite frankly, I was sick of it. I just wanted a normal relationship where I could go anywhere with her and not worry about someone seeing us.

"Having fun?" Ally asked as she sat down beside me in the sand.

"Tons."

"Please contain your enthusiasm," she replied sarcastically.

"Sorry. I'm not in that great of a mood."

"There's a shocker. What's wrong?"

"Emma."

"Trouble in paradise? Did she get mad because you couldn't afford a 10,000 dollar purse or something?"

I shot her a glare. "I don't need your mouth tonight, Ally."

"Okay, gesh. What's wrong?"

"Everything. I won't ever measure up to the standards that she's used to."

"Why do you say that?"

"Look at my life, and then look at hers. We're from totally different worlds. I can't give her that kind of life. I'm the flat-ass broke kid from the trailer park."

"Who gives a shit if you can't give her a mansion and a Ferrari? If she loves you, what you have to offer should be enough. I know you've realized by now that I don't like her. She's a stuck-up twat who thinks she's better than me. But I don't like seeing you unhappy. If you really care about her, you can't let the obstacles get in your way."

"Of course I love her. But will she love me when she's living in a trailer park?"

"If that's what she's worried about, then she's a bigger bitch than I thought."

"It's not her who's worried about it. It's me." I stared at the fire in front of me that someone had started earlier.

Ally reached over and pushed my hair away from my face. "You're an amazing guy, Jesse. You just need to realize how lucky *she* is to have *you*."

"Thanks, kid. I mean it."

"I'm not a kid. I'm the same age as you."

"Yeah, yeah. Whatever." I grinned at her.

She threw her hands up in the air. "I'm tired of this moping shit. I'm going to go get a drink. You want another one?"

"Yeah, if you don't mind."

"I'll be right back."

I watched her as she walked away. I wished that Emma could be Ally. Then, she would be a part of my life, and I wouldn't have to feel the guilt that I was feeling now. Ally would never question the life that I could give her because she knew nothing else—unlike Emma, who was used to the finest of everything.

I spent the rest of the night drinking beer after beer until the fire in front of me started to spin. I cursed myself as I tried to focus. I had planned on driving back to my house in Andy's car, but now, it looked like I would need to find a ride since both of us had been drinking way too much.

Lying down in the sand, I stared at a pair of feet that had come into my range of vision.

"You okay?" Ally asked as she bent down in front of me.

"Fine, but I need to find a ride home."

"I can take you. I only had one beer, so I'm fine."

"Thanks. Can you help me up?"

She laughed as she grabbed my arm and hauled me to my feet. I leaned into her as she led us to the rocks.

"You're really out of it."

"I'm fine," I mumbled as she helped me climb over the rocks. *Damn, the girl is strong.*

"Sure you are."

She somehow managed to get me back down the trail and into her car. She closed my door, and before I even realized she wasn't standing beside me, she was already in the driver's seat.

"Holy fuck, you're fast," I slurred as the car started moving.

I must have dozed off because before I knew it, we were in front of my house, and Ally was trying to get me out of the car. I stumbled and nearly fell, but she caught me and continued dragging me to the door.

"Where are your keys?" she asked.

I tried to get them out of my pocket, but for some reason, I couldn't get my hand inside my shorts.

"Oh, for heaven's sake, I'll get them." She moved my hand away and started digging for my keys. As soon as she had them, she unlocked the door and led me inside.

I didn't know how she was getting me to my room with the way I was staggering, but somehow, she did. I fell down onto my bed and buried my head under my pillow, willing the world to stop spinning so fast.

"I think I drank too much."

Ally snorted. "Ya think?"

I took the pillow off my head and tried to focus on her. "Thanks for bringing me home. I'll see you tomorrow."

"I'm not leaving just yet. I don't want you to choke on your own vomit or something like that."

"Gee, thanks," I mumbled as I closed my eyes.

Everything went black.

SHATTERED TIES

Emma

I'd spent the entire night worrying about Jesse, and I couldn't stand it anymore. I'd tried to call and text him over and over, but he'd apparently shut off his phone because it always went straight to voice mail. I'd went over our last conversation over and over in my head, trying to understand what had happened to make him snap, but I couldn't figure it out. I knew what my mom said had hurt him, but I didn't think it was enough for him to leave me over. From the beginning, he had known just what kind of person she was.

I had hoped that we'd worked things out at his house, but that obviously wasn't the case. I knew he was stressed over his mom trying to get him to move, and I was hoping that his outburst was because of that. I didn't want to lose him. I couldn't. I loved him.

Unable to sit around and wait any longer, I grabbed my keys and crept quietly to the garage where I'd parked my car the night before. I knew I was taking a chance on my mother catching me, but I didn't care. I had to find Jesse and tell him that none of that stuff mattered to me. We could be together in a tent for all I cared—as long as I had him by my side.

I broke several traffic laws on my way to his house, and I was surprised that I hadn't gotten pulled over. As soon as I parked my car outside of his house, I was out and running for the door. When I noticed Ally's car parked next to Jesse's, my stomach instantly dropped. At least, I thought it was her car. I'd only seen it once when we first met outside the dinner. *What is she doing here so early?*

I knocked on the door, but no one answered, so I tried the knob. The door was unlocked, and I let myself in. I glanced around for signs of life, but there were none. Trish apparently wasn't home since her car wasn't outside, and Jesse was nowhere to be seen either. The place was eerily quiet.

I walked through the living room and down the hall to his room. His door was closed, and I hesitated before opening it. As soon as the door opened, I wished that I'd left it closed. Jesse was in his bed in only his boxers with his arm wrapped around Ally. I felt like I was going to vomit when she opened her eyes and gave me a triumphant grin. She'd won. She'd finally taken him from me.

"No," I whispered.

Ally held a finger up to her lips. "Shh, he had a long night. You don't want to wake him."

At the sound of her voice, Jesse groaned and opened his eyes just barely. "Ally? What are you doing here?"

"You don't remember last night?" she asked sweetly.

I was going to be sick. *How could he do this to me?*

"I didn't mean to interrupt anything. I just wanted to make sure you were okay," I said in a shaky voice.

"Emma?" Jesse's eyes opened wider as he took in Ally in bed with him and me standing by the door. "What the…oh shit. Emma, it's not what you think!"

"I'm not stupid, Jesse. We had a fight last night, and then I walk in to see you in bed with someone else the next morning. It's not hard to put two and two together."

"Let me explain! I was drunk, and Ally brought me home. I don't know how she ended up in my bed, but I swear, nothing happened." He looked down at Ally with pleading eyes. "Ally, please. Tell her nothing happened."

She turned away from him, so he couldn't see her facial expression as she smiled at me again and winked. "Emma, nothing happened."

"I can't…I have to go." I turned and ran from the room.

I threw the front door open and rushed to my car. I really was going to be sick. I stopped beside my car and started throwing up violently. *Dear God, why did he have to do this?* We could have worked everything out. I would have stood up to my mom and told her that I loved Jesse and that I was going to be with him. I would have put it on a billboard if he wanted me to. But now…everything was ruined. *Everything.*

"Emma, wait!" Jesse yelled as he ran out of the trailer.

"Please. Just leave me alone," I managed to gasp out as sobs wracked my body.

"I swear, nothing happened. Ally is just my friend. That's it."

"A friend you sleep almost naked with?"

"I don't know how I ended up like this, but I know I didn't cheat. No matter how drunk I was, I would never do that to you."

"I'm sorry, but I don't believe you. We're done, Jesse. I can't even stand to look at you."

"You don't mean that," he pleaded.

"I do. I never want to see you again. I think you should move with your mom because I don't think I could stomach the sight of you at school." Now that I'd stopped vomiting, I opened my car door and got in. "Good-bye, Jesse. Please don't try to contact me again."

I cried the entire way home. I cried like I'd lost my best friend…because really, I had. Jesse had been everything to me, and he'd tossed me aside like I didn't even matter. He'd begged me to believe him. *But how could I when I walked in on him and Ally?* There was no coming back from this. I'd given him everything, including my virginity, and now, I had nothing left—nothing.

True love doesn't exist.

Jesse

I watched her car disappear around the corner, taking everything that mattered to me with it. *How did this happen to us?* I knew from the pain in her eyes that she was truly gone. *I didn't cheat. I know I didn't.* No matter how drunk I was, I would never betray her like that. Despite my insecurities from the night before, I still wanted to be with her.

It took everything I had not to chase after her. I couldn't let her go. I couldn't let her think the worst of me. Maybe if I gave her a few days to calm down, she would see reason and know that I didn't cheat. Needing some kind of outlet for the emotions running through me, I slammed my fist into the side of the trailer before I walked inside. I went back to my room where Ally was still in my bed.

"Why were you in bed with me?" I asked.

"I'm sorry. I got tired while I was watching you. I must have fallen asleep."

"How did I end up in only my boxers?"

"I took off your clothes for you while you were sleeping. I thought you might be uncomfortable."

I sighed. "I wish you didn't. It looked really bad when Emma came in here."

"So what? I thought you were done with her."

"I never said that. I was just confused and upset over some stuff her mom had said. Now, it looks like she's done with me. She told me to stay away from her."

"I wish I could say I was sorry, but I'm not. It's time you moved on from her. She's not the right girl for you."

"How can you even say that? You know nothing about her," I said angrily.

"But I know you. You could do so much better, Jesse. Why can't you see that?"

"I don't want anyone else!"

"Not even me?" she whispered.

"What?" I asked incredulously.

"You heard me. You can't pretend that you don't know how I feel about you."

I wasn't pretending. I had no idea where this was coming from. Ally had never even hinted that she felt that way about me.

"I honestly have no idea what you're talking about."

Apparently, that was the wrong thing to say. Her face twisted in anger as she spit out her next words. "Of course you don't. You've been so wrapped up in her that you can't even see what's right in front of you."

"I—"

"Just don't even say a word. I should have known better than to hope for something between us." She stomped past me and out the door.

I stood there with my mouth hanging open, trying to process what had just happened. *Ally wants me? When did that happen?* I walked over to my bed and fell down onto it. My head was pounding like hell, and my world had gone to shit in just twenty minutes. *Why the fuck do I even try?* I closed my eyes, letting the world fade away.

I wasn't sure how long I'd slept, but I woke up to someone tossing my ass out of bed.

"What the fuck?" I groaned.

"Get up, asshole," Andy said.

"What the hell is your problem?" I asked. Apparently, today was shit-on-Jesse day.

"Ally just came home, crying her eyes out. I can't believe you would do that to her!"

"Do what?" Now, I really was confused.

"Sleep with her, and then kick her out. I thought you were better than that. We've been best friends for years, and she's my sister!"

"Whoa, wait a minute. I never slept with Ally, I swear."

"Well, that's not what she's saying, and I'm taking her word over yours. Stay the fuck away from us, or I'll kick your ass. I mean it."

"Andy, I swear, I didn't!"

"Whatever. Just stay away from us."

He turned and stormed out of my room. *Jesus, could anything else go wrong today?* I'd lost Emma, Ally, and Andy in the span of a few hours.

"Jesse, why are you on the floor?" my mom asked from the doorway.

I looked up to see her staring at me with concern. "It doesn't matter. Is your offer to go with you still open?"

Her eyes widened in surprise. "Of course it is, honey. What happened to make you change your mind?"

I ignored her question. "I can have all of my stuff packed by morning."

Yeah, I know I'm running, but I don't care. Obviously, my word is shit to everyone around here, so what does it matter if I'm here or on the other side of the country? I'm done with all of it, all of them.

I spent the rest of the day and the night packing.

When Mark pulled up the next morning with the U-Haul, I didn't hesitate to load my stuff first. After we had everything loaded and my mom's car attached to the back of the U-Haul, I hopped into my Jeep, and I didn't look back as I followed them onto the interstate and away from everything and everyone I loved.

EPILOGUE
TWO YEARS LATER

Life sucks. It had taken me a while to realize that, but it finally hit me like a ton of bricks. *The only positive is that you learn from your experiences, and you grow.*

Two years ago, I'd certainly grown up when I walked in on the boy I thought I loved in bed with one of his best friends. I'd learned to let him go as time passed—or at least I thought I had.

Now, I wasn't so sure. *There are people who pass through your life who forever change you and everything you thought you knew about yourself and the world.* Jesse was one of them.

It had been two years since I left him standing in his driveway, but I'd never been able to let him go completely.

I'd debated this decision for months. I'd told myself over and over that it was stupid and pointless, but I always knew that I would end up here. I knew that Jesse had been a part of my old life, my old self, but I couldn't get my heart to accept that little fact.

I gripped the steering wheel tightly as I drove down I-79 from the Pittsburgh airport to my new school. Up ahead, I saw the sign welcoming me to my new home. It was ridiculous to be nervous at the sight of a simple sign. The chances of him ending up at the same school as me were slim to none. *Then, why am I here?*

I took a deep breath as I glanced up at the sign just before I drove past it. *Welcome to West Virginia.*

ARE JESSE AND EMMA FINISHED?
OR WILL FATE BRING THEM TOGETHER AGAIN?
FIND OUT IN 2014.

SHATTERED
TIES
BOOK TWO

RELEASE DATE TO BE ANNOUNCED SOON.
CHECK WWW.FACEBOOK.COM/KAROBINSON13
FOR THE LATEST UPDATES.

ACKNOWLEDGMENTS

I don't even know where to begin. There are so many people who made this book possible.

First, I want to thank my fans for standing behind me. You guys are incredible, and I feel blessed to have every single one of you.

To my friends: Katelynn, Sophie, Amber, Tijan, Tabatha, Lesley, Heidi, and so many more—You've listened to my rants, helped me when I was struggling, and made me laugh when I wanted to cry. I love every single one of you.

To my husband—You've stuck by me through all the craziness that began with *Torn*. None of this would be possible without you.

To my parents—You've helped me and listened to my endless rants. You've helped me to grow as a person over the years, and I wouldn't be who I am today without your guidance. I love you so much.

To my son—Your smile is what gets me through the tough days. I cherish every day that I have with you.

ABOUT THE AUTHOR

K.A. Robinson is the *New York Times* and *USA Today* Bestselling Author of The Torn Series. She lives in a small town in West Virginia with her husband and son.

For more information, check out:

Facebook: www.facebook.com/karobinson13
Twitter: @karobinsonautho
Blog: authorkarobinson.blogspot.com

CPSIA information can be obtained at www.ICGtesting.com
Printed in the USA
LVOW08s1819290914

406397LV00010BA/141/P